SEREN

A GRAYSON GODS NOVEL

J. NATHAN

*For my wonderful son.
May you find a passion in life that
brings you as much joy as writing brings me.*

CHAPTER 1

Grace

My mom's headlights cast the only light on the winding, tree-lined New Hampshire road. I toyed with the silver ring on my right ring finger, spinning it around and around. It was looser now. Lack of food would do that to a person.

"This isn't going to be so bad," my mom said softly from the driver's seat.

Wasn't going to be so bad? My dad just died, and I was being forced to relocate to Grayson Manor where my mom had been a housekeeper for over eighteen years—an hour away from my home. She might not have minded spending her week away from the common people of Coopersville. But, I was a few months shy of graduating. I had friends and a life in Coopersville. "I just don't understand why I couldn't stay with Holly or Laney until you're home on the weekends."

She sighed, and I hated that a sigh could carry so much meaning. Hated that after everything she'd been through—*we'd* been through—I was still giving her grief over moving to the manor.

"You and this job are all I have left," she said. "We're both grieving, Grace. You need me as much as I need you." She reached over and placed her frail hand on top of mine, causing me to stop spinning the ring my dad had given me. "This is what compromise looks like. We move here and you still get to graduate from Coopersville High. This way we both get what we want—at least until you leave for college in the fall."

I heaved a sigh. I *had* agreed to stay at the manor where she'd lived during the week for my entire life. Though now she wouldn't be home for weekends. She'd stay here indefinitely. I understood with my dad gone she wouldn't allow a seventeen-year-old to stay home alone for weeks at a time. I just wished she agreed to let me stay with one of my friends because the hour ride in every morning and afternoon was surely going to suck.

My mom hit her blinker which was unnecessary given we were the only car on the stretch of dark road. We entered a neighborhood with high walls surrounding the properties. No houses were visible from the road, and I wondered if it was due to the darkness or if daylight would bring the same scenery. I knew my mother worked for a rich family, but from the looks of the walls, the people in these neighborhoods were beyond rich.

My mom turned off the main road and onto another. The brick wall surrounding this property continued for what felt like a mile. It was clear that only one house sat on this stretch of road. We pulled to a stop at an entrance blocked by an elaborate wrought-iron gate. My mom put down her window, and I watched her punch a code onto a discreet number pad set into a stone pillar. The gate in front of us slid aside as she put up her window and drove up the long winding drive. I peered into the darkness ahead waiting for the big reveal. Because I was certain there *would* be a big reveal.

And, Grayson Manor did not disappoint.

As our car moved closer, the vastness of the property became apparent. It was as sprawling and grand as my mom had described it. The old cobblestone façade was a thing of beauty, even in the darkness. The chimneys. The gargoyles looking down. The circular drive with elaborate water fountain. This home was exquisite…and a little creepy. "They've got *this* big of a place and you stay in the basement?"

"It's not the basement. It's the helps' quarters."

I rolled my eyes. "The help? You grew up with Maureen. She refers to you as the help?"

She shrugged, and I knew it had to bother her. She and "the lady of the house" were best friends growing up in Coopersville. But one lucky blind date set Maureen on a road to riches and my mom to a life of servitude. Maureen thought she'd done my mother a favor by giving her the job. But what she didn't realize was my mom saw it as a favor to Maureen, always keeping an eye out for her once-best friend. When you had money, people used you. And my mother hated seeing that happen to Maureen. And, even when Maureen lost her husband to a heart attack three years ago, my mother was the only one to be there for her and her three sons— well, my mom *and* Mr. Grayson's business partner Martine who was now her new husband.

My mom pulled the car to a stop around the side of the house. There was a six-car garage set apart from the main house, but she parked beside the garage so that her car was concealed by the darkness of the nearby trees. She switched off the engine, yet she didn't make a move to get out. Silence filled the car telling me what I already knew. Our lives were going to be irreparably changed once we moved into the manor.

Knowing someone had to go first, I opened my door. The squeak of the older door broke the silence. I stepped out and the cool April night air bit at my skin as I circled to the trunk. As I waited for my mother to pop it open for me, I glanced at the manor, unable to believe the curveball life had thrown us. A curtain moved in a window on the second floor, catching my attention. I squinted into the darkness but saw nothing but a shadow.

Great.

As if life hadn't been brutal enough, now I'd be dealing with ghosts.

CHAPTER 2

Grace

I tossed in bed all through the night, unable to get comfortable on the new mattress. If I'd slept more than three hours, it would've been a miracle. Like my appetite these days, my sleep pattern was out of whack. I glanced at my phone on the nightstand noting it was almost eight o'clock. Sleeping in the basement apartment with no windows would either be a blessing or a curse.

I sat up, stretching my arms above my head and twisting my long dark hair back into the hairband it had come loose from. The only bright side to my new situation was that it was spring break which gave me time to unpack, explore the house and grounds, and get acclimated to my new surroundings.

I'd expected Maureen to greet us when we'd arrived the previous night, but she was nowhere to be found as we made our way to "the helps' quarters" which were indeed the basement. My mom's apartment was homier and more modern than the older exterior of the house would suggest. She had two bedrooms, a kitchen area with nice marble countertops, and a bathroom with a spa tub and glass shower. My mom's bedroom had a flat-screen on the wall and a queen-sized bed with a pretty lace comforter.

Maureen had made sure a bed was there when I arrived and had even decorated my new room with a pastel plaid comforter and matching throw pillows, a flat-screen, and a sleek white desk. I wondered if she was happy to have a girl in the house to balance out the testosterone of her three teenage boys. It wasn't like I expected to see her often since the unspoken line had been drawn long ago between her and my mom. But, despite their change in status over the years, I still respected the fact that Maureen had suggested we move to Grayson Manor. She even handled selling our home so my mom didn't have to. I guess she figured my mom didn't need a mortgage to pay on her own now that my dad was gone.

My mom's footsteps in the kitchen drew my attention to my closed bedroom door. I loved her with all I had, but for almost eighteen years, I only had her on weekends. During the week, my dad and I would fend for ourselves. Now, the notion that I'd be with her every day held a tinge of sadness, reaffirming the reason why. Tears stung my eyes. I wondered when the pain would stop hurting so much.

I crawled out of bed and opened my door, finding my mom in an outfit straight out of some historical British drama. "Oh, my God."

"What?"

My eyes drifted over the one-piece, black, polyester dress with frilly white apron. "Maureen seriously makes you wear that?"

"She was a bit obsessed with *Downton Abbey*."

I shook my head, unable to look at her with a straight face. No wonder why she never brought her uniforms home. My dad and I never would've let her live it down. "Please tell me she doesn't make you use a feather duster."

Laughter tumbled out of her. "No."

"Good," I said, loving that she could still laugh after everything we'd been through. There was hope for me yet.

"How'd you sleep?" she asked.

"I'd be lying if I said good."

Her lips twisted in disappointment. "Is there anything I can do?"

I shook my head. "It's gonna take time."

She walked over and wrapped her arms around me. "For both of us."

I relaxed into her hug, wishing a hug didn't feel so necessary.

She inevitably released me and stepped back, straightening her uniform.

"Would it be okay if I explore the grounds or do they have security—or vicious dogs—patrolling the premise to keep the riff-raff out?"

She smirked, knowing my dad and I had teased her for years about the hoity-toity place she worked. "Everyone knows you're here now. They'll leave you alone. Just be sure not to wear a ski mask or press your back against the wall and act suspicious."

I laughed. "I think I can handle that."

"Oh," she said abruptly. "The boys will be at school until two-thirty."

"They're not on spring break?"

She shook her head. "They had it last week and spent it in Mexico. But when they do get home, stay away from them."

My brows knitted together. "Why?"

She pursed her lips as if she didn't know how to verbalize what she wanted to say. "They…" she began. "They haven't been the same since their father died."

"What does that mean?"

"It means…their idea of a good time is not the same as yours."

"Could you be any more cryptic?" I asked.

She heaved a sigh. "Trust me, Grace. They enjoy hurting others. Let me rephrase that. They enjoy *watching* other people get hurt. They've changed over the past three years and neither Maureen nor Martine can control them."

"Okay. No fraternizing with twisted rich boys who torture others. Got it."

"I'm not joking," my mother warned as she grabbed her phone from the counter and tucked it into her frilly white apron. "Stay away from them," she said as she moved to the door and opened it. "Call me if you need me."

"You mean if I get lost?"

She rolled her eyes before closing the door behind her, probably knowing that me getting lost on the property was a true possibility.

* * *

I sat under one of many beautiful flowering trees trying to read a book on my phone. Since my dad died, I couldn't finish a chapter without my mind wandering back to him—his laugh, his advice, his amazing hugs. I switched over to social media, scanning my news feeds for anything to make me feel as though I hadn't been ripped away from my town. I hadn't seen most of my friends since the funeral. And, I really needed my friends. Sure, we talked every day, but it wasn't the same. I couldn't wait to be back at school on Monday.

My finger lingered over my photos app. I desperately needed to see my dad, but I couldn't bring myself to look at photos or videos of him yet.

"Oh my God!"

I looked around, searching for the girl whose voice had carried across the property.

"Oh my God!" she yelled again.

Goosebumps popped up all over my body, and I jumped to my feet, bolting a hundred yards across the lawn to the pool house where the voice seemed to carry from. I couldn't run fast enough to reach the voice. My breath heaved as I approached the front door. I grasped the knob and pulled, but it was locked. I hurried to one of the floor-to-ceiling windows and cupped my eyes to keep out the sun's glare so I could peer inside. I scanned the furnished sitting room and the kitchen area. Everything appeared silent and still.

I turned back toward the pool, thinking maybe the sound had come from there or the outdoor patio.

"*Seren!*" she said, but she no longer sounded scared. More like she was urging someone on. And it *was* coming from inside the pool house.

"You like that?" a deep voice asked, causing the hair on my arms to stand on end.

"Yes," she said all breathy and unafraid.

I took another look into the window and spotted two people in the corner of the room. A shirtless guy with his back to me had his hands splayed on the wall above his head with a girl caged between him and the wall. I couldn't see beyond the sofa blocking my view but from what I could gather, his hips were moving.

"Just like that," she begged.

Shit.

I'd seen enough to know what was happening. And I'd been *very* wrong.

I removed my hands from the window to get away from the embarrassing situation, but my elbow knocked against the glass.

I froze and my eyes widened.

The guy looked over his shoulder, locking his eyes on me. I winced, hoping my features conveyed my apology for stumbling upon the two of them. I expected him to stop what he was doing, but he didn't. He kept me locked in his cold emotionless glare as he continued thrusting into the girl.

As much as I needed to move away from the window, my feet wouldn't budge. I feared that when I moved, he'd see all of me. And the way he wouldn't allow me to move from that spot told me he was used to doing what he wanted and to hell with everyone else.

I finally unfroze and spun away from the window, running back to the main house as quickly as I could. I didn't turn back for fear of finding those cold emotionless eyes still on me. Because I knew, with much certainty, that he'd still be watching me.

CHAPTER 3

Seren

I left Kiki in the pool house and made my way into the main house, down the second-floor hallway, and to my mother's closed bedroom door. I pounded twice on it before entering, not wanting to catch her and my stepfather in the act. Been there. Done that. Got the visual scars to prove it.

"Who the hell's the girl?" I demanded.

"What girl?" she asked focused on her reflection in her vanity mirror. She was applying something to her face—the one that already had more surgeries than I could count. I think she thought by altering the outside, she'd be able to alter the inside. But she'd sold her soul to the devil a long time ago, and there was no redemption on the horizon.

"Don't play coy with me, Mother."

"*Ohhhhhh.* You mean Grace?"

"Who's Grace?" I asked, wanting to know more about the girl who didn't cower when I glared.

My mother swiveled on her pillow-topped seat. I found myself searching for traces of the mother I once knew under all the changes she'd made to her appearance. Gone was the distinct nose like mine—replaced by an upturned one. Gone was the dark hair my brothers and I had—replaced by platinum blonde extensions. Gone was the Cupid's bow lips girls loved about me—replaced by filled-in bubble lips. Even our family's signature green eyes had been swapped out with blue contacts. "Don't you listen when I tell you things?" she asked.

I pushed away the thoughts and steeled my features. "No."

My mother sighed. "She's Rosalie's daughter. I told you she'd be moving into the helps' quarters with Rosalie until she leaves for college in the fall."

"I would've remembered something like that," I clipped.

Confusion crossed my mother's face. "Wait a minute. What time is it?"

"I don't know. One."

"Why aren't you at school?" she asked, pretending to be the attentive mother she knew she wasn't.

"I needed the day off."

"You're a senior in high school. What could you know about needing a day off?"

I ignored her dig. As if her life was so damn difficult. "Hire her."

"What?"

"Grace. I want you to offer her a job. Say you think it'll lighten Rosalie's load or something. She can clean my room."

"Your room?" she asked, waiting for the punchline.

"She just lost her dad, right?" I asked.

Her brows would've lifted had it not been for all the filler injected into her forehead. "You *were* listening."

"She probably needs something to help get her mind off that shit."

"Mouth, Seren!" my mother reprimanded.

I rolled my eyes. Now wasn't the time to start mothering me. I was eighteen. Not twelve.

"That's a nice gesture. I think I will offer her a job," she said before spinning back around to look at herself in the mirror.

Nice gesture?

She had no idea.

CHAPTER 4

Grace

"Grace?" my mother called.

I glanced up from the floor of my room where I was on my hands and knees searching under my bed. "Have you seen my ring?"

She was still in her uniform as she stepped into my doorway, looking exhausted. "When was the last time you had it on?"

"I took it off before I took a shower and put it on the nightstand. But now it's not there." I couldn't lose that ring. It was the last gift my father had given me. "I don't know where it went."

"Don't worry, sweetie. It'll turn up." She turned to walk away then stopped and looked back at me. "Maureen asked if you'd be interested in helping me out around here."

"Helping you out?" I asked.

"Well, not for free. A part-time job. You were saying a few weeks ago that you wanted to start saving for Tampa," she reminded me.

"What would I have to do?"

She laughed. "Whatever I don't want to do."

I rolled my eyes. "Sounds like a dream."

"Come on. It won't be too bad. I'm a great boss."

I smiled, feeling for the first time since my dad died that I could actually smile with my mom again and mean it. "Yeah. Okay."

* * *

When I said I'd work with my mom, I didn't know she meant the next day or that I'd have to wear one of her ridiculous uniforms. But, there I stood outside a closed second-floor bedroom door decked out in a scratchy black polyester dress with a frilly white apron.

"Just make the bed," my mother said, stepping up beside me. "Fold any clothes strewn about. The cleaning supplies are in the bathroom, so just clean in there and then move on to the next room."

I nodded as I slipped on the rubber gloves she'd given me. "Okay."

"Just call me if you have any questions."

I opened the closed door, finding a boy's bedroom with navy walls. A poster of Miami's quarterback, Caden Brooks, was tacked to the wall behind the unmade bed. A red comforter lay partially on the bed and partially on the floor. I made the bed quickly, then moved on to the attached bathroom. I wiped down the glass shower door and walls then used the cleaning supplies from under the sink to clean the counter and sink. I saved the toilet for last, holding my breath while I tackled it.

I was about to hurry out of the room when I spotted a picture on the nightstand of a man and three young boys. I knew the man had to be Maureen's late husband and the boys had to be her three sons. The tallest one beside the dad caught my attention. *Those green eyes*. Each of the boys had them, but the tallest boy possessed the familiar ones I'd seen in the pool house. The ones that held something I couldn't quite read. Secrets? Indifference? Rage? The other two boys were a little shorter, but all were broad-shouldered and good-looking. They would've been taller and bigger now since their father passed away three years ago. They all had perfectly styled short dark hair in the photo. I wondered if they looked so put together in real-life.

Realizing I was snooping around whichever boy's room this was, I turned and made my way out, moving to the next one. This room was similar to the first, though these walls were lighter, giving the room an airy beachy feel. This boy was neat, making his own bed and leaving nothing on the floor. I moved quickly through the room and made my way to the third room.

I opened the door and stepped inside, freezing when I saw the mess I was facing. "Jesus Christ," I mumbled, taken aback by the disaster and having no idea where to even begin. Clothes were strewn on every surface, dishes with half-eaten food and cups half-filled with liquid sat on the nightstand. The comforter was halfway to the bathroom door as if it had been dragged. I didn't dare look in the bathroom. I'd tackle that if I managed to get to it. I picked up the comforter and shook it out, moving it back to the bed. That's when I spotted the note on the pillow. *Change these sheets. The threesome got a little sweaty.*

My eyes widened. Without having met any of the Grayson boys, there was no doubt in my mind who this room belonged to.

I went into the hall in search of my mom. I found her in the master bedroom. "Hey, where do I find new sheets?"

Her forehead creased. "New sheets? Those don't get changed until Friday."

"There was a note asking for them."

"A note?" she asked as if that was a strange request. Had no one left *her* a note before? I guess it was better I received the lewd request than her anyway. "They're in the closet at the end of the third-floor hallway," she said, pointing in the direction of the stairs. "How's everything going?" she asked as she fluffed the throw pillows on the bed.

"The first two rooms took no time. But this one looks like it's going to take me a lot longer."

She snickered. "Yes. Seren is a bit messy."

"He's the tall one?"

Her brows furrowed. "How do you know that?"

"I saw a photo in one of the rooms of the boys with their dad."

"Oh, yes. Sawyer has the photo beside his bed," she said.

I motioned toward the door. "Well, I've gotta get moving if I want to finish his room by dinner time."

"That's a little dramatic," my mother laughed. "Besides, you're done after that room."

"Seriously?"

"What type of boss do you think I am?"

"The amazing type, obviously." I smiled before moving upstairs. The hallway looked exactly like the second-floor hallway with its dark wood-paneled walls and closed doors, but it was darker—almost lifeless. A cold shiver rushed up my spine as each of my steps seemed to creak the old wooden floor beneath my feet. I stopped at the closet door that practically blended into the wood-paneled walls. I retrieved new sheets and pillowcases. They were as soft as the ones in the other two rooms and probably cost a fortune.

"I told you I needed time!" a deep voice with an Italian accent bellowed from behind one of the closed doors.

I froze mid-step. It must've been the boys' stepfather, Martine.

"These things take fucking time!" he yelled followed by what sounded like his fist slamming down hard on something. "Give me a couple of months. It will all be over in a couple of months."

Silence followed and I didn't want to get caught in the hallway eavesdropping, so I hurried back downstairs, feeling more at ease on the second floor where I knew my mom was.

I returned to Seren's room, changing the sheets quickly and making his bed with the black comforter at the foot of his bed. I grabbed the clothes thrown on his dresser, desk, and chair and folded them, unable to ignore the expensive scent wafting off them. I snatched any clothes still on the floor and tossed them into the laundry basket in the corner of his room.

I took the dishes and cups from the nightstand and dresser and placed them on the cart in the hallway. His room looked neat compared to the mess it had been, but I'd yet to check the bathroom. I pulled open the door to find towels all over the floor and bottles of deodorant and cologne on the countertop. Yup, expensive designer stuff.

I reached under the sink to grab the cleaning supplies and discovered a huge half-empty box of condoms. Of course he'd be stocked up. I reached behind the box and grabbed what I needed, cleaning the bathroom as quickly as I could.

By the time I finished in there, I was wiped out. I said goodbye to my mom and hurried down to our basement apartment. I stripped out of the ugly uniform and jumped into the shower, ridding myself of the dirty feeling I got from being in Seren's room.

After dressing in jeans, a hoodie, and my Chucks, I walked around the grounds to get some fresh air. I texted with Holly and Laney before stopping by the pool. I crouched at the side and glided my fingertips over the cool water. I couldn't wait for the day when I'd be working by the ocean as a marine biologist. And, if things went my way and I got the summer internship at the Tampa Marine Life Rescue Center, that day would come even sooner.

I stood up and eyed the lounge chairs on the patio. It wouldn't hurt to soak up a little sun before retiring to the basement, so I lay down on one of the chairs and closed my eyes. Lawnmowers hummed in the distance as the bright afternoon sun warmed my otherwise cool body.

The morning hadn't been so bad. Sure, cleaning other people's rooms wasn't the ideal job, but it made me money for college and cut down on my mom's workload. Besides, once I returned to school next week, I'd be moving to the kitchen to assist during dinner.

"What the fuck?"

My eyes shot open.

Seren and a skinny blonde girl stared down at me. He looked different than he looked all dressed up in the photo in his brother's room but just as cold as he had when I found him in the pool house. The same glare was firmly in place on his surly face. "The help isn't allowed on the grounds," he said.

I jumped up. "Sorry. I must've dozed off."

"Who is *she*?" the girl asked him.

"The creeper from yesterday," he informed her.

A cold chill rushed over my body. "Creeper?"

"Yeah," he said, pegging me with his eyes. "The one watching us in the pool house window."

My mouth dropped open. "I was *not* watching you. I thought you were assaulting her."

He scoffed before his eyes cut to hers. "Was I assaulting you, Kiki?"

"Only in the best possible way," she assured him.

Poor pathetic fool. He'll clearly dump you for the next best thing. "Well, moving forward I'll be sure to stay away from people who seemed to be calling for help."

"You best keep your eyes and ears to yourself around here," Seren warned, his green eyes boring into mine.

"Is that your idea of a threat?" I asked, totally unaffected by his attempt to intimidate me.

"Yes," he said matter-of-factly.

Kiki snickered, and I suddenly felt like I was caught in the middle of some bad teen movie.

"The help's quarters are that way," Seren said, pointing toward the house and dismissing me.

My eyes narrowed. "I'm well aware of where the *basement* is." I spun away from them and walked toward the house in no hurry at all. Let them look. I wasn't intimidated by rich assholes.

CHAPTER 5

Grace

The following day there was another note on Seren's unmade bed. *Scrub the shower. Wouldn't want tonight's brunette to find last night's blonde hair in there.*

Was this guy for real?

I cleaned his room in record time, paying extra attention to the shower per his request. Thankfully, I didn't find any blonde hair, and now his latest conquest would be none the wiser.

* * *

The next day, per his third note, I entered the pool house. My eyes scanned the spotless living room and kitchen, and I was glad that I wouldn't need to clean in there. I moved down the small hallway to the bedroom in the back of the house. True to what Seren had written in his note, this was a disaster. Handcuffs, petroleum jelly, and lingerie were strewn on the unmade bed. *Gross.* I quickly changed the sheets, straightened up the room, and threw out the garbage and accessories. This kid was eighteen, but it was like he was a porn star.

I hurried to our apartment, never feeling dirtier in my life. I showered, washing all the icky-ness of that pool house off me. I went to my room with a towel wrapped around my body and my wet hair up in a knot. I dropped onto my stomach on the bed and grabbed my phone. I checked my newsfeed. And, before I could even stop myself, I searched Seren Grayson. He didn't have any social media accounts, but that didn't stop people from creating their own "fan" sites or hashtagging him in their posts. Most of the photos that appeared were recent and there were girls in many of them. Blondes, brunettes, pink-haired beauties. And despite *their* wide smiles, he didn't smile in even one of the photos. His emotionless eyes stared straight at the camera, eerie and cold. A shiver raced up my spine. He wasn't who people thought he was. There was something else there. I just couldn't put my finger on it.

In between photos of him with girls at parties or in the hallway at school, there were photos of him in his navy and white football uniform with the number twenty-five on his chest. There were some of him standing on the sideline during practice with sweaty hair and red cheeks and lots of him throwing footballs during games. There were also some of him with his brothers, all tagged #GraysonGods. In some, they wore football uniforms and in others, they posed at charity events. I wondered how many fundraisers Maureen dragged them to.

I didn't know what I thought I'd learn about Seren by stalking him on social media, but what I found didn't shed any light on who he was. I wondered if I'd ever learn or if all our interactions would be via note or cold uncomfortable run-ins.

* * *

Loud music reverberated off our walls Friday night. You'd think the old stone exterior of the manor would've kept the noise out, but between the screaming girls jumping into the pool and the loud music, it was difficult to concentrate on the book I still couldn't finish on my phone. I crawled off my bed and stopped in my mom's open doorway. "Can we expect a party every weekend?"

My mom glanced at me from her bed where she'd been watching television. "Not my business."

"Well, did you have to clean up after them?"

"The weekend staff handles weekends. I'm usually long gone by the time Friday night rolls around."

"So, do you think they do this every time Maureen and Martine are out of town?"

She shrugged, but something in her features said she knew. Wasn't it a foregone conclusion that the help always stayed quiet but gossiped behind closed doors?

"Night," I said before returning to my room.

With all the noise, I knew I wouldn't be able to read…or sleep. So, once I was sure my mom had fallen asleep, I tiptoed to the front door and slipped out. I needed to see this party for myself.

Expensive cars, jeeps, and SUVs lined the driveway. Some people walked about the grounds, but most mingled by the pool and pool house. I really didn't want to catch anyone's attention, especially after the way things went down with Seren and that girl by the pool the other day. So, I made my way across the grounds, moving from tree to tree as if on a clandestine mission.

Out of nowhere, a hand clasped my mouth from behind, stealing my breath away. Fear grabbed hold of me as I struggled against the hand, only to be pulled back against a strong body.

"*Shhhh.* I'm not gonna hurt you," a deep voice promised.

"L…e….t…g…oooo," I struggled to say against the hand.

"I'm gonna let go," he assured me. "Just promise you won't yell."

I nodded, willing to agree to anything for him to release me.

Slowly the hand released my mouth and I spun around ready to unleash my wrath on whoever had touched me. My head hitched back at the sight of one of the Grayson boys standing in front of me, tall and handsome, his green gaze capturing mine. His lips slipped into a small smile. I knew him from the photo, but I wasn't sure if he was Saint or Sawyer. "You must be Grace," he said, his eyes drifting over my jeans and hoodie.

Feeling uncomfortable under his appraisal, I crossed my arms.

"No wonder your mom kept you away from here," he said.

"What's that mean?"

"My brothers would definitely eat you up and spit you out," he assured me with a laugh.

"Excuse me?" I asked, annoyed by his words.

As if remembering his manners, he shook his head. "I'm sorry. I'm Sawyer."

"Maureen's youngest son?"

He grinned. "My reputation precedes me?"

"My mom might've mentioned it."

"Before she threatened you to stay away from us?"

My eyes narrowed.

"I knew it!" he said, my expression giving me away. "She was smart to keep you away," he said, burying his hands in the pockets of his jeans. "We are trouble."

"*You're* trouble?" I asked, unable to believe it given his baby face.

"Well, maybe not me. But Seren and Saint are. So, as far as everyone in town's concerned, I'm guilty by association."

"Sounds crummy."

He shrugged like it was no big deal.

"If you've got this whole party going on at your house, why're you lurking around in the shadows?"

He chuckled and the soft sound was endearing. "There's a lot to see and hear in the shadows."

Screams from the pool caused both of us to glance over.

"Do you want me to introduce you to some people?" he offered.

"No. I was just checking out what all the noise was." My eyes snagged on a few people stumbling across the lawn and a tinge of longing to be back home with my friends hit me in the center of my chest. I glanced back to Sawyer. "Do you guys throw parties every weekend?"

He shook his head. "Not every weekend. And it's not my party. It's Saint's."

"So, these aren't your friends?"

He shrugged. "I'm only a sophomore. Some of them are only nice to me because they're scared of my brothers."

"*Should* they be scared of your brothers?" I asked.

He thought for a minute. "Probably."

"Well, I wouldn't be so sure these people aren't your friends, too. You seem like a pretty nice guy to me."

"Are you enrolling at Windham Prep?" Sawyer asked.

I shook my head. "I'm graduating with my friends in Coopersville."

"That's cool."

I smiled, happy that my mother had been wrong about at least one of the Grayson boys. "I'll let you get back to your party—I mean, your *brother's* party."

"Don't go," he said. "This is the most fun I've had all night."

I laughed. "You can always find me in the basement."

He looked down at his feet, and I could tell he was embarrassed about my living quarters.

"I'm just kidding. It's actually really nice down there."

His eyes lifted to mine and apology filled them. "At least it's only for a little while, right?"

For me. But my mom was there for as long as she decided to stay. "Good point."

"Sawyer!" someone called.

Sawyer and I turned in the direction of the voice.

Seren stood in the distance under a tree with his arms crossed. His harsh glare was undeniable even several yards away. "What the hell are you doing talking to the help?"

The way he called me *the help* again pissed me the hell off. "What's your problem?" I called to him.

Sawyer touched my arm as if to quiet me down—or protect me. I couldn't be sure.

Seren's eyes narrowed.

"I was just getting to know Grace," Sawyer explained as a way of settling down his fiery brother who was now stalking toward us.

"What's to know?" Seren asked.

"I hate your brother," I grumbled under my breath.

"He's not always this—"

"Get your ass to the pool," Seren ordered Sawyer. "Someone's gotta watch the drunk girls."

Sawyer glanced at me. "Duty calls. See you around." He took off toward the pool.

Seren remained where he stood staring me down.

Why was he such a jerk? "No worries," I said. "I know where I belong, and some lame rich kid's party isn't it." I spun away from him and headed back to the basement—away from him and his stupid glare.

CHAPTER 6

Seren

"What the hell were you talking to her for?" I spat at Sawyer when I found him leaving his room the next morning.

"What are you talking about?" he asked, his hair all ruffled and his eyes sleepy.

"The help."

"Fuck off, Seren. She's nice."

"Nice?" I growled. "She's not one of us. Don't make her think she is."

Sawyer rolled his eyes and walked past me toward the stairs. "Dude, you've got issues."

I grabbed the front of his shirt and slammed him into the hallway wall, holding him there with the palm of my hand as he tried to push me off. I was three inches taller and had at least ten pounds on him. "*I've* got issues?"

"You need help. Now, get the hell off me and get it."

Despite the rage his words elicited in me, I released him.

He straightened out his T-shirt and glared at me as if he could actually take me in a fight.

"Stay away from her," I warned.

"Take your own advice," he grumbled as he headed toward the stairs.

"Excuse me?"

He stopped and looked at me. "I'm not stupid. I know you're the reason Mom hired her."

"Prove it."

He rolled his eyes and disappeared downstairs.

I watched long after he left. It wasn't like I hadn't gotten help after my father died. All three of us had seen a shrink. I'd heard what she said. But she wasn't telling me anything I didn't already know. Normal teenage things lost meaning once he died. Parties. Friends. Even girls. My life was a series of monotonous events. Each more unfulfilling than the last. Though, like sex, football served as a release for me. I could unleash the rage I tried to harness in other areas of my life on the field. I hated to think how bad things would've been if I didn't play.

I headed toward our home gym, knowing I needed to work out or else the anger and misery that normally consumed my life would take over again.

Grace

Sitting in Mr. Adams Calculus class normally would've put me to sleep, but not today. Not when I was back home where I belonged surrounded by the people who cared about me. The hour drive to school sucked, and so did waking up at five to get on the road by five forty-five, but it was all worth it to be back in Coopersville.

I needed normal back in my life.

"Grace?" Mr. Adams called as I gathered my things from my desk at the bell. "A word?"

I swung my backpack onto my back, and, as the rest of my class filed out the door, I approached his desk.

"I just wanted to ask how you're doing," he explained.

I tried spinning the ring on my finger that still wasn't there. "I'm okay. Glad to be back," I said, omitting the fact that I wasn't actually back in Coopersville since living in another town wasn't allowed.

"Well, please know we're all here for you," he said.

I nodded. "I know. Thank you."

* * *

"So?" Holly asked as she braided her blonde hair.

"So, what?" I replied from across the lunch table.

"Tell us about living in that mansion," Laney, our raven-haired counterpart, added from beside me.

"It's big," I explained. "But I live in the basement."

"Now a prince can come to rescue you," Laney said.

"Not in *this* fairy tale," I said.

"There are three guys living there," Holly added. "So, you never know."

"Not likely. The only nice one is a sophomore."

"Fresh meat," Laney said with intrigued eyes. She'd never been one to shy away from the younger guys, while Holly and I always fell for the older ones.

I laughed. "Oh, Sawyer's good-looking. All three Graysons are. But from what he tells me—and from what I've seen, the older ones are a little twisted."

"Seriously?" Holly asked, all wide-eyed and intrigued. "You didn't tell me that."

I nodded as I sipped my drink.

"Twisted how?" Laney asked.

I shrugged, not mentioning the notes Seren had been leaving for me. "Both Sawyer and my mom warned me to stay away from them. So, there's got to be something to it."

"Why are we just learning this *now*?" Holly asked. "Your mom's worked there your whole life."

"She kept that part of her life separate from mine."

"Oh my friggin' Lord," Laney said. She held up her phone, displaying a photo of the Grayson boys in their football uniforms with black paint under their eyes.

"Holy hotness," Holly said.

"You need to introduce us," Laney demanded.

I stared at the photo. There was no doubt they were good-looking guys. But even in the picture, it was clear that both Seren and Saint hid something behind their vacant green eyes. Sawyer was the only one who smiled and seemed to mean it.

"Which one's the young one?" Laney asked.

I pointed to Sawyer.

"Yup. He'll do," Laney agreed.

I laughed.

"A triple date it is," Holly added.

"Which twisted brother are you getting?" I asked her.

"Whichever one will have me."

We all burst out laughing. It felt so good to be laughing with my friends. I didn't realize how much I needed that.

* * *

I pulled into the driveway around four-thirty, after hanging out in the school parking lot for a while before getting on the road. I punched in the code my mom had given me and pulled up the driveway. I parked to the side of the six-car garage where my mom had parked the car.

As soon as I stepped out, I heard a basketball bouncing off the pavement nearby. I grabbed my backpack and shut the car door. When I turned, I spotted all three Graysons playing basketball on the court at the far end of the driveway. I stilled, admiring the sight of them shirtless and laughing. The conversation with the girls at lunch sat heavy in my mind. I was living under the same roof as the hottest guys I'd ever actually seen in person. I was seventeen. I was single. I had eyes.

"Hey!" Sawyer called when he spotted me.

Inwardly, I cringed, hoping I hadn't been caught gawking. I waved then headed toward the basement door.

"Where're you going? Come here!" he called as he walked off the court toward me.

Dammit. I pulled in a breath and reluctantly headed toward him.

Saint and Seren hadn't stopped shooting, but Sawyer chugged a stream of water from his water bottle as he met me halfway.

"I thought you played football," I said.

He smirked. "Have you been stalking me?"

"Obviously. You're a babe."

He threw back his head and laughed. "Football season's over. Luckily, spring practices are starting next week."

The basketball bounced off the rim and rolled toward us. I bent and picked it up, tossing it in the direction of the others. Seren nabbed it. His eyes locked on mine, and I wasn't about to back down so I stared back at him. Our stare-down lasted longer than expected, but I wouldn't be the one to break our eye contact first.

"Aw, fuck," Saint said. "Big brother's met his match."

Seren's eyes cut to Saint and only then did I look away, releasing the breath I'd been holding. Latching onto Seren's cold gaze was hard. But he couldn't think he could do what he wanted, and I'd cower and disappear.

Saint approached Sawyer and me. "Sawyer, introduce me to your friend."

"I'm Grace," I said, not needing Sawyer to talk for me.

"You're the princess being held in the dungeon?" Saint asked, his eyes sweeping over me in an uncomfortable appraisal.

"Let's go!" Seren demanded from the court. Saint looked to him. "Why are you wasting your time with her?"

Anger swelled in my chest. No one elicited the rage in me I felt whenever Seren spoke.

"Just bullshitting with the help," Saint called before he turned and walked back over to him. "You know, you gotta keep them happy so they take good care of you."

My stomach dropped as I glanced to Sawyer who'd yet to follow him. I could see he knew I'd been fooled by Saint's fake kindness.

"See you later, princess," Sawyer offered apologetically before returning to his brothers.

I turned back to the house as they started dribbling again. They carried on as if I'd never interrupted. As if I didn't even exist.

CHAPTER 7

Grace

Darkness shrouded the manor as I hurried to my mom's car the next morning. Before I could open the driver's door, I froze.

No. No. Noooooo.

I circled the car, my hands tunneling through my hair.

Not *one* tire was flat. All *four* tires were flat.

I spun toward the manor. This was no accident. I looked around, but I stood all alone out there. I glanced up at the manor—all dark and cold like some of its occupants. A curtain on the second floor fluttered like it had the night I arrived. I stared up at the window, shooting daggers at the person who'd undoubtedly done it.

Screw it.

I stormed into the house, making my way up the main staircase. I made it to the second floor, passing Sawyer's room and then Saint's. I grabbed the knob on Seren's door and threw it open. I expected him to be in bed, pretending not to have been watching me, but he wasn't. He stood by the window with his arms crossed wearing nothing but black boxer briefs.

"You did that to my tires," I spat.

"Don't know what you're talking about," he said.

I shook my head, my blood boiling. "What's your problem?"

"Well, for starters, having the help barge into my room without knocking is unacceptable."

I narrowed my eyes.

"So is spying on me in the pool house."

My head dropped back. "I told you. I thought someone was being hurt."

"Fucked. She was being *fucked*. Do you not know what that sounds like?" he asked condescendingly.

"Excuse me?" I said aghast.

"You heard me. Don't you let boys back in Coopersville touch you like that?"

My teeth clenched, grinding together as I spoke. "Who do you think you are saying that to me?"

"Oh, so you're a prude," he said.

Ignoring his insult, I held out the palm of my hand. "Give me your car keys."

Humorless laughter burst out of him. "Like hell I'm giving you my car."

"Well, you fucked mine up!"

"Prove it."

Frustration grabbed hold of my body. "How am I supposed to get to school?"

"Not my problem."

Rage flared inside of me. "I will find a ride to school and when I get back, my tires will be fixed."

He moved toward me, closing the distance between us until his toes nearly touched the tips of my sneakers.

He glared down at me. "Do you have any idea who you're messing with?"

"Do you have any idea who *you're* messing with?"

He scoffed. "I've done things that would make your prudish blood run cold."

I swallowed around the lump in my throat, trying to keep up my bravado. "You don't scare me, Seren."

"Then you're a fool."

"Fix my tires," I demanded before spinning away from him and hurrying into the hallway. I dashed toward Sawyer's room, slipping inside quietly. He lay sound asleep beneath his covers looking so peaceful—such a stark contrast to his cold brother. I sat down on the edge of his bed and gently rubbed his arm. "Sawyer?" I whispered.

He stirred.

"I need your help."

His eyes cracked open. "What's wrong?"

"My tires are flat and I need to get to school."

"Flat?"

"Yes."

"I don't have my license yet," he said.

"There's a six-car garage out there. Surely, there's a car that no one uses."

"Keys are in a bowl in the kitchen cabinet above the toaster. Grab the one with the ruby keychain. They're for the Jeep. It might need gas."

I patted his arm. "You're a lifesaver." I jumped to my feet and snuck out of his room, making sure no one heard me creep down the stairs.

I grabbed the keys from the kitchen then found the Jeep in the garage amidst a black Land Rover, a motorcycle, and some black SUVs. The tank was half full which was more than enough to get me to and from school. As I backed out of the garage, I glanced to the second floor where the curtain was pulled back and Seren stood glaring at me. I flashed him my middle finger before taking off for the one place I belonged.

Seren

My pulse pounded in my temples as I raced out of my room and tore down the hallway. How the hell had Grace gotten the Jeep? Scratch that. I knew how she'd gotten the Jeep, but why hadn't I anticipated her move? I prided myself on being a step ahead of everyone. If you didn't know someone's move, they were dangerous. And, since I was the most dangerous person in any room, that shit was not going to fly. Grace needed to know who was in charge. And it wasn't her.

I slammed open Sawyer's door. "Why the fuck did you give her the Jeep?"

He sat on the edge of his bed, rubbing his eyes with the palms of his hands. "Because somehow her tires ended up flat. Don't think I don't know it was you."

"Why does everyone think it was me?" I growled.

"Because you can't stand it when someone isn't fazed by you. You can't understand why your cold demeanor isn't making her fall at your feet."

"Watch yourself, brother."

"Dude, normal people talk if they want to get to know someone. They don't flatten all their tires."

"I don't want to get to know her," I snared.

"*Right.*"

"She's the fucking help!"

"Get over yourself, man. She can't stand you and you hate it."

I pegged him with serious eyes. "You will not help her again."

"You're not my father," Sawyer said.

The hair on the back of my neck stood on end. Sawyer should've looked up to me after our father died, but all I'd done was given him reason to be put off by me. "Yeah. He's dead. And I'm all you've got."

Sawyer's eyes drifted from mine and he shook his head, disgusted by my words. By my actions. By me.

I twisted away from Sawyer and stormed out of his room.

I wanted to be left the fuck alone.

CHAPTER 8

Grace

I hit the garage door opener and pulled the Jeep inside after school. I cut the engine, thankful that all the other vehicles were not in there. I hopped out and went to check my tires. All four were still flat. My heart wilted. I didn't know why I thought Seren would do the right thing. Why I thought he'd reconsider his actions and make things right. But that clearly wasn't who Seren Grayson was.

I hurried into the kitchen and put the keys back into the bowl where I'd gotten them, then I went down to the apartment. My mom was still working. And as much as I wanted to confide in her, I knew that she had a lot on her mind and really wanted our living arrangement to work out. I couldn't let her know that things were not going as planned—at least for me.

I walked into my room and dropped onto my bed. I moved to my closet and pushed my clothes all the way to the left, hesitating before reaching in and pulling the powder blue sweater at the far-right side off its hanger. Tears pricked my eyes as I brought it to my nose and inhaled. My dad's spicy scent still clung to it, so I closed my eyes and breathed it in, imagining him standing beside me. Tears escaped my closed eyes because, just for a moment, it felt like he was really there with me. I missed him so damn much. I couldn't imagine anything hurting worse than the knowledge that I'd never hug him again. Never hear him tell me he loved me. Never be on the receiving end of his bad jokes. Never walk down the aisle beside him on my wedding day. I gave myself over to the grief for a few minutes. But that's all I'd give it. Otherwise, I risked getting lost in it, and that wasn't a place I wanted to stay.

I returned my dad's sweater to its spot in the closet before freshening up my tear-stained face. Then, unsure if the air had been let out of my tires *or* if they'd been slashed, I made a call to an auto shop to come check my tires. They couldn't make it out to the manor until the following day, so it looked like I'd be taking the Jeep again in the morning.

Just before five, I got dressed in my ridiculous uniform and hurried to the manor's kitchen through the back door. Since spring break had ended, I'd begun helping with dinner prep clean-up. I could hear a lively conversation filtering in from the dining room as soon as I took my spot at the sink. I slipped on my rubber gloves and began scrubbing the pots and pans piled up there.

"Then, Saint let the snake loose," Sawyer said, his voice carrying through the swinging door as Janette, the server, moved between the kitchen and dining room with trays of food. "It was hysterical. All the girls were screaming and jumping on their desks."

"*Saint!*" Maureen admonished.

"Someone had to make things interesting," Saint said.

Sawyer laughed.

"I can't believe I haven't gotten a call yet," Maureen said.

"You did. I intercepted it," Saint said as if it was no big deal. "Told them I was Martine and would handle it."

"Stay out of trouble, Saint. I'm warning you," Maureen said, though even I didn't believe her threat.

"What are you gonna do? Ground me?" Saint said.

"She might put you in the corner," Sawyer added.

"You're awfully quiet, Seren," Maureen observed.

I stopped scrubbing the pan and listened. Would he confess to what he'd done to me?

"Where's Martine tonight?" Seren asked, accusation heavy in his tone. "Late night at the office again?"

Silence filled the room. I wondered if he'd hit upon a sore subject or if he just had stepdaddy issues.

"Does that mean you don't know?" he continued prying.

"Let it go," Maureen said.

I could tell the discussion was over when I heard silverware clanking on a plate followed by a chair scraping away from the table. Footsteps neared the kitchen, so I quickly lowered my head and scrubbed away at the pan in the sink. The door swung open.

"Oh, hello," Maureen said.

I glanced over my shoulder hoping she was speaking to Chef, but I was the only one in the kitchen. She looked nothing like the younger photos I'd seen of her. She'd clearly had plastic surgery. "Hi."

"Oh my God." Her face lit up upon seeing me. "The resemblance is uncanny. You look just like your mother did when we were kids. My goodness, you're transporting me back to my days growing up in Coopersville."

I smiled, happy that she remembered she and my mom had once been friends and that my mom was more than just her housekeeper.

"I'm so sorry for your loss, honey," she offered. "I wish I could've made it to the services. I just haven't been feeling well lately."

"No worries. The flowers you sent were lovely," I assured her.

She nodded and an awkward silence passed between us.

"Thank you for setting up my room for me."

She smiled as if proud of her decorating abilities. "I never had a daughter, so shopping for a girl was so much fun."

I nodded. If my mother's relationship with her was any indication of how she interacted with the help, I knew better than to think there would ever be more than brief small talk. I began to turn back to the wet pan in my hands.

"Have you met my boys?" she asked.

I turned back, not sure how much to say. "Sawyer's very nice."

"Am I to take that to mean Saint and Seren aren't?" she asked.

I swallowed hard. "Oh…I just meant…"

She laughed. "I'm teasing you, Grace. My boys are all just as wonderful." And though she seemed like she wanted to believe that, her eyes deceived her. "Maybe you four will be as close as your mom and I were—are," she said, correcting herself.

I shrugged, knowing that was not going to happen. Maybe Sawyer and I would be friends. But definitely not Seren and Saint.

"Well, I'll let you get finished in here. Don't let Chef keep you too late," she said.

"I won't. Nice talking to you," I said.

"You too, honey."

When she left, I couldn't help but wonder what my life would have been like if my mom had been set up on a blind date with Mr. Grayson instead of Maureen. Would this have been my life? And would I have even wanted that?

CHAPTER 9

Grace

I stood beside my car the following morning. All four tires were still flat. So much for wishful thinking that Seren would do the right thing. I hurried back into the house and snuck into the kitchen, opening the cabinet above the toaster and grabbing for the keys to the Jeep. The keys that were no longer in there.

"Looking for something?"

I sucked in a breath and spun around. Seren stood there shirtless and in boxers with sleepy morning eyes and the keys dangling from his finger. If I didn't hate him so much, I may have appreciated the view more, but since the mere sight of him caused nausea to swirl up inside me, I didn't.

"You can put your tongue back in your mouth," he said. "Your ogling's embarrassing."

I opened my mouth to respond but thought better of it since I needed those keys. "Give them to me."

He scoffed. "Should I tell my mother you're stealing our car?"

"Should I tell her you flattened my tires?"

He yawned. "This conversation again? How boring."

I hated this guy so damn much. "Sawyer lent me the car."

"*Yesterday.* Did you ask to borrow it today?" he countered.

I said nothing, the anger swelling inside me becoming almost too much to contain.

"Exactly what I thought."

I was stuck. I had no way to get to school if he didn't hand over the keys. Then, I'd have to tell my mom the truth. She'd talk to Maureen who'd likely believe her son over me. Nothing good could come from telling the truth.

"What's going on?" Sawyer asked as he stepped into the kitchen.

Relief washed over me at the sight of him.

"I was just talking to this thief," Seren said.

Sawyer snatched the keys from Seren's hand and tossed them across the room to me. Luckily, I caught them. "I said she could borrow it." He looked to me with conspiratorial eyes. "Your car's getting fixed today, right?"

I smiled, loving this kid more than I could explain. "Yup. This afternoon."

"Great. So, it's settled." Sawyer glanced at Seren. "Grace is borrowing the Jeep for the last time today. No biggie."

Seren's laser-sharp glare could have cut through a pane of glass, but it didn't scare me. I had the keys.

"See you later, Sawyer." I hurried out of the kitchen and outside the manor. The sun was getting higher and I knew I was gonna be late for school if I didn't hurry. And, at least there, I'd have familiar faces to greet me.

Seren

"Are we partying at your house this weekend or is the wicked witch around?" Christa asked from behind me in physics class.

I shrugged, not sure what the weekend would bring.

"Kiki said you've got a new roommate," she continued.

I spun around, my eyes narrowed. "What?"

"She said she has free reign of the manor." Christa was a shit-stirrer, so she knew exactly what she was fishing for by bringing up Grace.

"She's the help."

Christa twisted a lock of her long red hair around her finger. "That's what Kiki said, but she also said she's hot."

"I don't think she swings that way," I clipped. "And, for future reference, who lives at my house isn't anyone's business."

"Is she staying in your room?" she asked.

Now she was pissing me off. "No one stays in my room."

She held up her palms as if not to push me. "Just asking. Your fans deserve to know the truth about their hero."

I turned back around. "Fuck you, Christa."

"Oh, but you've already been there and done that."

I hated Windham Prep. Scratch that, Windham, New Hampshire. I couldn't wait to get the hell away from this town. In the fall, I'd be playing football in Alabama and be far from the gossip. Far from my mother. Far from my name.

* * *

When I pulled into the garage after playing a pick-up game of football with some of the guys after school, the Jeep was back in its spot where it belonged. I stepped outside and saw that Grace's tires were fixed. The sight pissed me off.

I walked into the house and went right upstairs.

"Seren? Is that you?" my mother called.

I ignored her irritating voice and walked into my room, slamming the door behind me. I slipped my backpack off and hung it on the back of my desk chair, knowing I wouldn't be opening it again until first period tomorrow. Alabama didn't care about my grades now. I was attending for my QB skills. Not because I was a scholar—though I was a lot smarter than most people thought. Sure, I was fucking rich, but that's not what I cared about. I wanted to play football.

Something on my desk caught my eye. The keychain with the crystal ruby on it. Why were the Jeep's keys in my room? Had Grace been in here? I glanced around half expecting her to still be there. I picked up the keys and saw that a piece of paper lay beneath them. Words scrolled in girl's handwriting read: *Thanks so much for your kindness. I left a small token of my appreciation in the bathroom for you. -The Help*

My eyes narrowed as I ventured into the bathroom, immediately spotting my box of condoms on the counter. As I moved closer, I noticed another note with an open safety pin on top of it. *Choose wisely…*

She *wouldn't?*

My lips twitched as I stared down at the safety pin. She was funnier than I expected.

But she wasn't in Coopersville anymore. And she clearly didn't know who she was messing with. If she thought she could get to me that easily, she needed a stark reminder that I could just as easily get to her.

CHAPTER 10

Grace

I woke with a jolt, turning my head on the pillow and grabbing my phone. 4:58. *Shit!* I jumped up, grabbing my uniform from my chair, but something shiny caught my eye on the corner of my desk. *My ring!* I grabbed it, tightening it in my palm and holding it as if it would somehow disappear again if I let it go. It hadn't been there when I'd fallen asleep. I would have seen it. I *know* I would have seen it.

I opened my hand and checked the inside of the ring to be sure it was mine. *My Girl* was engraved in script. A moment of nostalgia washed over me. A moment of peace. A moment of sadness. I'd been trying to occupy my mind with anything but thoughts of my dad. I knew it's what I needed to do to move on. I wasn't trying to forget him. Far from it. I was trying to survive this trauma, and dwelling on something I couldn't change was not healthy.

I slipped the ring back onto my finger where it belonged, promising myself I'd never take it off again. It hadn't been there when I'd searched high and low for it. And, it hadn't been there when I'd fallen asleep. My mom must've found it and placed it there for me to see when

I woke up. The elation of having my ring back almost made me forget I needed to get to work.

"You're late," Chef said as I dashed inside the kitchen. "That's unacceptable."

"I'm so sorry. I fell asleep."

He huffed. "I've got something I need you to do tonight."

"What?" I asked.

"Janette's sick. I need you to serve the food."

"Serve the food?" I repeated.

"Someone needs to," he said.

Inwardly, I cringed knowing I'd have to face Seren.

Chef pointed to a tray that held four bowls of soup on the far end of the center island. "Start with the soup."

"Just so you know, I've never been a waitress," I explained.

"Then don't carry the tray. Just carry two bowls out at a time."

I could handle that. I picked up two bowls and used my butt to push open the swinging door. Maureen and the boys sat around the dining room table, each on their own side. I could feel their eyes on me as I entered, but I kept my eyes down and moved to Maureen. "Excuse me," I said as I placed the soup carefully down in front of her, spilling a tiny bit on the table cloth.

"Where's Janette?" she asked.

"Not feeling well," I explained as I moved to Sawyer to her left and placed a bowl in front of him.

"Thanks, Grace," he said.

Back in the kitchen, I grabbed the other two bowls. My hands began to shake slightly as I carried them into the dining room. Saint said nothing as I placed his bowl down, and then I moved to Seren at the opposite end of the table from Maureen.

As I placed the bowl down in front of him, he whispered, "Nice ring."

Why was he complimenting my ring? Unless…

I stumbled back, unable to believe I hadn't considered it before. Had Seren taken my ring? I hurried back to the kitchen, dragging in a few deep breaths.

"Everything okay?" Chef asked.

"Yup," I lied.

"Well, give them a few minutes to finish the soup then you can go collect their bowls and bring out the antipasto."

I went to the sink and began washing the pans. Why would Seren sneak into my room to steal my ring? What would he gain from having it? I exhaled a long breath. Maybe I was just jumping to conclusions. Maybe, despite our disastrous interactions thus far, he was just being nice for a change and noticed my ring. It wasn't like I'd been wearing it since it went missing.

"Head back in, Grace," Chef said after a few minutes.

I put down the clean pan on the drying rack and walked back into the dining room. I avoided eye contact as I made my way around the table, removing the empty soup bowls in the same order I'd delivered them and finishing with Seren.

"My girl?" he whispered as I leaned in to pick up his bowl. "Interesting sentiment."

A cold chill rushed up my spine. That son of a bitch *had* taken my ring. *And*, he'd snuck into my room to return it—*while* I was sleeping. I hurried back to the kitchen with the bowls.

Was he trying to scare me? Was he trying to show me he could get into my room whenever he wanted to? Get to *me* whenever he wanted to?

"Grab the antipasto," Chef said.

My entire body quivered with anger as I picked up the antipasto dishes from the center island. I balanced all four in my hands and carried them into the dining room, circling the table and serving Maureen, Sawyer, and Saint. I was about to place Seren's dish down when he whispered, "Did some Coopersville loser give it to you?"

That did it. I tipped the dish so the antipasto slipped off it and right into his lap.

He jumped up with lettuce and dressing dripping down the front of his shirt and jeans. "What the fuck?"

"Language!" Maureen ordered.

My hands cupped my mouth, concealing a smile. "Oh, my goodness."

Seren tossed pieces of antipasto back onto his plate.

"Let me get you another one," I offered.

"I don't want it," he spat.

"You sure?" I said, leveling him with my eyes. "Everyone should get what they have coming to them."

He glared at me and, for the first time since I'd arrived at Grayson Manor, I felt like I held the upper hand.

"Honey, it was an accident," Maureen assured him, as if apologizing for me. "That isn't the first accident we've had, and it certainly won't be the last."

"I really am sorry," I said to Seren with a smirk that only he could see. Then I grabbed his dish and went back to the kitchen.

"What happened?" Chef asked as I emptied the remnants of the antipasto into the garbage.

"Just a little accident," I assured him as I put the dish into the dishwasher.

"Well, I'm done with dinner, so wash the rest of the pans and I'll serve the main course."

"You sure?" I asked.

"Positive," he said.

I tried not to giggle as I started cleaning the pans. And as the high from putting Seren in his place slowly began to wear off, the realization hit me. I'd won the fight, but I might've just started a war.

CHAPTER 11

Seren

"What are you doing?" Sawyer asked, startling the hell out of me.

I glanced up from behind Martine's desk in his third-floor office.

"You know you're not supposed to be in here," he said as he stepped inside and closed the door.

"This is our house. Not his," I reminded him.

"You sound childish."

"Spoken by the sixteen-year-old," I countered.

He rolled his eyes.

"What do you want?" I asked, annoyed by his intrusion.

"Just making sure you're not planning on doing anything stupid."

My brows inverted. "Anything stupid?"

"To Grace. You know, after she spilled the antipasto all over you."

The thought of her purposely spilling food on me sent anger coursing through my veins. No one tried to one-up me. But she seemed to keep doing it. And I'd be lying if I said I wasn't curious to see what she did next. "Why do you think I'd do something to her?"

Sawyer cocked his head. "Because it's what you do. You don't let people play you and not pay the price."

"You make me sound diabolical."

"Not diabolical. Nuts."

I flipped him the bird.

He didn't laugh like he normally would. "She's nice, Seren. I don't want you messing with her the way you've messed with people in the past."

I *had* fucked with people in the past. But they'd all deserved it.

"I'll kick your ass if you hurt her," Sawyer warned.

I scoffed at the absurdity of his words. "Are you her bodyguard now?"

"Consider yourself warned," he said before opening the door.

"I don't take kindly to threats, little brother," I said.

He walked out, closing the door behind him.

I couldn't help but smile. I'd taught him well. No one wronged you without repercussions, and though I knew he wouldn't make good on his threat to me, at least he— as well as everyone else in this godforsaken town—knew, Seren Grayson was not someone to fuck with.

Grace

"So, how's life at the manor?" Holly asked from behind the wheel of her car Friday night.

"Different."

"Different good or different bad?" Laney asked from the backseat.

"Well…" I wasn't sure I wanted to tell my friends about the shitty stuff that had been happening. It was easier letting them believe everything was fine. "I'm just trying to find where I fit there."

"If you ask me, it's right between the two older brothers," Holly said.

I rolled my eyes. If she knew the truth, she wouldn't be saying that.

Laney laughed. "You still need to leave the young one for me."

"He's a sweetheart. I wouldn't want you ruining him," I joked.

"*Hey*," she said and we all laughed.

"I'm so happy I'm sleeping here tonight," I said.

"Yeah, I can see how you'd want to stay away from the mansion," Holly teased.

"Or, the male models who live there," Laney added.

"It sounds better than it actually is," I assured them.

The loud revving of motorcycles roared behind us, their blinding lights shining into the car and setting it aglow.

"What the hell?" Holly said, squinting into her rearview mirror.

Laney and I glanced over our shoulders. The lights from the motorcycles were moving closer to the back of Holly's car.

"Oh my God," Laney cried. "They're chasing us."

"Speed up," I urged.

Holly hit the gas. But, the motorcycles sped up too. I couldn't hear anything but the roar of their engines. Then, they swerved, speeding up on both sides of us, slowing once they were beside us. That's when their red and blue lights flashed.

"Dammit," Holly cursed, realizing we weren't being stalked by some road-raged bikers. We were being pulled over by the cops. She hit her blinker and pulled the car to the side of the road.

The cops stopped behind us, removing their helmets and slowly getting off their motorcycles. We sat in silence as one of them stayed at the back of the car while the other approached Holly's side and motioned for her to open the window. She did.

"License and registration," he said.

"Yes, sir." Holly popped open the glove compartment and grabbed her registration.

"Do you always speed up when you're being pulled over?" the cop asked Holly who handed him the registration then began searching in her wallet for her license.

"That was my fault, officer," I interjected. "I told her to speed up."

The cop leaned down and looked across Holly at me. He was younger than expected and had a distinct freckle above the right corner of his mouth. "Trying to evade the police is a felony, ma'am."

"We thought you were crazy stalkers," Laney added.

He looked at her in the backseat. "Do I look like a crazy stalker?"

"Your lights weren't flashing," Holly said to him.

"Step out of the vehicle," he said abruptly, standing up to his full height. "We've got a defiant one," he called to his partner behind the car.

Panic filled Holly's features. "What? I wasn't being defiant."

The cop pulled open her door. "I said, 'Step out of the vehicle.'"

My heart began to race as Holly frantically looked to me before stepping out.

The cop led her to the back of the car.

"Shit," I said.

"This is our fault," Laney said.

The other cop stuck his head in the open door, startling the hell out of us. He said nothing, just opened the center console and rummaged through it. "Does she have any weapons in here?"

"Weapons? What? No!" I shrieked.

"Drugs?" he asked.

"Absolutely not," Laney added.

"How well do you know her?" the cop asked.

"We've known her since first grade. She would never purposely evade anyone," I assured him. My eyes shot to the back window where the other cop now had Holly behind the car. "Please let us go. This was a big misunderstanding."

Laney chimed in. "We thought we were being followed and—"

"The speed limit's thirty-five on this road. She was going seventy. She was jeopardizing your lives and the lives of other drivers," he explained before closing the door and joining his partner at the rear of Holly's car.

We sat there for what felt like hours, our legs bouncing beneath us.

"Can you see anything?" Laney asked, sitting like a statue in the backseat afraid to move.

I looked from my side mirror to Holly's. "No. Why are they holding her there for so long?"

I turned to see what was happening behind the car. The flashing lights continued to fill the car and guilt consumed me. I'd told her to speed up. I all but forced her to do it. Now she was taking the blame.

I turned back around facing the long stretch of road ahead of us. I wanted to help but was unsure what to do. I felt so helpless.

Eventually, the driver's door opened and Holly slipped into her seat.

Relief washed over me. "Are you okay?"

"That was fun," she said.

"Seriously. Are you okay?" Laney asked.

"I'm fine."

"Did they give you a ticket?" I asked.

She shook her head. "They debated it, but, in the end, they just threatened me to keep an eye on you guys at the party."

My eyes widened. "Keep an eye on *us*?"

She shrugged. "Did you see how hot they were?"

Laney laughed and I slouched in my seat, so happy my night in Coopersville wasn't ruined before it even began.

* * *

We arrived at Jeff's backyard party and grabbed drinks, needing to calm the nerves that had minutes before consumed us. A few of our guy friends pulled Laney and me into a game of beer pong. It was so great to be home with people I'd grown up with. People who wouldn't purposely hurt me. I desperately needed this night.

We played a few rounds of beer pong. Laney and I dominated the table until silence swept over the party and everyone seemed to stop what they were doing.

Motorcycles roared in the front of Jeff's house.

"Cops!" someone yelled.

Again?

Everyone scrambled, dumping their cups of beer and rushing to their cars in the front yard before the cops started checking IDs. I looked around, searching for Holly.

Laney grabbed my arm and pulled me toward the gate as the cops killed their engines. We hurried toward Holly's car a few houses down from Jeff's. I twisted back to see how many cops had broken up the party. There were only two. I squinted into the darkness as they removed their helmets. My stomach dropped. The same two cops who'd pulled us over stood there looking proud of themselves for breaking up our fun.

"This is messed up," Holly said as she caught up with us and yanked open the door to her car. "Cops never break up our parties."

I hopped into the passenger seat and looked at her with raised brows. "Exactly."

"Do you think they followed us?" Laney asked.

"Dammit," Holly cursed, just realizing we'd led them to the party.

"Yup," I said.

"If either of you tell anyone," Holly warned.

"Girls night!" Laney proclaimed, causing us to break into laughter.

"Pizza and movies?" Holly asked.

"Sounds perfect," I assured them.

CHAPTER 12

Grace

I pulled into the driveway of the manor the next afternoon. I'd gone from hanging out with friends and being around people who cared about me, to a place I didn't belong. I parked the car beside the six-car garage, a constant reminder that I was inferior to the Graysons.

As I stepped out of the car, I couldn't help but notice all the vibrant flowers blooming in massive pots along the exterior of the mansion. It was as if they'd flowered overnight. I wondered if they smelled just as beautiful as they looked.

"Hey!"

I twisted to find Sawyer heading my way in basketball shorts and a T-shirt. "Hi."

"How was your night away from this place?"

My eyes narrowed. "How'd you know I wasn't here?"

"You didn't serve dinner. At first, I thought you got fired for the antipasto thing. But then Chef said you had the night off."

"Would you have fought to get me my job back?"

He laughed. "Well, do you plan on dropping food in *my* lap?"

"Only if you deserve it."

He laughed even harder. "I *knew* you did it on purpose."

I shrugged. "I have no idea what you're talking about."

His smile faded. "Be careful, Grace. Seren doesn't like it when people try to make him look stupid."

"Consider me warned. No more antipasto in his lap."

"Just know, with Seren, there's a fine line between love and hate," Sawyer added.

"What's that supposed to mean?"

"Boys always pick on the girls they secretly like," he said.

Humorless laughter shot out of me. "You think that's why your brother and I don't get along?"

He shrugged. "I've never seen him this focused on someone before."

"Well, how do I shake his attention because I assure you, it's unwanted."

His lips twisted regrettably. "When Seren wants something, he usually gets it."

Seren

I stood watching out the window of the pool house as my brother spoke to the help like she was one of us. I should've stopped my mother when she said she was going to offer Rosalie a place for her daughter to live. I knew nothing good could come from her being here.

"What are you doing?" Kiki asked, stepping up beside me.

I turned away from the window.

"Oh," Kiki said, spotting Grace in the driveway. "She's always around, isn't she?"

"She lives here."

"She needs to know her place," Kiki said as if *she* lived at the manor.

"She's well aware of her place," I assured her.

"I'm not so sure she does," Kiki muttered as she moved away from the window and slipped off her shirt.

"Put your shirt back on," I said.

"Excuse me?"

"You heard me."

She didn't listen, moving behind me and kissing my neck.

I pulled away, feeling the nothingness of her lips on my skin. "I'm not interested."

She laughed. "Seren Grayson's not interested? Has hell frozen over?"

"Just not feeling it," I said as I walked away from the window, leaving her standing there.

Her gaze drifted back toward Grace and Sawyer. "You were feeling it before *she* arrived."

I ignored her dig, but she wasn't wrong. Since Grace arrived at the manor, I'd been feeling all sorts of things. And I had no idea what to do with that.

Grace

Sunday, I drove into town to do some shopping at the quaint shops that lined Main Street. I bought a pair of earrings and then stopped at a café for a latte. When I returned to the manor, I parked the car beside the garage and stepped out, noticing a shirtless Seren tossing a football with someone at the far end of the driveway. Something about the way he ignored me pissed me off. So did the fact that someone so mean could be graced with such a great body.

The guy tossing the football with him missed the pass and turned my way to fetch it.

I froze.

So did he when he spotted me.

Why was Seren hanging out with the cop who pulled me and my friends over? The same one who broke up the party?

Oh my *God.*

Anger flared inside me. That son of a bitch. He'd taken things way too far. I stormed across the driveway, past the cop, and stopped in front of Seren. "You're an asshole!"

He glowered at me as if I was nothing more than mud on his expensive sneakers.

I pointed to his friend. "He pulled me and my friends over because *you* told him to."

Seren's head hitched back. "*I* told him to?"

The cop tried to conceal his laughter but failed miserably.

I glared at Seren. "I'm not stupid."

"Could've fooled me." He looked to the cop and held up his hands. The cop threw Seren the football.

Seren prepared to throw the football back, but I'd had enough.

I grabbed the ball out of his hand. "Stop this shit!"

Seren reached for the ball, but I held it away from him.

"I said, '*Stop!*'"

He crossed his arms over his bare chest feigning boredom.

"You had him ruin my night. Why?" I demanded.

"While we're throwing questions out there, why'd you drop food in my lap?"

"That's what this is? Payback?"

"I'll give you guys a minute," the cop said, taking off toward the manor.

"Dude," Seren called to him. "The conversation's over."

"The conversation's far from over," I said through clenched teeth as the cop disappeared inside.

Seren scoffed.

"Answer me!"

His eyes narrowed. I knew he didn't like being told what to do. "You're the help. I asked *you* a question. If you want to keep your job, answer *me*."

"I don't care about the stupid job. You can have it. I'm out of this town in a few months and you'll never have to see me again."

He looked as if I'd slapped him across the face.

"This isn't the olden days. People don't have to pay because you *think* they've wronged you. It's messed up. *You're* messed up."

He didn't say anything but his clenched jaw was ticking. I was fairly certain he wanted to tell me to fuck off.

I shook my head and dropped the football. "Have a great life being a cold angry asshole. It looks good on you." I turned and walked back to the manor. I half expected to take a football to the back of the head. Luckily, I returned to our apartment unscathed, having said my peace.

CHAPTER 13

Grace

"Grace?"

I glanced up from my computer screen on Monday afternoon and looked at my teacher.

"They need you in the office."

I looked at the clock. Class was over in ten minutes, so I closed my laptop and stuffed it into my backpack, slinging it over my shoulder. I mouthed goodbye to Holly then walked out of class into the empty hallway and hurried to the office. The secretary smiled when she saw me. "Hi, Grace. Principal Arnold is waiting for you."

"Thanks." I moved to the open door beyond her confused as to why I'd been called there in the first place.

Principal Arnold sat in his high-back leather chair, looking tired and ready to retire. "Come on in, Grace," he said, and I could tell his smile was forced.

I sat down in the chair opposite him and teetered on the edge, not wanting to get too comfortable. "What's going on?" I asked.

"Well. It's been brought to my attention that you no longer live in Coopersville."

My stomach dropped.

"I hate to have to do this to you—especially after all you've been through, but given that you no longer reside in town, you can no longer be enrolled at Coopersville High."

"But—"

"I know this is the last thing you want to hear from me, but it's the rule. And if ever I could make an exception, it would be for you. But I can't."

"Graduation is less than two months away," I argued.

"I know. I brought it to the school committee hoping they'd hear me out, but they feel as if they make an exception this time, they'll be setting themselves up for more requests. They don't want to set a precedence."

Tears pooled in my eyes.

"You need to have your mother call the school to have your transcript sent to your new school."

My new school?

I didn't reply, just stood from the chair trance-like and walked out of his office, not bothering to go back to class. I walked out the front doors and straight to my car. Once inside, I dropped my forehead to the steering wheel and tears poured out of me.

Now, I'd lost everything.

CHAPTER 14

Seren

I leaned against my Land Rover in the school parking lot, waiting to go in. Clouds had moved in, bringing some gloom to the otherwise promising morning.

Christa stepped up beside me. "What are you doing?"

"Just chillin' before heading in," I said.

"What's *she* doing here?" Kiki clipped as she joined us.

I followed Kiki's glare.

Grace, wearing Windham Prep's navy top and pleated navy and green plaid skirt, looked out of place walking through the parking lot filled with expensive cars. But, if I was being honest, she looked better than the other girls in this place. She hadn't been tainted by money and a false sense of superiority. She didn't try so hard to look good. She just naturally did.

Fuck.

I shook off the notion because she'd soon find out for herself that she wasn't like the rest of the girls here. And that realization would come with a price.

"Apparently, her school found out she didn't live in Coopersville anymore," I said.

"Well, this is gonna be interesting," Christa said.

Kiki laughed, and I knew it was only a matter of time before the fun began.

I took off for the building, and like the minions they were, Kiki and Christa followed me.

"You gonna show her around?" Kiki asked.

"I figured I'd leave that job for you," I said. "I know you're interested in her."

"Oh, allow me," Christa chimed in. "I'm a lot nicer than Kiki."

"Hey," Kiki said, pretending to be insulted. "I pride myself on not being nice at all."

Christa laughed, and I left for first period, getting far away from the two of them.

Grace

I wanted to crawl into a ball and disappear as I sat in chemistry class. Who starts a new school the last week of April of their senior year?

I glanced around the classroom. Most of the other students were on their phones as the teacher droned on about element seventy-five on the periodic table: Rhenium. After a painful hour of sitting in a room full of strangers listening to material I'd learned when I was a sophomore, the bell rang. The teacher was still talking but everyone started leaving the classroom. I wanted to ask someone how I could find my next class, but literally everyone was on their phones.

I stepped out into the busy hallway, more confused than ever.

A pretty redhead smiled at me. "You lost?"

"How could you tell?" I asked.

"Well, I know everyone at this school, so I know you're new and chances are you don't know your way around yet."

"Good observation," I said.

She laughed. "I'm Christa."

"Grace."

"Well, allow me to welcome you to Windham Prep. Home of the rich, famous, and ridiculously over-privileged."

I smiled.

"Where're you headed?"

I looked at my schedule. "Room one twenty-two. English."

She ticked her head to the right. "Follow me."

"Thanks."

"What year are you?" she asked as we walked through the crowded hallway.

"Senior. You?"

"Junior. It's kinda late to be transferring," she said, the question evident in her statement.

"My dad died, so I had to move here."

"Oh, I'm sorry," she said.

I shrugged since there wasn't much else to do when people showed you sympathy.

She stopped and extended her arm toward a doorway. "Here's your class."

"Thanks for this."

"I'll look for you at lunch," she offered.

"That would be great. See ya later." I went into the classroom and approached the teacher, introducing myself. She gave me a book and told me to take the first seat in the last row by the windows.

When the bell rang, she began her lecture on *Pride and Prejudice*. Since I'd read the book at least twenty times and seen the movie just as many, I knew I wouldn't be lost—at least in this class.

"What's the biggest problem between Elizabeth and Mr. Darcy?" the teacher asked.

I knew the answer but waited to see what my classmates would say.

When no one offered a response, she pried, "Anyone?"

"Elizabeth had a chip on her shoulder," a familiar voice said from the back of the classroom.

The hairs on my arms stood on end. Not only was Seren somewhere in the classroom, but, of course, he would see Elizabeth as the one to blame for their appalling initial interaction.

"Care to elaborate?" the teacher asked Seren.

"She's like every other girl. She thinks her pride is hurt and hates *him* for it when she should really be hating herself for her reaction. He didn't make her hate him. She *chose* to hate him. You know, free will and all that."

"Wow," the teacher observed. "Most don't interpret it that way."

"How do they interpret it?" he asked condescendingly.

"Any ladies in the class care to answer that?"

I waited. I really did. But no one responded. My arm shot into the air.

"Grace," the teacher said. "You've read the book?"

I nodded. "It's one of my favorites."

"Of course it is," Seren grumbled.

"The initial interaction between Elizabeth and Mr. Darcy is normal human nature," I began. "He knows deep down that he can't have her, therefore, he detests her for *his* feelings. She has every right to hate him for his judgment of her and his appalling behavior toward her. What woman wouldn't? Just like men, women are strong, independent, and proud. If someone challenges that and minimizes our feelings, it's human nature to be angry at that."

I sat back in my seat, kind of expecting a round of applause after that off-the-cuff, yet powerful, monologue, but the room was dead silent. Did the other girls not agree?

"Thank you, Grace," the teacher said. Her warm smile told me *she* at least agreed with me. "That was a great analysis from a woman's point of view." She continued lecturing on the book, noting other instances where maintaining one's pride became an issue.

"Note to the new girl," the girl behind me whispered. "Never challenge Seren Grayson. It never ends well."

The high from my response wore off, and the reality hit me that I was yet again in Grayson territory.

When the bell rang to dismiss class, I took my time leaving so I wouldn't have to face Seren. Not because I was scared of him. But because I just wanted to get through the day unscathed and go home. Sadly, even that notion didn't bring me comfort because it wasn't *my* home.

At lunch, I searched the faces, hoping for a familiar one preferably Sawyer's. Unfortunately, I didn't see him. I did see Christa and breathed a sigh of relief before walking over to her.

"Hi," I said with a smile as I reached her table.

She looked at me as though we'd never met.

"Grace," I reminded her.

"Sorry, no seats at this table," she said coldly.

Heat spread over me, likely radiating from my cheeks.

"There are plenty of seats over there." I recognized Kiki, the blonde from the Grayson's pool house, as she pointed to a table in the corner. "With the other poor kids."

I swallowed the lump in my throat. This had to be some kind of sick joke. People didn't actually behave this way. Did they?

I turned away from them and went to the table she'd pointed out. At least I knew I wouldn't be taking anyone's seat if I sat there. I slipped onto the end of the bench seat and pulled my phone and lunch from my backpack. Holly had already texted ten times to check on me. I couldn't even bring myself to text her back, so I ate my lunch in silence. I'd never felt so alone in a room full of people.

I was glad that gym was my last class of the day. The gym teacher gave me a Windham Prep gym uniform that had the school's logo on it. I changed then joined the rest of the girls in the gym. To my surprise, no one wore the shorts, and very few even changed into the top. *Awesome.*

The teacher directed me to the small group walking the perimeter of the gym while a game of basketball took place on the main court in the center. Since I knew no one, I walked alone. It gave me time to count down the number of school days I had left. Nineteen. I could do nineteen days at Windham Prep. If I could pick up and move to the manor, I could do this. I mentally made a list of all the positives of attending Windham Prep.

One. Short commute.

Two. I could sleep later.

Three. More free time before work.

Four…I'd have to think of a four…

"*Owww,*" I cried before keeling over and clutching my stomach. The basketball that had knocked the wind right out of me, bounced away.

"Oops."

I glanced up.

Kiki stood there with her hands on her hips. "My bad."

I stood up, disguising the pain. "No worries. It takes more than that to bring me down."

"We'll see about that," she said.

I willed myself to shake it off as I continued walking the perimeter of the gym. I kept an eye on Kiki, though, making sure she wouldn't get another chance to hit me.

"Head back to the locker room," the gym teacher called with five minutes left in the school day.

Relief swept over me. I couldn't get back to the locker room quickly enough. I returned to my changing cubby and pulled off my new gym T-shirt, slipping my navy uniform shirt back over my head. Then, slipped off the shorts and shimmied back into the skirt. I grabbed my backpack just as the bell rang and hurried out to the parking lot.

I hadn't realized how much I needed the fresh air. So, I breathed it in as I headed to the back of the parking lot where I'd parked. I stopped short a few yards away from my car. *What the hell?* The entire thing was wrapped in plastic wrap. And not just one layer. It looked as though it had been swallowed by bubble wrap. A sign wrapped underneath on my driver's window read: *Welcome to Windham Prep*

People gathered around my car, laughing and taking photos of it. As soon as someone spotted me, people turned and filmed my reaction. I tried to laugh. Tried to act like I thought it was funny. But it wasn't funny. And, I had no idea how I'd ever be able to unwrap it on my own.

"Did someone call for some scissors?"

I exhaled, relieved to hear a familiar voice.

"Sorry, Grace. These people suck," Sawyer said as he handed me a pair of scissors. "It's better if you do it yourself," he whispered. "Let them think you love it." And then he was gone.

I approached my car and began cutting into the plastic wrap. More photos were snapped, but eventually, the crowd dissipated. Apparently, it wasn't as entertaining to watch me undo their hard work as it was to set up the prank.

After most of the cars had left the lot, I sat down on the curb near my half-wrapped car and waited until every car was gone. I sat until I knew tears wouldn't fall. I sat until I knew I could get all the plastic wrap off without breaking down.

And then I did.

I unwrapped the entire car and drove back to the manor now more than ever determined to prove that I could handle whatever they threw my way.

CHAPTER 15

Seren

"I'm glad you could all finally make it," Arthur Andrews, my dad's lawyer, said as he glanced to my brothers, my mother, Martine, and me seated around the large boardroom table at Grayson Industries.

I leaned back in my swivel chair, taking in the lifeless room. Over the past three years, Martine had taken down the portraits my father had commissioned of our family. My father wanted this company to be our legacy. It felt odd to be there without him. Probably the reason I'd been putting off this meeting. Because I *was* the reason the meeting hadn't happened sooner. And everyone knew it.

"As you know," Arthur continued, "Your father left fifty-one percent of Grayson Industries to his wife, Maureen, until his first-born son turned eighteen and was deemed capable of running the company."

All eyes moved to me. I remained stoic. What were they expecting? This wasn't news to me. I was there when his will was read three years ago. Should anything happen to my father, his business would go to my mother until I turned eighteen. Then, if she thought I was responsible enough, I'd gain control of fifty-one percent of Grayson's Industries, with Martine maintaining his forty-nine percent. Yeah, the guy nearly fell out of his fucking chair when he heard he'd be owning less of the company than me. Apparently, my dad kept that bit of information close to the chest, and Martine only learned of it when we did. Served the douchebag right for taking his dead partner's wife.

"You've been eighteen since September, Seren," Arthur continued. "And you've yet to announce if you'll be accepting your role at Grayson Industries."

I was appreciative that my dad thought I could handle such a huge undertaking—at eighteen. But, I had no intention of taking over Grayson Industries.

"That's because he's playing football in Alabama," my mother explained.

"Well, if that's the case, we have some logistics to work out," Arthur explained.

"What happens if I don't accept my position?" I asked.

"Grayson Industries stays with your mother," he explained.

"What about Saint and Sawyer?" I asked.

"His *first-born* son," Arthur explained, reading from the will in front of him. "If you do not follow through with his wishes, the fifty-one percent stays with your mother who could do what she sees fit with the company."

I glared at my mother. "Would you sell it?"

"Well…I don't know," she said, which told me she totally would. "If you don't want it—"

"After all the hard work dad put into building the company from the ground up, you'd be selfish enough to take the money, wouldn't you? Jesus. Don't you have enough money?"

She said nothing, nor did anyone else in the room.

"Martine stands to lose just as much as us if you sell." I glanced to Martine, who averted his gaze. He'd become such a damn puppet to my mother. "Would you fuck him over too?" I asked her.

"Mouth, Seren," she admonished.

"I'm sure these men have heard worse," I clipped.

"Do you ever intend to work at Grayson Industries, Mr. Grayson?" Arthur asked, redirecting my attention to him.

"I want to play football. I haven't given anything after that a thought." That was a lie. I'd been thinking about what I was gonna do since I'd heard the company was ultimately mine three years ago. Talk about a lot of fucking pressure on a fifteen-year-old who loved football and dreamed of going pro.

"No one faults you for that," Arthur said. "I just have an obligation to your father to see to it that his wishes are met."

"If the company's ultimately mine—"

"Fifty-one percent is yours," Martine quickly corrected me.

Prick.

"Could I give it to my brothers?"

"Your father made it clear in no uncertain terms that his wishes were for *you* to be the principal owner of the company. You knew your father as well as I did. He was stubborn when it came to what he wanted. But underneath all that passionate determination, he always had a huge heart that did the right thing when push came to shove. He knew what he wanted. He wanted *you* to have his company. And he asked that I carry out those wishes if God forbid anything happened to him."

Everyone grew silent because something did happen to him. He lost his life way too soon.

"He wanted this business to remain in the family with you at the helm."

Nothing like trying to guilt me into accepting something I didn't want. I glanced around the table taking in the disappointed faces of my brothers. I was a selfish bastard. Everyone knew that. But they didn't deserve for me to be left the business and act like an unappreciative prick by not accepting it. I glanced to my mother and Martine who were impossible to read before glancing back to Arthur. "It's mine whenever I want it, right?"

"Yes," he agreed. "Unless your mother decides to sell it."

"Seren, you and your brothers will continue to earn money from Grayson Industries whether you accept ownership or not," my mother added. "And if I did sell it at some point—which I have no plans to do, the money would be dispersed to the three of you."

Money wasn't the issue. My father left all three of us more money than we knew what to do with. It was more the idea that I'd lost my father. I didn't want to lose the one thing he'd put his whole heart into creating. It felt wrong. But so did giving up on *my* dream.

I glanced at my brothers. I wished I knew what they were thinking. Sawyer was only sixteen. And though he was the smartest of the three of us, there was no telling where his future would take him. He never once said he wanted to work for Grayson Industries. Saint, on the other hand, was a year younger than me, but he barely managed to pass his classes. And, he was a loose cannon who didn't like being told what to do. Him struggling to hold a job was a legit possibility, but Grayson Industries ensured he'd always be employed.

"Seren?" Martine interrupted my thoughts. "Grayson Industries has been making tremendous strides with our surveillance technology and have prototypes being considered by the military that would prove beyond lucrative for all of us. Selling it now would be absurd and your mother knows this."

At least there was that buying me time. "Well, then. I don't have to commit to anything today now do I?" I jumped to my feet. "I'd say we're done here."

"Are we?" Arthur asked.

Ignoring his question and the eyes of everyone in that stifling room, I walked out. I didn't need to stick around to hear anymore. Because I knew the truth. I couldn't give up my chance at playing football for something that was never my dream.

I was way too selfish for that.

CHAPTER 16

Grace

I wasn't exactly in a rush to get dressed to head back to Windham Prep the following day, but I tossed my backpack on my back and headed out to my car. The cool early morning air hit me, giving me a push to keep a positive attitude, despite the previous day. I opened the driver's door and slipped off my backpack.

"Can I get a ride?"

I glanced over my shoulder at Sawyer heading my way with a big grin. "Where are your brothers?"

"Saint rides his motorcycle, and Seren took off early."

"You sure you wanna be seen with me? I may bring down your popularity."

He laughed as he pulled open the passenger door. "I'm not worried about that. Besides, the saran wrap prank is just a first day thing."

Thank *God*. I slipped into the car and Sawyer did the same. "You sure it won't look like I need a bodyguard?"

"Would me being your bodyguard be a bad thing?"

I thought for a moment then started my engine. "Nope. Not at all."

"Then let's go," he said.

Having Sawyer with me definitely eased my trepidation about going back to Windham Prep. Though,

I wondered if he'd purposely driven with me to be sure I actually made it there.

We parted ways once we entered the front doors of the school, Sawyer heading to the sophomore wing and me to the senior wing on the far end of the building. I walked toward my locker, relieved I'd found my way in the maze of unfamiliar hallways. As I neared my locker, I noticed people looking at me. A pit formed in my stomach. Something was off. It couldn't just be my car that caused their attention. That's when I spotted my locker. The words *Protection from the Grayson Gods* were etched in black marker on the outside of it.

Having no clue what that meant, I ignored all their eyes and unlocked the lock. I pulled open the door and hundreds of condom packets spilled out, piling onto the floor at my feet. Howls of laughter erupted around me. I had no idea how I did it, but I steeled my features, grabbed the books I needed from inside, and slammed the door shut. I headed toward my first class, shutting out the eyes on me and the voices around me. I couldn't get to chemistry class fast enough.

Inside the classroom, the whispering and laughter continued. Luckily, the teacher began his lecture on element seventy-six on the periodic table: Osmium, and the chatter subsided.

I made it through first period without further incident. Once the bell rang and I stepped into the hallway, Christa greeted me. "Hey, you."

I spun around, searching for the person she was speaking to because it *clearly* couldn't be me after the way she'd treated me the previous day.

"*You*, Grace. I was speaking to you," she assured me.

I kept walking as she kept pace with me. "That's surprising. Yesterday you didn't even know me in the cafeteria."

"Oh, you know how things go."

"No. Actually, I don't." I walked faster, trying to lose her but she sped up.

"Careful, Grace. You need friends in a place like this," she warned.

"Yeah, well yesterday I realized we weren't going to be friends."

"Fine." She stopped walking and called, "Fend for yourself, bitch."

Yup. Like I said. We were never going to be friends.

I entered English class and took my seat. I didn't answer any questions because I didn't need to draw any more attention to myself. I'd received enough to last a lifetime, and it wasn't even noon.

I finished the day with my head held high even though inside I was dying to get out of there. Sawyer had football practice, so I'd be driving home alone. I reached my car in the parking lot, expecting something to have been done to it. But, by the grace of God, it was untouched. At least on the surface. I pushed the key into the ignition and held my breath until the car purred to life without some kind of explosion happening. I released a sigh of relief and drove out of the parking lot as quickly as I could.

Seren

Spring football practice had begun after school for the guys playing next year, so Coach had me working with Kramer, the sophomore who'd be the new starting quarterback. Between Grace showing up at school and having to figure out what to do about my father's company, I was having a shitty week. And, since I felt my best when I was on a football field, helping out was a no-brainer.

"Funny prank on the new girl today," Kramer said while we played catch on the sideline, warming up his arm.

"I wouldn't know," I lied.

"I'd hook up with her," Kramer continued.

I clenched my teeth as I caught his pass. "She's our housekeeper's daughter."

"I'm not opposed to slumming it," he said.

A flicker of anger pricked my insides.

"Especially when she's got a tight little body like that," he continued.

The flicker no longer pricked my insides, it spread like a motherfucking blaze. I fired the football into his gut, hoping it took him down.

"*Oomph*," he gasped as the football ricocheted off him and bounced to the ground.

"Keep your hands ready at all times," I barked, equally pissed at him for being a douche *and* me for reacting to him like that.

"Dude, you hummed it at me," he whined.

"A good quarterback is always ready for the unexpected."

He rolled his eyes before grabbing the football off the ground.

I should've taken my own advice because nothing could've prepared me for the jealousy that nearly knocked me on my ass.

CHAPTER 17

Grace

I managed to stay off everyone's radar the next day. At least I hoped I had. At lunch, I found my spot at the "poor kid" table. They didn't whisper or laugh when I sat down. They didn't even acknowledge that I sat there, which was fine by me. I texted with Holly, knowing she would make me laugh. And her texts always made me laugh. In between texts with her, I checked my email to see if there was anything from the Tampa Marine Life Rescue Center regarding the summer internship I applied for. But just like every other day, there wasn't.

The cafeteria began to buzz around me. I glance up from my phone to find too many people looking at me. I glanced behind me hoping they were looking at someone else, but those people looked my way too.

"Grace," someone whisper-shouted.

I spotted Sawyer standing just outside the doorway. He looked nervous and gestured me over. I left my lunch on the table and hurried out of the cafeteria to him. "What's up?"

"You can't freak out," he said.

"About what?"

"Just promise you won't freak out," he pleaded, his eyes concealing something I couldn't discern.

My nerves flared to life. "Okay, you're scaring me."

He clutched his phone in his hand. "Just know this could be a hundred times worse."

"What could?"

He held out his phone and a video of me pulling off my gym shirt in the changing room played on loop to a song that was likely the background music for a stripper's grand finale.

A cold chill rushed up my spine. "Where did that come from?"

"Someone posted it online."

"Well, take it down!" I demanded.

"I didn't post it."

"Well, who did? We need to find them." I was beginning to get frantic. "You can make them take it down. You're a Grayson, right?"

He shook his head, the regret heavy in his eyes. "I'm sorry, Grace. Unless I know who did it—which I don't, it's out there."

"I hate these people," I said, wishing I was anywhere but there.

"Me, too." Sawyer dug his hands into his pockets. He didn't know what to say. My world was continuing to unravel and there was nothing he or I could do to stop it. "I don't want to leave you, Grace, but I was in the middle of a test and pretended I needed to puke. I really need to get back, but I wanted to be the one to tell you. I didn't want you to find out from someone else."

"Thanks," I said, but I didn't know why I was thanking him for bringing me shitty news.

Once Sawyer headed back to class, I returned to the cafeteria to grab my stuff. The attention had grown. Had they all seen the video? I glanced over at Christa and Kiki. They smiled in my direction.

Bitches.

Beside them, Seren stared at me. He wasn't smiling like the girls were. His eyes were narrowed on me like he couldn't fathom why I wasn't falling to pieces.

It's gonna take more than that, asshole.

* * *

In no rush to get back to the manor, I took a detour, pulling off the road at one of the mountain overlooks meant for tourists who needed to stretch their legs amidst God's greatness. Though I lived in New Hampshire all my life, I wasn't immune to the grandeur of the mountains. The lofty peaks held snow even in the spring. The green treetops covered the mountains like a perfect grove. The clouds sat midway up the mountains, giving the impression of heaven on Earth.

I climbed out of my car and sat down on a cobblestone rock wall, just needing time to think. Time to decompress. Time to hate everyone. How could the people in Windham be so different from the people in Coopersville? Sure, they had money. But money didn't automatically create assholes. Sawyer was rich and a sweetheart. Had he just not been tainted yet? Was it just a matter of time before he became cold like his older brothers?

I inhaled a breath of fresh air and tried to clear my mind. The view surrounding me was breathtaking and just what I needed to come down from such a shitty start to my time in Windham. Hell, my entire senior year had sucked. Even back home, once my father became ill and we knew there were no other treatments to save him, life had taken a turn for the worse.

I spun the ring on my finger. It made me feel closer to my dad. And if ever there was a time I needed him, it was now. I pulled out my phone and tapped on my photos. I had to scroll back a bit, but I found what I was looking for—what I was *finally* ready to watch. I tapped on the video and it began to play.

"Shut that camera off, Gracie," my dad said on the screen, looking so young and healthy.

Tears pricked my eyes like I knew they would.

"Not until you tell me I'm your favorite daughter," I said in the video, my voice a little squeakier given I was five years younger.

Laughter tumbled out of my dad and the sound hit me deep, making it difficult to see the screen with the tears glazing my eyes. "Of course you're my favorite daughter. You're my only daughter."

"*Hey*! Is that the only reason?" I asked.

"Come on now. You know better than that."

"Do I?" I asked, totally fishing for compliments.

"You're beautiful," he began.

"Go on."

"You're smart," he continued, causing tears to fall from my eyes as I continued to watch.

"Keep going," I laughed.

"You're talented."

"And?"

He chuckled. "And, you're going to make an amazing marine biologist someday."

"Oh yeah? Why's that?" I asked.

"Because I've seen firsthand how animals are drawn to you. Hell, everyone's drawn to you," he assured me. "Because they can sense they can trust you."

"I love you, Dad."

"I love you more, Gracie," he said, smiling into the camera.

Tears streamed down my cheeks as the video ended. As hard as it was to watch, I needed to see it. Because no matter what these rich kids in Windham threw my way, I'd handle it. I'd learned from the best. My dad had been a fighter. All the way to the bitter end, he'd fought. Fought to stay here for me. Fought to stay here for my mom. Fought until he couldn't fight anymore.

Sure, I'd been through hell. But, nothing these people did would make me cower. I'd fight like my dad fought. He wouldn't expect anything less from me.

Seren

I stormed into the house after a bad fucking day at school. I hated when things were out of my control, and things at school suddenly felt like they'd taken an unexpected turn—without my permission.

"Oh, Seren. I didn't know you were home already." My mother stood at the kitchen island, dark circles plaguing the areas beneath her eyes.

"You look like shit."

"Mouth, Seren," she reprimanded. "I don't feel well. I'm having those sharp stomach pains again. I was up all night."

"Don't you think you should see a doctor?" I paused. "Actually, it didn't help dad, so you'll probably end up like him whether you go or not."

"You *would* like that, wouldn't you?" she snapped. "Me six feet under?"

I shrugged. "You'd be reunited with your one true love, wouldn't you?"

She rolled her eyes. "Another dig at Martine? *Really*? I thought you'd gotten past your animosity toward him."

"Never happening," I assured her.

"Oh, that's right. You've got it all figured out."

"That's right, *Mother*." The word dripped off my tongue with disdain. She was anything but a mother. "I know all your secrets."

"Try thinking of someone other than yourself for a change," she spat.

Her words stung, especially since she was the most selfish person I knew—and that was saying a lot given I lived in Windham.

"Did you want me to grow old alone?" she asked, laying on the drama. "Would that have made the almighty Seren Grayson happy?"

"Nothing makes me happy. Thanks for that." I turned away and walked out. The sight of her made me sick.

Grace

I arrived back at the manor shortly before my shift in the kitchen and spotted Seren shooting baskets alone. I ignored him and headed toward the house.

"What? No tongue lashing?" he called. "Is your *pride* too hurt?"

I stopped in my tracks, turning slowly toward him. "You would be enjoying this."

"Enjoying what? Watching my people remind you of your place?" He shot a basket as if he hadn't just started the conversation.

"I'm glad you lump yourself together with them. You're just as much of an asshole."

"Never said I wasn't."

Something about the cavalier way he said it struck me. "Oh, my God." How had I not realized it? "*You* called my school."

His eyes narrowed. "What?"

"You told my school that I moved here."

"I have no idea what you're talking about."

A humorless laugh escaped me as I examined his face, looking for even the slightest show of remorse. I found nothing. "Why are you trying to destroy my life? Because I found you in the pool house with some whore? It's not like you try to hide it. Or, was it the food in your lap? Because I've gotta tell you, what you're doing to me is a hundred times worse."

His teeth clenched and his jaw ticked but he didn't respond.

Well, if he wanted to keep playing his games and acting like I was the crazy one, I had news for him. He'd never break me. "Is your life so boring—so unfulfilling—that you need to mess with mine?"

He just stared at me, and his silence pissed me off even more.

"Why are you like this?"

Seren

I stared at the hate in Grace's eyes. It was a hell of a question she'd asked. But did she really want to know the answer?

I contemplated telling her the truth. Telling her she was all wrong about me? Telling her it was my mother's fault I was like this. Telling her that the two of us weren't that different? But, would she believe me? Or, was it safer to keep letting her believe the lies?

I didn't like Windham any more than she did. I saw these fake people for what they were.

And, though her question still hung in the air and she awaited a response, I did what Seren Grayson always did when challenged. I glared across the space between us like all of this was her fault.

As if she was wrong for wanting to know.

As if she started this back-and-forth between us in the first place.

As if she was beneath me.

"I hate you," she scowled, before spinning away from me and hurrying to the dungeon.

She should hate me.

It was better that way.

I was a selfish bastard who hadn't felt anything since the day his father died.

Scratch that…since Grace first stepped foot at Grayson Manor.

CHAPTER 18

Seren

At lunch the next day, I straddled the bench seat at my table watching all the insecure wannabes posting selfies to social media while the people around me talked about ridiculous nonsense that wouldn't matter in a year from now—hell, it didn't matter now.

Everyone started to whisper.

I twisted on my seat.

Grace entered the cafeteria with her head held high, like the room wasn't filled with a swarm of piranhas eyeing her—and likely envisioning her in her bra. She lifted her chin and straightened her spine as if these people couldn't touch her. But they could. People always targeted those they saw as weaker than them. *Beneath* them.

I knew the day had already sucked for Grace. She couldn't enter a single class without guys whistling or playing the music from the video for all to hear. I knew it could've been worse. She wasn't naked and ultimately wore what she would've worn to the beach. But, the accompanying music and the slow-mo effect made it look a hundred times worse. And, despite me allowing her to hate me, the knowledge that people were spreading the video around like it was funny to them, had me on edge.

"Nice rack!" a guy shouted across the room.

The room erupted in laughter. Grace winced for a beat but her steps never faltered as she made a beeline for her normal table in no-man's land.

The music from the video played loudly and there was more laughter.

My stomach churned.

"Shake 'em," a guy shouted from somewhere else.

Rage flared inside me like it had when Kramer brought up Grace. I tried squashing it, but it took hold of my legs, and I jumped to my feet. "Shut the fuck up!" My voice reverberated around the room silencing everyone.

People swiveled in their seats to see who'd yelled, but my eyes were on Grace who'd stopped in her tracks. You could hear a fucking pin drop.

"Knock this shit off!" I continued, the anger in my voice leaving no room for confusion.

Grace continued walking to her table and sat down.

The normal buzz in the cafeteria eventually resumed, but I was pretty confident everyone was talking about my outburst.

I kept my eyes on Grace. Her eyes averted mine which pissed me the hell off. I'd just helped her, and she showed nothing. Not appreciation. Not relief. Nothing.

So much for taking my mother's advice and thinking of someone other than myself.

Instead of sitting back down, I stormed out of the cafeteria, needing to clear my head because I knew full well why I'd stood up for her, and that shit was not going away.

I'd been the king of hazing at Windham Prep, but it all just felt empty. Now, Grace had become a pawn in the immature game I'd started in a desperate attempt to feel something after my father died.

I thrust open the exit door and walked out into the parking lot. The cool air couldn't touch the heat coursing through my veins. My day was over, and I needed to be out of that place. It had suddenly become too small for both Grace and me, and I didn't know what to do with that.

Grace

I picked at my sandwich, furious that the one person I hated the most in this town had come to my rescue. There had to be something to it. He'd probably be expecting something from me in return. Something he could hold over me. *As if I owed him anything.* He was the one who wanted me here. He wanted this. So why stop it?

When the bell rang, I headed into the hallway and right out the exit door. I hadn't planned on skipping the rest of my classes, but what were they gonna do? Kick me out with a month left?

The cool air was a welcome sensation. I couldn't get to my car fast enough and was shocked to see Seren leaning against the hood. Had he expected me to run like I had? "Get away from my car."

"Is that any way to treat the person who just saved your ass?"

"Saved my ass? It wouldn't have been necessary if you hadn't brought me to your school in the first place."

Anger tightened his features.

"What? Did you think it would be more fun watching me get bullied by your rich friends?"

His eyes narrowed.

"Are you disappointed that I haven't shed tears in a room full of vipers? Are you not getting the response you hoped for? Tell me, Seren. What more do you want from me?"

His eyes itched to pull away from mine, but I could tell the internal battle to hold his own raged within him.

"I thought my dad dying was as bad as it could get," I said, exhausted by everything that happened to me. "But then I had to move here." My arms spread, indicating the grounds around me. "I got torn away from the only friends I'd ever known. Now, I've got to endure entitled assholes who want to hurt me for no reason other than it's entertaining for them. How much more should I have to take?"

Seren's eyes dropped away from mine, focusing on his expensive sneakers.

"What's wrong? Did you forget I might actually have feelings?"

"Stop!" His eyes lifted to mine. They were cold and empty and impossible to read.

I crossed my arms. "You first."

"Whatever." He pushed off my hood and walked away, leaving me standing alone in the parking lot wondering what I'd have to endure next.

CHAPTER 19

Grace

I didn't go straight to the manor. Instead, I headed back to the overlook to clear my head. My phone rang and it was Holly. I lifted the video call and saw Laney and Holly in the frame.

"Hi," they sang, excited to see me.

I smiled because they were the two people in this world that made me the happiest. "Hi."

"How's it going?" Laney asked.

"I miss you guys," I said, trying to deflect the conversation so I didn't have to explain how it was really going.

"We miss you," they said.

"I miss you more."

After chatting for a few minutes and getting filled in on all the Coopersville gossip, we said goodbye and I headed back to the manor. I pulled into the driveway a little before four and was relieved to see no one playing basketball. I parked the car, stepped out, and headed for the manor.

"Got a minute?"

I tensed, the sound of Seren's voice sending a cold shiver skimming down my spine. He was on the bench by the door, his elbows on his thighs and his hands linked in front of him. He looked like any other hot guy. So athletic. So good-looking. So normal. But Seren Grayson was anything but normal.

"I didn't tell your school you lived here," he explained.

My head hitched back, confused by his sudden confession. "Who did?"

He shrugged. "Maybe some of those people you call friends back home."

"They wouldn't do that."

"Assholes don't only live in this town."

I crossed my arms, not sure what else to do.

Seren stood up and ticked his head toward the back lawn. "Walk with me."

My forehead creased. "Why?"

"Because I want to talk."

I scoffed. "I'm not going anywhere with you."

"Why not?"

"Because I don't owe you," I said.

"Owe me?"

"Isn't that why you yelled at everyone?"

"So, you'd owe me," he repeated for clarification.

"Yes," I said.

"You've got nothing I want," he said, his dismissive tone reminding me why I hated him so much.

"Well, if I've got nothing you want, there's no need for me to go anywhere with you." I turned and began walking toward the manor. *He had some freaking nerve.*

"Please, Grace," he said, his voice low and regretful. "Don't go."

CHAPTER 20

Grace

I made it three steps before Seren's words stopped me in my tracks. It was the first time I'd heard Seren beg anyone for anything.

His footsteps moved closer until he stepped beside me. "Just give me a few minutes."

"Why should I?"

"Because I need to talk to you," he said.

I didn't want to walk with him. I didn't want to spend time with him at all. He'd made my life miserable from day one. But, if I didn't listen to him, I'd always wonder. And who knew? Maybe we'd somehow come to a compromise, and I'd be able to finish school without any more issues. I relented on a sigh. "Fine."

He didn't give me a chance to change my mind. He took off toward the back lawn. He was taller than me by a foot, but I managed to keep pace with his long strides. We walked down the brick path. Beautiful pink flowering bushes encased us on either side. I expected him to stop in the pool area or at the pool house, but he kept walking past them. Our footsteps were the only sounds as we ventured further away from the manor. When he took a turn at the edge of the property where the beautifully manicured lawn met the dirt of the bordering woods, I realized where he'd taken me.

"Wow," I said, stopping and tipping my head back so I could admire the well-constructed treehouse up in one of the massive trees. "Did you build this?"

"With my dad."

"Can we go up?"

"Would you like to?" he asked, surprised by my request.

"Obviously."

He gestured toward the five wooden planks nailed into the tree trunk. I climbed up first, pushing on the trap door at the base of the house and folding it over. I climbed inside. The enormous tree trunk grew through the center of the treehouse. I spun around, taking in all the cool features they'd built. Seren joined me inside and watched as I admired the layout. Glass windows were on two of the walls. Benches were nailed around all four walls. One windowless wall had old pictures tacked to it.

I glanced to Seren standing across the treehouse. "This is the coolest thing I've ever seen."

He nodded, agreeing with my appraisal.

I moved to the wall of photos, examining them closely. All three boys and their dad were in them. They were so young and innocent. So happy. A knot twisted in my stomach seeing their smiling faces. I was in their shoes. And, those authentic smiles disappeared with the death of a parent. Sure, they were replaced at times with forced smiles and fake happiness, but the authentic ones were gone forever. "I wish I had a cool place like this when I was younger."

"Yeah. We were lucky my dad knew a thing or two about construction."

"And technology?" I said, knowing Grayson Industries was a tech company.

"Yeah, his company's cutting edge."

I turned slowly and met his gaze. "I'm sorry you lost him."

"We thought he was a racehorse. Turns out even racehorses can fall." He was quiet for a moment before he added, "I'm sorry you lost yours."

I pulled in a silent breath, unprepared for kindness of any sort coming from Seren. Why had he taken me to this place that held memories for him? I turned back to the wall of photos. Sawyer had been so small. And, Seren had always been broad. And their eyes. Those green eyes were so otherworldly.

"If you ever need to get away, you can come up here," he offered.

"I won't need to get away if you stop giving me reasons to," I said.

He didn't respond, so I glanced over my shoulder at him.

Coldness had overtaken his eyes. "I had nothing to do with any of that stuff at school."

I turned to face him. "Bullshit."

"I'm serious. I knew something would happen because you're new—and since girls are jealous that you're living here, but I didn't do any of it."

"Prove it."

"How would you like me to do that? All I have is my word." There was honesty in his response that I *almost* believed.

"Then, what *did* you do?"

He dragged his teeth over his bottom lip, likely considering if he should fess up or not. "Let the air out of your tires."

"Why?"

He shook his head, averting my eyes. "It was stupid."

"Why, Seren?" I demanded. "What would you gain from flattening my tires?"

He was quiet for a moment. Then, his eyes cut to mine. "You'd need me."

My head flinched back. "Need you?"

He cocked his head, his eyes trying to convey something I just couldn't understand. "I would've gotten to spend time with you," he admitted, his words coming out pained as if he hated hearing himself say it aloud.

"But you hate me," I said, completely confused by what he'd revealed.

"I hate the way you look at me."

My brain fought to catch up with his words. "I'm just giving you back what you give to me."

Indecision mixed with regret clouded his eyes. I couldn't fathom why the truth would affect him. "You would've seen I wasn't such an asshole if I was the one driving you to school. You'd get to know the real me. But then Sawyer offered you the Jeep, and that just made me hate you more because you clearly didn't need me."

My mind spun. He hated me. Then he didn't hate me. Then he did? I could barely keep up with the craziness. "I came to your room that morning," I reminded him. "You could've offered me a ride then."

"I don't like being accused of something."

"Accused of something *you* did!" I closed my eyes and shook my head, feeling completely exasperated. "You're not making any sense."

"Jesus Christ, Grace. Do you need me to fucking spell it out for you?"

Was he seriously getting annoyed with *me*? "No. I don't need anything spelled out for me. Because I don't need anything from you."

He growled deep in his throat as he stalked toward me, causing me to backpedal until I bumped into the wall behind me. He pressed his hands to the wall on either side of my head, caging me in.

My eyes widened as my heart nearly jumped out of my freaking rib cage. Did I call for help? Scream bloody murder?

"I cannot stop thinking about you, Grace."

It was as if his words sucked all the air right out of the treehouse.

"You're on my mind from the second I wake up until the second I fall asleep."

What. The. Hell?

"I've tried hating you for it. I've tried avoiding you. I've tried making you hate me. But none of it makes it go away."

I swallowed the lump in my throat. "But you hate me," I repeated because what he was saying, and the way he was currently gazing down at me, did not align with the cold, heartless way he'd treated me up to this point.

"Didn't you hear me? I don't hate you, Grace. I hate everything you're making me feel, and I wish I could just snap my fingers and make it all disappear."

"Do you want it to disappear?" I asked, my voice a mere whisper.

"Do *you*?" His eyes riveted between mine as if trying to read my reaction.

Good luck with that because my mind was reeling like a loose kite string. Our heaving chests mirrored one another as thick tension closed in around us. His proximity caused me to inhale his expensive cologne. It smelled the way every hot guy should smell—heavenly. "I'm definitely confused right now."

His eyes didn't waver from mine.

"You do realize you just dropped a whole lot on me, right?"

"So?"

"So? You don't even know me."

"I know after I was a complete asshole to you, you charged into my room to call me out on my shit. I know you wouldn't let some stupid pranks stop you from walking into school every day with your head held high like a badass. I know when girls are bitches you put them in their places. I *know* you, Grace. And, I like what I know."

"Well, I don't know you," I countered, feeling overwhelmed, confused, and at a loss for how I should feel.

"What do you want to know?" he asked as if he was willing to lay it all out on the table for me.

"I'm gonna need more than that."

He inched closer to my face, taking that as an invitation.

I sucked in a sharp breath, knowing it wasn't an invitation. On the contrary, it was the truth. I didn't know him. And, what I did know, I didn't like. I needed to get out of the treehouse. I needed time to process what he'd said and try to wrap my head around how I felt about it.

His lips inched dangerously close to mine. "Tell me to stop."

"Stop," I said.

"You don't sound so sure about that," he goaded. "Tell me to leave."

"Leave," I said, knowing my tone didn't hold much conviction. In my defense, having a hot guy admit he wanted me the way Seren just had was unnerving and over-freaking-whelming. And, I wasn't immune to his good looks.

His lips quirked. "You sure that's what you want?"

"Would a knee to the balls convince you?"

He laughed. "It would certainly kill the mood."

I hated the way the sound of his laughter burrowed its way deep inside my chest since it was the exact opposite of how our interactions usually ended. I wanted to know who the real Seren was. Because the things he'd said made me want to believe there was more to him than I initially thought. "You show me the real Seren, and I'll consider what you said." I quickly slipped out from beneath his arms and moved toward the tree trunk. I needed to get down the steps and as far away from him as I could.

"Grace, wait," he said.

"No, I need to go," I said before stepping through the trap door and climbing down the plank steps, careful not to miss one. I dashed away from the treehouse and hurried back out onto the path and toward the house.

What the hell just happened in there?

Since arriving at Grayson Manor, Seren had been awful to me. His words. His actions. His disdain for all things me. *And,* he admitted he'd let the air out of my tires then hated me for blaming him for it. *Who did that?* But, now I had insight into why he'd acted that way. But did it make it better? Or, did it just prove he was more whacked-out than I initially thought? Yes, he was gorgeous beyond reason. But that's where the attraction ended for me. There couldn't be anything worth salvaging because we had nothing.

The sound of Seren's shoes on the path behind me neared. "Grace!"

Shit.

I considered picking up the pace and ducking into the manor before he could reach me, but I wasn't a child. I could face my issues head-on. And Seren was *definitely* an issue. I stopped and twisted around.

He stopped in front of me, and for a moment I allowed myself to see him in a different light. He wasn't a cold-hearted guy. He'd lost a father and just dealt with his issues unlike anyone else I knew. But now he'd been honest. Was that enough to make me want to know him?

"What?" I asked.

Instead of responding with words, his lips crashed down on mine. Heat spread over my body, and a tingling I'd never experienced before numbed my lips. He slipped his arms around my hips, pulling me against his rock-hard chest and fitting me against him as if I belonged there. But I didn't belong there. I pressed my hands to his chest, ready to push him away, but I couldn't bring myself to do it just yet. He kissed me as if starved for the taste. His tongue slid between my lips and parted them effortlessly. I opened slightly, and we became all tongues and teeth and lips, a perfect collision of hate and heat. It was intoxicating and all-consuming. I felt the kiss everywhere. I felt *Seren* everywhere. Before I knew what was happening, he pulled away leaving me breathless.

Stunned and a little dazed, I looked to him for an explanation. But instead, a smirk crawled into his cheek. Anger flared inside me, and I shoved him away from me with all my might.

He barely stumbled back and his smirk remained firmly in place.

"You can't just do that!" I admonished.

"You said to show you the real me."

"I didn't mean like *that*." My exasperation was palpable.

Dimples dug into his cheeks. "You should've specified."

I wasn't sure if I was pissed or relieved that the uptight and normally cold Seren Grayson morphed into someone young and carefree right before my eyes. And, the fact that he was an amazing kisser didn't hurt either. I shook off the thoughts. "You can't just take what you want when you want it."

"Why not?" he asked so casually that I knew he meant it.

"That's not how it works. You need to earn it. You need to get to know someone."

He buried his hands casually in his pockets. "That's what I was trying to do."

I growled in frustration.

"And so you know, that was only a glimpse of how I really wanted to kiss you, Grace."

Ugh. Why did I like the way my name rolled off his tongue? I needed to fix this, and I needed to fix it fast. "Well, now that you got it out of your system, we can go back to hating each other." I turned to walk away, but his hand shot out and caught my wrist, stopping me. I didn't dare turn around as my heartbeat drummed faster, betraying me on so many levels.

"That didn't come close to getting it out of my system," he said, the rasp in his voice telling me he was serious. "And, I don't want to hate you anymore."

I closed my eyes, *really* needing to be away from him so I could process the craziness that just went down.

He finally released my wrist, but his grasp branded my skin like a hot vise grip and I couldn't shake the feeling of it despite how hard I tried. I hurried up to the manor, and this time he didn't follow me.

Had he really been treating me coldly because the alternative was falling for me? All of it seemed so outrageous. But I wasn't in Coopersville anymore. People in Windham controlled other people better than they controlled their own emotions. And, apparently, I was the chink in Seren Grayson's armor.

CHAPTER 21

Grace

I'd stayed in Coopersville at Holly's, needing the weekend away from Grayson Manor to think about what had happened with Seren. To rethink the kiss, my reaction to the kiss, and my confusion over his one-eighty. Holly and Laney were all #TeamSeren, loving that he'd saved me in the cafeteria and then declared his actual feelings for me. They hung on every word of my story like it was some kind of fairy tale. But nothing about my time around Seren had felt like a fairy tale.

Maybe I wasn't being fair.

Sure, he and I had gotten off on the wrong foot when I arrived at the manor, but maybe I'd misread everything. I'd seen it one way, and he'd been seeing it differently because he was coming at it from another place. A place I'd never even considered.

I'd assumed he'd done all the crappy stuff to me, but I'd been wrong. Maybe I needed to forgive his actual indiscretions because now I knew they were done out of feelings he was having for me that he didn't want to be having. Maybe I never met the real Seren until now.

I wasn't Elizabeth Bennet from *Pride and Prejudice*. I could admit when I may have been wrong. I could move past the bad and see the good. Maybe I'd been ignoring all the good things about Seren. He *had* stuck up for me in front of the entire cafeteria. He *had* tried to get me to need him to drive me to Coopersville (albeit in a screwed-up way). He *had* tried to push me away because he knew he was no good for me. He *had* admitted he'd done some messed-up stuff.

Maybe forgiveness was what I needed to take away from my time in Windham. And, maybe I needed to start with Seren.

*　*　*

At school on Monday, most people looked away as I passed by. No laughter or whispering followed me down the hallways. It seemed as though Seren's threat in the cafeteria had worked.

I spotted Seren standing by his locker on my way to chemistry. My anxiousness about seeing him after what happened quickly morphed into a pit in my stomach. Kiki stood plastered to his side, her arms wrapped around his hips from the side as she whispered into his ear. She wasn't hanging on him the way a friend would. She was hanging on to him the way a girlfriend would.

"Bitch," Christa called as I moved by them.

Kiki pulled her attention away from Seren long enough to add, "Whore."

Whore?

Did they know what happened with Seren and me? I looked to Seren, hoping to find an explanation behind his eyes, but he avoided my stare.

What the hell?

Kiki reached up and tunneled her fingers into the back of his hair. I was about to avert my gaze when she pulled his mouth down to hers.

That caused me to look away as my stomach roiled. My heartbeat thrashed off the wall of my chest as I hurried to class. My mind whirled as I wove myself through the crowded hallway. Had I really been that stupid? That gullible? That naïve?

He played me.

Again.

And I let him.

I gave everything he'd said in the treehouse credence. And it all ended up being a lie—another way to pay for my "crimes" against him.

And I fell for it.

Hook. Line. And sinker.

I struggled to focus on the teacher's lecture on element eighty on the periodic table: Mercury. He had all sorts of show-and-tell objects including large thermometers and fluorescent lamps, but his words were a jumble of discernable sounds.

The good thing about being blindsided by the truth was that I didn't even care about anyone around me as I walked down the crowded hallway toward English class the following period. I wondered who knew about what happened in the treehouse. Had that been recorded like my "strip show" had been?

I noticed a huge sign over the hallway doorway: *Prom Countdown*. A number twelve flapped to the side of the words. Beneath it must've been the remaining numbers so they could be torn off to assist with the big countdown. I wondered if anyone planned to ask me to the Coopersville prom because now, more than ever, I needed to be around people I could trust.

I slipped into my seat in English class, avoiding looking to the back of the classroom. I couldn't stomach the sight of Seren. How could someone be so deceitful? So cruel?

He entered the classroom just as the teacher stood behind her podium shuffling through papers, but instead of walking to his seat in the back of the room, he crossed in front of the teacher and walked right over to me. "We need to talk."

"No, we don't," I said, not bothering to look at him.

"It wasn't how it looked," he explained.

I kept my eyes down. "It has nothing to do with me."

"I pushed her away," he explained with desperation in his voice.

I glanced up. "Good for you."

He growled, but instead of causing more of a scene, he trudged to his seat.

"Settle in everyone," the teacher said. "Today, I want to discuss character motivation. Mr. Darcy came to Elizabeth's aid when she needed his help. She didn't ask for it, nor would she have ever expected it, but he assisted in bringing dignity back to the Bennet name after Lydia's actions with Wickham would have dishonored them all. The question is why? After everything that happened between Elizabeth and Mr. Darcy, what motivated him to come to her rescue?" She waited for a response from the class, but as usual, the class was silent.

"Because he cares about her," Seren said.

Goosebumps raced up my arms at the sound of his voice. I hated my body's reaction almost as much as I hated myself for wanting to believe he wasn't just speaking about the book.

"He didn't always know how to show it based on their different places in society," Seren explained. "He was at odds with himself for falling for her in the first place. He knew it was wrong, but he just couldn't help himself."

If he'd actually been being truthful in the treehouse, there would've been an undeniable parallel between the novel and our situation. But since it had all been a lie, we were more like Mr. Wickham and Elizabeth. Destined to be enemies.

"So, you're saying actions spoke louder than words when it came to Darcy and Elizabeth's relationship?" the teacher asked Seren.

"I don't know. I just know the guy had it bad for her. But, he sucked at communicating that without pissing her the hell off. He figured why not try another approach to make things right between them."

The teacher stared in Seren's direction for a long moment before breaking into a grin. "Good answer, Mr. Grayson."

It *was* a good answer. Too bad it didn't fix our situation. He'd lied. And I was too smart to fall for his lies again.

* * *

I hurried toward the kitchen, still tying the ridiculous apron around my waist as I rushed through the open door. "*Oof,*" I cried as I slammed into someone and fell back, landing on my ass.

"Oh, no. Let me help you," a man with an Italian accent said as he reached for my hand and pulled me to my feet. "Are you okay?"

I nodded, realizing I'd literally run into Martine, Maureen's husband—and Seren's stepfather.

"You must be new," he said. "I would've remembered such a pretty face."

"I'm Grace."

His eyes narrowed as if he was trying to figure out how he knew that name.

"Rosalie's daughter," I explained.

"Ah. Yes. Maureen said you moved in. I didn't realize you were working here, too."

"Just saving money until I leave for college."

"This fall?" he asked.

I nodded. "I was accepted to the University of Tampa."

"That's wonderful."

"Yeah. I'm hoping to go early if I get the internship at the Tampa Marine Life Rescue Center I applied for."

His eyes widened, intrigued. "Sounds exciting."

Chef entered through the swinging door between the dining room and kitchen. "Oh, good. You're here," he said to me. "Good evening, Sir," he said once he noticed Martine.

"Chef," Martine acknowledged him as he picked up a mug of steaming hot tea from the center island. "It was nice meeting you, Grace," he said before moving into the dining room.

"What did he want?" Chef asked me once Martine had disappeared.

I shrugged. "Tea?"

Chef busied himself at the oven while I pulled on my yellow rubber gloves and began scrubbing the pans.

The door flew open. I looked over my shoulder as Seren stalked toward me. "I need to talk to you."

I continued scrubbing my pans. "I'm working."

"Chef, I need her for a second," Seren demanded.

Chef shooed me away with the back of his hand.

"Who will clean these pans?" I argued, my wide eyes pleading with him to make me stay.

"Go," Chef said.

I cursed under my breath as I tugged off my rubber gloves and slapped them down on the counter.

Seren moved to the kitchen door that led outside. I begrudgingly followed him out, stopping a few feet away from the door as he kept walking out onto the back patio. He quickly spun around, capturing me in his gaze. "What did he say to you?"

"What?"

"*Martine.* What did he say to you?" he demanded.

"You stormed in there to ask what Martine said? *Really?*"

"Yes."

I spun away from him, heading back to the door. "You've got some nerve."

"Grace."

I kept walking.

"Grace, I'm sorry."

I stopped, inhaling a deep breath before spinning around to face him. "For what?"

He at least had the decency to look remorseful. "Today."

"Were you trying to make me look like a fool?"

"No."

"Were all of your friends laughing at me for thinking you'd actually been truthful with me?"

"I *was* truthful with you."

"Right. You know, I'm not even disgusted with you because you did what Seren Grayson does. I'm disgusted with myself for actually believing you. And, *God*," I winced. "You kissed me then turned around and kissed *her*."

His teeth ground together. "I told you. Kiki tried to kiss me but you didn't stick around long enough to see me push her off me."

I rolled my eyes.

"I screwed up today."

I crossed my arms because what came next was bound to be enlightening. "According to you, you didn't. It was all Kiki."

He huffed his frustration. "I hadn't thought about how people would react if we…if they found out the two of us…well, if they thought I…"

"I'll save you the confusion. There's nothing for them to react to because there's nothing going on with us. Problem solved." I turned back around to head to the kitchen.

"*Fuuuuuck!*" Seren screamed into the night air.

His outburst caused me to jump, but I kept moving and walked back inside the kitchen.

"Next time, don't let me go," I said to Chef as I pulled my rubber gloves back on at the sink.

"Does your mother know?" he said, not bothering to look at me as he prepared something on the stovetop.

"There's nothing to know."

He didn't respond, and I hoped he forgot he saw or heard anything because *nothing* was going on between Seren and me.

CHAPTER 22

Grace

I headed to chemistry class with my head held high. I avoided walking by Seren's locker, but I couldn't avoid being in English class with him. I sensed the moment he walked into the classroom, and I knew his eyes were on me. But unlike yesterday, he walked straight to his seat.

The teacher's lecture revolved around Elizabeth walking a very fine line by omitting truths to her family as well as Mr. Darcy. The idea started a class debate about omitting truths being lying. The discussion could not have been more apropos. And while many students voiced their opinions on the topic during the debate, both Seren and I remained silent. Clearly, we'd said all that needed to be said.

At the bell, I stuffed my things into my backpack, purposely taking my time so I didn't have to deal with him. But it didn't matter. He slipped out the back door and didn't wait for me. Why would he? He was doing what I wanted him to do and leaving me alone.

After school, I worked on my homework and then dragged myself to the kitchen. I made sure I stayed at the sink and kept my head down. I didn't want to have to talk to Chef about anything, nor did I want to risk running into Seren.

"Oh, hello," Martine said when he found me alone in the kitchen at the sink. Janette was serving the meal in the dining room, and Chef had run to the pantry.

I glanced over my shoulder. "Hi." I turned to face him, noticing the teacup in his hand with the tea bag already in it. "Can I get you some hot water?"

"No, I can get it myself," he said as he moved to the teapot on the stovetop. "I've just got to get *mi amore* her tea." He poured the water into the cup. "What kind of husband would I be if I didn't keep her happy?" he said with a smile as he returned the teapot to the stovetop.

"Happy wife, happy life," I said, having heard that saying somewhere before.

"That's right," he laughed. "Be sure *you* choose someone who lives by those words. Makes for a much easier life," he assured me before moving to the dining room door. "Good night."

"Good night," I said as he disappeared into the dining room.

A little after seven, I stepped into our apartment. I couldn't wait to get out of my ridiculous uniform and into the shower. There was a note on the counter from my mom. *Ran to the market.*

I spent the next half an hour in the shower, enjoying the soothing sound of the water until my fingertips turned to prunes. I switched off the water and grabbed a towel from the back of the door. I wrapped it around my body, my wet hair hanging loose. I tossed my clothes in the laundry basket in the hallway closet then went to my room. I switched on the lights and screamed, my heartbeat nearly crashing out of my chest. "What the hell are you doing in here?!"

Seren's eyes drank me in as he sat on the edge of my bed. "Well, you wouldn't listen to me anywhere else, so..."

I pointed toward the door with my heartbeat still racing. "You need to leave. This is breaking and entering."

He held up his index finger with a keyring dangling from it. "Not when I have the key."

"You may have the key, but you have no right to come in here when we're not home."

"You were home," he countered.

"I was in the *shower!*"

"I needed to talk to you."

"Talk to me?" I shrieked. "You scared the hell out of me!"

His eyes cast down.

"My mother will be home any minute and kill me if she finds you in here."

"Would finding me in here *really* be that bad?"

I cocked my head. "Your reputation precedes you."

His lips twisted in contemplation.

"I'm serious, Seren. You need to leave."

He stood up. His height, mixed with the knowledge that I wore solely a towel, made the room feel smaller and the walls feel as though they were about to close in around us. "I wanted to make things right between us."

"There's no us."

He stepped closer.

I moved back until the wall behind me stopped me.

"I want there to be."

"You don't know what you want."

He moved closer, his chest pressing against me and caging me to the wall. "I want you."

My mind spun. I didn't know what was up or down when it came to Seren. One minute he seemed like there may be redemption in him after all, and then the next he was acting crazy. "Right *now* you do. What about tomorrow at school? What about when Kiki shoves her tongue down your throat? Will you then?"

His eyes drifted from mine.

I scoffed as I pushed at his chest, causing him to step back from me. "I can't keep up with you. And, after yesterday, I don't want to."

He met my gaze, and regret hung heavy in his eyes. "That's probably best. I'm fucked up, Grace. A lot's happened since my dad died. Stuff I don't talk to anyone about."

"Then see a psychiatrist."

His eyes narrowed and the cold Seren appeared. "That's harsh."

I scoffed. "Kind of ironic coming from you." When he didn't respond, I huffed my frustration. "What do you want from me?"

"I want to know you, Grace."

"Why?" I asked, truly perplexed by his infatuation with me.

"Because despite how it may seem, we're more alike than you think."

Right.

"I never want to let anyone in, but I have this strange desire to tell you things. Things I don't tell anyone else," he said. "But I'm just doing the opposite and screwing everything up."

"Then stop screwing things up."

He said nothing, but the far-off look in his eyes told me he'd heard me and was contemplating the notion. It didn't seem tough to me, but for someone as cold and angry as Seren, maybe it wasn't as easy. He didn't say another word before he turned away from me and walked out of my room. I heard the front door open and close, and then there was silence.

I dropped down onto my bed, releasing a long breath. At least he had the decency to leave before my mother got home. Too bad I wasn't any closer to understanding what the hell was going on with him. What was it about me that made him want to let me in? And, what could he possibly want to tell me that he didn't tell anyone else?

CHAPTER 23

Seren

"What are we doing tonight?" Kiki asked as we walked into the cafeteria on Friday.

My eyes swept the room, searching the tables for Grace. *Stop screwing things up*, she'd said. Like it would be so easy. I often wondered what it would've been like if my father hadn't died. Would I still have ended up angry and callous?

"Hello?" Kiki waved her palm in front of my face, trying to get my attention.

"What?" I asked as I straddled the bench seat at our normal table, still looking for Grace. I'd been giving her space since Tuesday because I wanted her to know I heard everything she said about not screwing up, getting to know someone the right way, and not being a dick for more than one day at a time.

Kiki grabbed my chin and turned my face to look at her. "I asked you a question."

I pulled my face from her hand. "Get your hand off me."

"Someone's in a bad mood." Her head whipped around, following the direction of my eyes. "Looking for someone?"

"Nope."

She turned back around and pulled out a container of yogurt. "Are we partying at your house tonight?"

"Nope."

"Why not?"

I shrugged. "I'm just over it."

"Over partying?"

"Over everything," I said.

"You weren't before *she* moved in," Kiki said.

"Don't bring her up," I warned.

"*Ohhhh*. Did I hit on a sore subject? If I didn't know any better, I'd think you're crushing on the poor girl."

"Fuck off."

"Watch it, Seren," Kiki warned. "You may have everyone in this school fearing you, but I can be a crazy bitch when I wanna be."

"What's that supposed to mean?"

She shrugged coyly. "Just reminding you, that's all." And just like that, her tone changed, and she was talking about a show on Netflix with someone on the other side of her.

Kiki had always been a bitch, but since I was the school's leading asshole, we just fit. But things needed to change. I wasn't about to become some saint, but I needed to shed some of the excess baggage weighing me down over the last three years. I stood up and took off across the cafeteria.

"Seren!" Kiki called, her voice getting lost in the noisy room as I walked out of it.

I strolled down the deserted school halls, passing classes in session. I had no real destination, but I knew I needed to be away from the people who brought me down. I made my way outside the building and headed toward the parking lot, walking through the rows of cars. I neared Grace's car in the corner of the lot and circled to the back. Grace sat on the ground, leaning against the back of her car. She was reading something on her phone with earbuds in her ears.

Trying not to frighten her, I sat on the ground opposite her.

She appeared startled when she saw me, quickly tugging her earbuds out of her ears. "What are you doing?"

"I could ask you the same question?" I said lamely.

Her eyes jumped around as if half-expecting more people to approach. "Aren't your friends gonna miss you inside?"

I shrugged. "Who cares?"

"Well, you do. You wouldn't want to be seen with me. Right?"

I hated that she had this way of throwing my words and actions back in my face. Not only did it piss me the hell off, but it also stung since I knew she was right. I was an asshole. "I'm serious. Why are you out here all by yourself?" I persisted.

"Wasn't in the mood to deal today."

I didn't blame her. The people in that school prided themselves on their parents' wealth and thought that somehow made *them* better than everyone else. I'd become one of those people. I was entitled. I was cruel. I was a dick. But what did it matter when everyone else bowed down to me because of it. It was a powerful feeling to be feared. "Good thing you'll be out of this place soon, huh?"

She nodded.

"Where are you going next year?" I asked, realizing I didn't actually know.

"Tampa."

"What's in Tampa?"

"I'm studying marine biology."

"Why marine biology?" I asked.

Her eyes became distant. "Because I told my dad I would."

I said nothing because what did you say to something like that? A promise made to a dead parent was like an oath made in blood. That's why my own selfishness when it came to my father's wishes for Grayson Industries hurt like a motherfucker.

"I was only seven when I said it," she explained. "But even at seven, I knew." She spun the ring on her finger, which I realized now was something she did when she was nervous or uncomfortable.

I was about to say something to change the subject when she continued.

"My dad would take me to the aquarium every year, and I'd stand by the glass of the dolphin exhibit and hold my hands up to it. Then, like clockwork, the dolphins would swim by slowly like they were letting me pet them through the glass. They'd make a few passes and then they almost stopped in front of me, looking at me, as if they were trying to communicate with me. Like I could read them and they could read me."

"Sounds cool," I said.

"Yeah. People even gathered around to watch them interact with me. The trainers said they'd never seen anything like it. When they wrangled them in for their next show, my dad and I would hurry in to watch the dolphin show. When I saw them with the trainers, I just knew it was what I wanted to do when I got older. Not necessarily helping them perform, but helping to rescue and rehabilitate the hurt ones. When my dad got sick, he made me promise to make my dream come true. It wasn't a difficult promise since I knew it's what I want to do."

Well, fuck me.

"How about you?" she said, clearly trying to change the subject. "Where are you going next year?"

"Alabama."

"Sawyer never mentioned that."

"He isn't always my biggest fan."

"Why's that?" she asked.

"Because I'm a prick."

Grace laughed out loud.

The sweet sound of her laughter brought a sense of happiness to my gut that I hadn't felt since she let me kiss her.

"I guess we agree on something," she said.

I smiled, hating the foreign feeling of it on my face. I'd worked so hard to perfect the stoic look I wore as a badge of honor. Then, one day, it just stuck. No matter the time or situation, I never let anyone see it falter…except Grace.

"Why Alabama?" she asked.

"They offered me a full ride to play football."

"That's awesome."

I waited for her to mention me not needing the full ride since I was rich, but she didn't. Unlike everyone else, she never mentioned our money.

"Are you gonna get to play?" she asked.

"Their quarterback's graduating next month. So, I'm hoping to beat out Kenyon, his backup."

"Do you have what it takes?" she asked.

I tipped my head to the side. "What do you think?"

She shrugged, completely unfazed by my arrogance.

"Well, my name means star, so…"

Her nose scrunched. "Does it really?"

"Come watch me and find out for yourself."

She rolled her eyes. "What are you majoring in?"

"Football."

She laughed again, and I was beginning to like knowing I was the cause of that laughter.

"You know, Florida's not that far from Alabama."

"Only like a thousand miles," she said.

"You could stream my games," I countered.

"Maybe."

"I'll take maybe," I said, hoping maybe turned into yes.

The bell inside the school rang. Grace climbed to her feet. "I'll see you later."

"Promise?" I said, standing up in front of her.

She stared up at me, the wheels in her head clearly turning as she considered her response carefully. "Maybe."

I smiled. "I'm starting to like maybe."

CHAPTER 24

Grace

I pulled off my rubber gloves and said goodbye to Chef, happy to be done for the night. I walked out the back door and onto the patio. The spring night air didn't hold the bitter chill of winter.

"Hey."

Seren was shooting baskets alone on the driveway court. "No party tonight?"

He shook his head. "Would you have come?"

"God, no."

He laughed, and I still couldn't get used to the foreign sound. "I don't blame you. They're a bunch of assholes."

I smiled, unsure what else to say since we both knew it was the truth.

"What are you doing tonight?" he asked between shots that he sank effortlessly.

"Well, I plan to get this awful uniform off and shower. Then maybe watch a movie or read the book I've been trying to finish."

"Trying to finish?"

"Yeah, since my dad died my focus has been shot."

His lips twisted regrettably.

"It's like my brain can only focus for so long and then poof. Nothing."

"I still struggle with that," he admitted. "But it's gotten a little better with time."

A long silence passed between us. I wanted to get out of my uniform, but I moved toward him and lifted my hands instead. Seren smirked and bounced the basketball to me. I dribbled a couple of steps before shooting the ball. It bounced off the rim.

"Almost," he assured me as he grabbed the loose ball and shot the ball from the three-point line. Of course he sank it.

"Show off."

He laughed as he nabbed the ball and tossed it back to me.

"I'm just getting warmed up, you know," I said before shooting the ball and making the basket.

"Nice shot," he said, grabbing the loose ball and turning to look at me. "You wanna get changed and grab some ice cream or something?"

"Ice cream?"

He shrugged. "Well, I'm not taking you to some Coopersville party."

I shook my head. "Did you need to remind me that you messed with my night?"

"I was jealous as hell," he admitted. "I wanted you to stay here. Not hang with some drunk guys where I couldn't keep an eye on you."

"That's not normal, you know that, right?"

He shrugged.

"If you want to spend time with someone, you ask them out. You don't have them pulled over by the cops and then have their party broken up."

His face hardened. "I needed that night to suck so you wouldn't need to keep going back there on the weekends."

"Well, you went to a lot of effort to be sure it did."

"I never said my actions weren't fucked up." Sensing my indecision over his sanity—or lack thereof, he moved closer to me. "Grace. I'm not gonna apologize for messing with your night. I'm happy it sucked. All I can say is I'm gonna try not to do anything like that again."

"You're gonna try?"

"That's all I've got," he said with sincerity in his eyes. "Go out with me tonight."

"People might see us together," I challenged.

"So? Let them."

* * *

New Hampshire's scenery blurred by as Seren took back roads through neighborhoods where each home was more breathtaking than the last. The close quarters in Seren's Land Rover overwhelmed my senses. His expensive cologne mixed with new-car smell filled the car, and the ease in which he drove with one hand resting on the steering wheel like the car drove itself was a sight to behold.

"Rap, huh?" I said, referencing the music playing in the car.

His eyes cut to mine. "Not a fan?"

I shrugged. "It's fine."

"What do you like?"

"Rock."

He reached for his phone and found rock music. Actions. He was giving me actions. And the butterflies fluttering deep in my stomach liked that.

Seren stopped at Brennan's Ice Cream Shop in the next town. I wondered if he purposely avoided Windham so no one would see us. He jumped out after asking what I wanted and returned with a chocolate shake for me and a cone of rocky road for himself. He drove as we enjoyed our ice cream, eventually stopping at the same mountain overlook I'd been stopping at after school.

He parked his car and cut the lights. Darkness surrounded us. I thought we'd sit inside since the darkness concealed the scenery, but he opened his door and stepped out. "Come on," he said before closing his door. I joined him in front of the car as he hopped up onto the hood. He offered me his hand, which I grabbed, and he pulled me up with his strong grasp until I was beside him. We both lay back against the windshield at the same time. The stars and full moon illuminated the otherwise dark night. Seren's car had been the only one I'd seen for miles, and I liked knowing we had the spot to ourselves.

"Sometimes I wonder if I really want to leave New England," he mused with his eyes focused on the star-speckled sky. "I think I take it for granted."

"New England?" I asked.

"Everything."

I let his words settle, wondering if I did the same. I'd certainly taken Coopersville for granted. And now that it was snatched away from me, I longed for the familiarity that filled me with so much happiness. "Why do you think you do that?"

I could feel his shrugging shoulder rub against my arm. "Because my life sucks."

"Doesn't everyone's?"

"I don't think so," he said. "I think there are people out there who get through life without shitty things happening to them."

My head fell to the side, and I took in his profile as he continued staring at the stars. "We all lose people we love. No one's immune to it."

"I think my mother killed my father."

Shock swept over me. "What?"

"He was healthy one minute then gone the next."

"Heart attacks come out of nowhere," I assured him.

He shook his head. "I thought the same thing until Martine started spending time at the manor. He was my dad's business partner and stepped in to take care of everything for my mother since she was apparently on the verge of a breakdown. I was fifteen, but I still found it strange that I never saw her cry. Not once. I could see her wanting to stay strong for me and my brothers, but she showed nothing. There was no breakdown. There was no mourning. There was no mention of my father after he died. It was like he never even existed."

"People handle death differently," I said, not knowing what else to say when I wanted to say, 'That doesn't really prove she killed him.'

"I think she was fucking Martine while my father was alive." He turned his head to look at me. "That's why she did it. She wanted Martine to replace my father. I'm just not sure if she slipped him something or she told him the truth and it literally broke his fucking heart."

I said nothing, realizing he truly believed his mother killed his father. I knew firsthand that grieving people always tried to find a reason for death. I did the same thing when my father was first diagnosed. I blamed everyone, from doctors for not treating him fast enough to my mother for being gone so much and not catching it sooner.

"There wasn't even an autopsy." Seren's words pulled me back. "My mother claimed we wouldn't have been able to have an open casket at the wake. But normal people would've wanted to be sure of the cause of death. Anyone who knew my dad knew he went to his doctor religiously and worked out like a fiend." Seren sat up, his elbows resting on his thighs as he wrung his hands in front of him. "The only plausible reason for not having the autopsy was because my mother already knew what killed him. She just didn't want anyone else to know."

I sat up beside him knowing there was nothing I could say to convince him that his theory was crazy.

"No one believes me. Not my brothers. Not the psychiatrist—which I did see, by the way."

I pressed my lips together, remembering that I'd told him he should see one. "Does your mother know you think she's the cause of his death?"

"She knows and denies it. I swear to God, I can't even look at her without wanting to put my fist through a wall. If she had nothing to do with it, how could she move on so fast?"

I wanted to assure him that these things happened. People became close when they shared a loss. As Mr. Grayson's business partner, Martine would've been grieving the loss of him, too. I kept those thoughts to myself knowing it wasn't why Seren was confiding in me. He just wanted someone on his side. "I'm sorry."

He shook his head, clearly not looking for my sympathy. "I just wanted you to know where my head's at most days. It's not on high school shit. It's like I'm going through the motions and trying to stop myself from flipping the fuck out. You've been a welcome distraction."

I bumped him gently with my shoulder. "Thanks for being honest with me."

"You're easy to talk to."

"Well, I'm here if you need to talk," I offered.

"I can think of a lot of other things I'd rather be doing with you."

"And, where would you like to do these other things? The pool house?"

"Nope. The pool house is reserved for people I don't care about."

"People who like handcuffs, petroleum jelly, and lingerie?" I probed.

He threw back his head and howled with laughter. I hadn't meant to be funny.

"Why are you laughing?"

"I totally forgot about that."

"About what?"

"Did you really believe all those notes?"

"Obviously."

"Jesus, Grace. I'm in high school. Sure, I've slept with girls, but not in the same week. I was trying to piss you off so you'd stay away from me."

I shook my head, constantly caught off guard by every new bit of information I learned from Seren.

"What?" he asked, his eyes riveting between mine.

"The guy I thought you were and the guy you're turning out to be aren't meshing in my brain. It's hard to sort through the lies to get to the truth."

He reached over and linked his fingers with mine. "I know I suck."

"You do…But I've also got a confession to make."

"Go on," he urged with a spark of intrigue in his eyes.

"My note wasn't real either."

His eyes widened. "You didn't use the safety pin?"

"And risk little versions of you running around? No way."

He laughed and I couldn't help but laugh too.

"I sure as hell didn't see you coming," he mused. "I wish I had. I would've been better prepared."

I cocked my head. "To push me away even harder?"

He shook his head. "To fall in love with you."

Butterflies fluttered in my stomach. *Damn them.* "You still don't know me."

"I know you, Grace. I'm just waiting for the day you'll know me and trust me."

"Trust takes time."

He squeezed my hand. "I'm not going anywhere." He sounded serious. He sounded like he hadn't had someone he could trust in a long time and, somehow, I fit the part. "You gonna let me kiss you good night?" he asked.

"You're gonna ask this time?"

He smirked. "I'm used to taking what I want."

"But we both know that doesn't work for me."

"That's why I asked."

He was certainly trying. I heaved a sigh. "Well, not at the manor. Wouldn't want anyone there seeing us."

"Works for me," he said, hopping off the hood and turning to face me. He fit himself between my knees and lifted his hands to my cheeks, cupping them gently as he gazed into my eyes. "Good night, Grace."

I stifled a smile, realizing what he was doing. "Good night, Seren."

His lips inched closer to mine, lingering for a long moment before they captured mine. He wasted no time. His tongue plunged between my lips. Our heads moved from side to side as our tongues fought for control, tangling and gliding against one another as if we couldn't get close enough. As soon as I draped my arms over his shoulders, his hands dropped from my cheeks to my hips, pulling me against his chest. My legs wrapped around him. His erection pressed between my thighs, and I couldn't stop myself from pushing against it as he devoured my lips. I felt him everywhere. I hated myself for giving in so easily, but everything about Seren—from his breathtaking looks to his vulnerability in telling me the truth—made me yearn to be closer.

Trying to regain some sense of balance, I pulled out of the kiss first. My breath was labored and my mind spun. Everything was happening so quickly. I needed to keep my wits about me before I did something foolish. Something I'd regret.

Seren dragged the back of his thumb along his bottom lip wearing a wicked grin. "Nope. Did *not* see you coming."

Once we returned to the manor, we went our separate ways in the driveway saying nothing more than *see you later*. But the look in Seren's eyes told me he was thinking about our kiss. If I was being honest with myself, I was too since I was unable to get the feel of it out of my head. I'd never been thoroughly kissed in my life. I could feel his need for me to trust him. His need for me to believe him. His need for me to be the one person to see the truth like he did.

I wondered if I could be that person for him.

If I'd be able to see his mother as a murderer.

If I'd be able to let myself fall for him the way he seemed to have fallen for me.

CHAPTER 25

Seren

I tossed the football around the driveway on Saturday with Sawyer and Saint. We'd taken off our T-shirts and played ball in our shorts since it was such a hot May day. I wondered if Grace planned to come out of hiding or if she was worried my brothers might sense something was going on with us if she came outside. Or, maybe, I scared her away by spewing all my shit to her. I still couldn't believe I told her so much. I guess I just needed to know if I could trust her the way everything inside of me was telling me I could. I wasn't lying when I said she was easy to talk to. She was not like the girls I was used to. They were all about money and status. Grace just wasn't.

Sawyer tossed a spiral that sailed over my head. I leaped for it, but it was out of my reach. It landed with a bounce ten feet behind me and rolled down the driveway and out of sight.

"Nice throw," I taunted. "Now, go get it."

Sawyer laughed. "I guess I don't know my own strength. I should be the QB."

"Fuck that," I said.

Sawyer jogged past me in search of the ball.

"Where were you last night?" Saint asked while we waited for Sawyer to return.

"Just drove around," I said.

"Alone?"

"What's it to you?"

"Not me. Kiki. She was all up in your business at Fiona's party," he explained.

"Fuck her."

"Dude, you've already done that. Now she thinks she's entitled to all things you."

Sawyer appeared with the football and a car following him up the driveway.

Saint and I squinted, trying to see who drove the old Honda. No one we knew owned a car older than their last birthday.

"Found these two lurking outside the gate," Sawyer explained as he directed the car to park in front of the last garage door.

Two girls stepped out. A leggy blonde held a bunch of pink and silver balloons and the one with black hair held a cake box. Both of them ogled us, giggling as they did.

"They're looking for Grace," Sawyer explained. "Turns out it's her birthday."

What the hell? Why hadn't she mentioned it?

"I'll go get her," I said, turning before anyone could follow me. I trekked into the house and down to the dungeon. I banged on her apartment door until it opened. I was about to ream her out for not telling me it was her birthday when I found her mother staring back at me.

"Can I help you, Seren?" she asked, clearly confused by my presence down there—especially all sweaty and shirtless. As far as she was concerned, I would never step foot down in the basement. It was beneath me.

"Grace's friends are here," I explained.

"Friends?" she asked.

"Two girls with balloons and a cake. I told them I'd get her."

She seemed annoyed by the notion of Grace getting visitors. But this was her home now. Why shouldn't she? "I'll send her up in a minute."

I nodded as she closed the door on me. I waited just inside the stairwell that led from the dungeon to the main floor. I heard footsteps a couple of minutes later, and Grace stepped into the stairwell. She yelped as I stepped in front of her and caged her against the wall.

She stared up at me, confused by my sudden appearance. "Hi," she said.

"Happy Birthday."

She smiled, ready to respond when I captured her mouth with my own. Her lips tasted like cherry lip gloss. I wanted to get lost in the kiss, but I was pissed she hadn't told me it was her birthday—not to mention jealous her friends got to spend her birthday with her.

I pulled out of the kiss first. "You should have told me."

"It's not until Tuesday, and it's no big deal," she said, all breathless.

"You'll be legal. Of course, it's a big deal. Now we can have some real fun and I won't get arrested."

"Oh, my God." She shook her head and rolled her eyes at the same time, likely not expecting my frankness. "My mom said I had visitors. *You're* the visitor?"

"No. Your friends are here."

Her face lit up, and I wished my presence elicited the same type of excitement. "Really?"

I motioned with my head toward the stairs. We climbed them to the main floor, and she rushed outside. As soon as she did, her friends shrieked and ran toward her. I moved away as the three of them hugged and jumped around. I'd never seen Grace so happy about anything before. I'd wasted a lot of time wanting to see her unhappy. This was a lot more enjoyable.

"Why didn't you call me?" she asked as they released her.

"Surprise!!" they squealed.

She was smiling from ear to ear when she noticed my brothers and me watching the whole scene play out. "Oh," she said to her friends. "Did you meet Sawyer and Saint?"

The girls nodded and giggled like they'd never seen three shirtless guys before.

"Holly and Laney, this is Seren," Grace motioned with her hand in my direction.

Their eyes drank me in. I was used to the attention, but I wondered if Grace had mentioned me to them.

"Show us around," one of them said to Grace.

"Let me go put my balloons away."

"I've got you," Sawyer said, taking the balloons and tying them to the arm of the nearby bench for her.

"Thanks, Sawyer." Without looking at me, Grace took off with them toward the back lawn.

I glanced at Sawyer who was giving me scheming eyes. "What?"

"There are three of them," he said with bouncing brows.

"So?" I said.

"There are three of us," he explained.

"If either of you touches Grace, I'll kill you," I warned.

Saint eyed me curiously.

"I knew it!" Sawyer said. "You've wanted her since the day she moved in."

"Have not," I said.

"She hates you," Saint added.

"She doesn't hate me," I countered.

Saint looked unconvinced.

Sawyer shook his head. "Girls always go for the dicks." He glanced at Saint. "You won't have any trouble getting one of them. You're more of a dick than Seren."

Both Saint and I flipped Sawyer the bird as he took off after them.

Grace

My heart was so full as I watched Holly and Laney laughing as Sawyer flipped into the pool and splashed them. Despite the warm temperature, the pool was still too cold for us to go in. We lounged on the poolside chairs and caught up with each other, eating the red velvet cake they'd brought me.

Throughout the day, I glanced over at the driveway hoping Seren would come outside. Saint had surprisingly joined us, keeping his distance as he played on his phone, but Seren hadn't.

"You hot for my brother?" Saint asked likely catching me.

"What?"

"Seren? You got a thing for him?" he asked.

"Do tell," Holly said, leaning closer as if we were talking about something juicy.

"You two would look hot together," Laney added.

"Oh…no…I don't…we don't even get along," I finally said.

"*Riiiight*," Sawyer chimed in from the pool where he hung onto the edge with his arms crossed on the brick patio.

"He's got a girlfriend, you know?" Saint added.

"*Saint*," Sawyer warned. "Kiki's not his girlfriend." He looked to me. "She wants to be, but he's made it clear that it's never happening."

I didn't say anything because I saw how successful he'd been at making it clear to her in the pool house that it wasn't happening.

"He needs someone like you, Grace," Sawyer said.

"Any guy would be lucky to have her," Laney added.

"Thanks for the vote of confidence, guys. But I'm not running for election here. And, my love life's not up for discussion."

"So, you admit you love my brother?" Saint said, a coolness to his tone.

My eyes widened. "What? No. I didn't say that."

"But you think he's hot," Sawyer added.

"What? No. I didn't say that either."

"What *did* you say?" Seren asked from behind me.

I froze as all of them burst out laughing except Saint who clearly just liked pushing buttons.

"You're all jerks. You know that, right?" I said, pegging each of them with my eyes.

"Sounds like I missed a good conversation," Seren said as he slowly walked over, stopping in front of me. He was shirtless like he'd been before, and I found it difficult not to relive what his chest felt like pressed to mine the night before.

He glanced at my phone on the chair beside me before meeting my gaze. I wondered what he'd do with all the prying eyes on us. Because they *were* on us. I didn't have to wait long. Seren leaned down and scooped me up in his arms. I yelped as he moved toward the pool. I held on to him for dear life. "Seren, don't!" I begged just as he jumped into the pool. I held my breath as we plunged underwater. The chill of the water bit away at my skin through my now drenched clothes. Then, Seren released me. We both resurfaced at the same time and everyone was laughing. I glanced over at Seren who waded water a few feet from me with a devilish smirk. "I hate you too," I assured him.

He laughed, and I knew I couldn't stay angry at him. He'd shown his playful side in front of other people. That was a huge step for him.

"Not nice, Seren," Sawyer called over.

Seren flipped him off.

"How's the water, Grace?" Laney asked

"Free-eee-zing," I said through chattering teeth as I moved to the side of the pool and climbed out while Seren stayed in. I grabbed a towel from the patio compartment and quickly wrapped it around my shivering body. I sat back down on my chair with my body shaking like crazy. It might've been warm out, but the water temperature was frigid.

"You girls staying the night?" Sawyer asked Laney and Holly.

"No. We have to get going soon. Laney has to work tonight and it's an hour drive back," Holly said.

Sadness welled in my chest. For a few hours, everything had felt normal. But the idea of them leaving made me feel an emptiness I wasn't sure I'd ever be able to fill.

"What the hell is this?"

We all turned to find Kiki standing at the edge of the patio eyeing us with daggers.

Her eyes cut to Seren's. "Did my invitation get lost somewhere?"

Holly and Laney glanced to me, their eyes relaying that they knew she must be the non-girlfriend Saint mentioned.

"Nope," Seren said, not bothering to look at her.

"Who are *they*?" she asked, looking at Holly and Laney.

"*They* have names," Holly snapped.

"*Ohhhhh.* These must be poor girl's friends," Kiki said, condescension dripping from her bright red lips. "Glad to see someone likes her."

I cringed, hating that my friends now had a glimpse into my life in Windham. It wasn't all pool parties with the Graysons. It was trying not to cross bitches like Kiki so I could just finish the year, graduate, and get the hell out of there.

Laney jumped to her feet. "You, *bitch.*"

Kiki looked her up and down in disdain, likely noting her old beat-up Chucks. "Please don't tell me you think I'll fight you. My manicure alone cost more than your outfit."

Holly stood up, ready to throw down. "You, *bitch.*"

"At least they're original," Kiki mused to herself.

I stood up and my towel dropped away as I turned to face my friends. "Ignore her. She's an evil troll."

"Says the drowned rat," Kiki balked.

A flash of rage rushed through me. It was one thing to embarrass me in front of strangers I didn't care about. But she'd crossed a line by doing it in front of my best friends. I harnessed all the self-control I was capable of and took a deep breath. "She's not worth it," I assured my friends loud enough for Kiki to hear.

"Damn straight she's not worth it," Laney said.

"Oh, I beg to differ. My daddy's net worth is over a hundred mill," Kiki added.

"*Mill?*" Laney shrieked. "Is that what obnoxious bitches say?"

"Come on," I said, not wanting them to go, but not wanting a big scene to break out either because that only meant I'd have to deal with the aftermath alone. "I'll walk you to the car." I led them away from the pool and past Kiki.

"Go back to the slums where you came from," Kiki called.

Laney and Holly both spun around. I seized their arms, dragging them away for the pool area and back toward the driveway. "Please, just keep walking."

"Grace, tell us you're not dealing with people like her?" Holly said as we headed toward their car.

My lips twisted, unwilling to lie to my friends.

"Jesus Christ, Grace. Come back to Coopersville," Laney said. "Stay with me for the rest of the school year."

"I wish I could. But I don't live there anymore."

Once we reached their car, I glanced back toward the pool. No one had followed us. I don't know why I thought they would. Kiki was one of them. And there was no denying that rich people stuck with rich people.

Holly and Laney wrapped their arms around me, hugging my wet body for a long time. I didn't want them to let go. Their presence felt like home to me.

"If she messes with you, I swear to God, Grace, I will kick the shit out of her," Laney said.

"And I'll break every one of her expensive manicured nails," Holly added.

I laughed, grateful for my friends. "Despite how it looked, I can handle her."

"We love you," Holly said.

"I love you guys, too."

"Seren wants you," Laney said as we stepped out of our hug.

"Bad," Holly added.

"How do you know?"

"He couldn't keep his eyes off you," Laney said as they moved to their respective car doors and opened them.

I rolled my eyes, wondering if that was the truth. "Thanks for making this a wonderful birthday," I said, hating that they had to go. "Be careful driving home."

"You be careful around here," Holly said sadly as her eyes moved over the manor one last time.

I held back the tears stinging my eyes until they'd waved goodbye, pulled down the driveway, and disappeared out of sight.

Without giving the pool area another look, I untied my balloons from the bench and carried them down to the apartment. My mother was cooking chicken on the stovetop when I entered.

"Did you have fun?" she asked without turning around.

"I had no idea they were coming. But I think I really needed to see them."

"They're good friends," she said.

They were, and the way they always had my back just proved it. "The best."

"Did you have fun with the boys?" she asked, still not facing me.

I swallowed hard, worried that she'd seen more than I thought she had. "Yeah, they're nice."

"I warned you about them," she said.

"Mom, I don't need a lecture. They're nice to me. I'd like to base my opinion on that and not what you think of them."

She spun around, her eyes drifting over my clothes. "Why are you soaked?"

I glanced down at my wet clothes. "Seren pushed me in the pool."

Her eyes clouded with disappointment. "I've been here for many years. You've been here for less than a month. I'd like to think I have a better grasp on this family than you do."

"You're right. I should value your opinion."

"Thank you."

"But if I want to hang around with people who I have something in common with, then I'm going to do it."

"What could you possibly have in common with those boys?"

"Well, for one, we all lost a father."

Her shoulders dropped as if she hadn't realized that commonality until now.

"I'll be eighteen in three days. You've got to give me more credit. I'm smart and won't let anyone hurt me." I nearly choked on my own words, but said them for her benefit, nonetheless.

"I don't have to like it," she said.

"Me being eighteen or me being friends with the Graysons?"

"Neither."

I walked over and wrapped my arms around her. She was frailer than I remembered. "Thanks for caring about me."

"More than anything in this world."

I knew she meant that. I was all she had left. But she had been wrong about Seren. And I think I'd been wrong too.

CHAPTER 26

Grace

Still reeling from Holly and Laney's visit *and* the run-in with Kiki, I didn't leave the apartment Sunday. On Monday, I hurried out to the car, running late and nearly dropping my bag onto the ground when I pulled it off my back.

"Can I have a ride?"

I glanced to my right to find Seren standing there wearing his backpack.

"What's wrong with your car?"

He shrugged. "Nothing."

I laughed as I gestured to the passenger side of my car. "You haven't ridden in style until you've been in this beauty."

He smiled, rounding the car to the passenger side and getting in.

I slipped into my seat and switched on the engine. Rock music played from my speakers as I reversed out of the driveway.

"I'm sorry about Kiki," he said.

"Yeah, that sucked."

"It would've made things worse if I said anything. I figured let her spew her hate and then I could just be done with her once and for all."

My eyes cut to his. "Sounds definite."

"I never should have…you know…"

Visions of them in the pool house flooded my brain. His cold glare as he watched me watching them. I needed to remember he wasn't as hateful as I thought. Guys slept with girls. He wasn't doing anything she didn't want him to do.

"Where'd you just go, Grace?" he asked, sensing my drifting thoughts.

I shook my head. "Windham's just a lot different from Coopersville."

"Why do you think I'm getting the hell out of here?" I laughed.

"Go out with me tonight."

I glanced to him. "I have to work."

"I can get you the night off."

"Where do you wanna go?" I asked.

"It's a surprise."

Surprise? "Can this surprise happen after my shift? I wouldn't want to let Chef down."

"Sure."

"Then okay."

"Okay," he repeated with a satisfied smile.

We arrived at school a few minutes later. I cut the engine then looked to him as he threw open his door. "You want me to wait a couple of minutes."

His brows furrowed. "What for?"

"So people don't see us together," I said, totally testing him.

A slow-spreading smile slipped across his lips. "Come on. This will be fun."

I opened my door and stepped out, pulling my backpack onto my shoulders.

Seren was at my side, slipping his hand into mine and squeezing it.

Oh, boy. This could go really well or really *really* badly because the repercussions could be vast. I did an internal sign of the cross and let him lead the way.

Heads turned as we passed people getting out of their cars in the parking lot. I cursed my corner spot because each step toward the school was steeped in quicksand, making it a slow trip to the front doors. People stopped talking and followed us with their eyes. I'd like to say I enjoyed the attention, but I didn't.

I could see the front doors of the school. Another fifty yards and we'd be there.

"What the fuck?" Kiki growled.

I noticed her stepping out of a car on our right.

Seren stopped. I pulled on his hand urging him to keep walking, but he wasn't someone you could make do anything. Without releasing my hand, he moved to Kiki. "You got something to say?"

Her eyes drifted to our joined hands. "What's this?"

"I think you're under the mistaken notion that I answer to you."

She burst out laughing. "So what? You spend time with poor girl and you think you've changed? People like us don't change, Seren. We stay with each other because we need each other."

"I sure as hell don't need someone like you," he assured her.

We walked away and made our way inside the building, getting just as many looks as we had in the parking lot.

"What do you have first?" Seren asked as we walked through the crowded hallway.

"Chemistry."

He laughed. "I took that sophomore year."

"Yeah, well, your school didn't have Chem two honors, so the guidance counselor just stuck me in there."

"So, you're pretty *and* smart."

I rolled my eyes.

Outside my class door, he moved in and I prepared for him to kiss me. But instead, he leaned into my ear and whispered, "Your car or the cafeteria?"

"What?"

"Where do you wanna eat lunch?"

"Well, I don't need any more attention on me today, so..."

He nodded his understanding as he stepped back. "See you in English." He spun away from me, disappearing into the sea of bodies rushing by us.

I found my seat in science class, overhearing girls around me talking about prom and their dresses.

"Today we're going to be discussing element eighty-one on the periodic table: Thallium," the teacher began. "Thallium is a post-transition metal made famous for its ability to poison and potentially kill by simply touching it in its metal form."

Everyone quieted down, tucked their phones away, and faced the front of the room. Apparently, this was an interesting element.

"Sounds like bull," a kid in the back of the class called out.

"I'm deathly serious—pun intended," the teacher said. With a rubber glove on his hand, he lifted a small see-through plastic capsule that held a two-inch-sized piece of silver-looking metal. "This is Thallium. I keep it locked up for fear of it getting into the wrong hands. I'm gonna call you up row by row to get a closer look."

As he called the rows, students gathered around his front lab table for a quick peek before returning to their seats.

"Thallium in this form is dangerous, but what if ingested? In its powder form, it was used in rat poison until it was outlawed in the United States."

"Can you be arrested for having it?" a girl in the front asked.

He laughed. "Only if I try to poison someone with it."

The class laughed.

"In its powder form, it can be used in lights and some medicines, but in the wrong hands...well, you know."

When the bell rang to dismiss class, I packed my things and headed to the hallway, eager to get to English. I arrived before Seren but, as usual, I could tell when he arrived because my skin prickled with awareness.

"Can we all agree, Elizabeth and Mr. Darcy should have just talked about how they were feeling in the first place?" a girl in the back asked during our class discussion.

"Maybe they needed to do it in their own time," Seren added, silencing the class.

I stifled a smile.

"Maybe Darcy just needed time to get his shit together—"

"Mr. *Grayson*," the teacher warned.

"Sorry," he grumbled.

"I agree," I said. "Maybe Darcy needed to see that someone like Elizabeth was good for him. She challenged him and he needed that." I glanced over my shoulder and met Seren's eyes.

His lips twitched. "She definitely did that. If she'd just done what other more agreeable girls would've done, it could've saved them both a lot of aggravation."

"But where would the fun in that be?" I said, turning back to face the teacher so she didn't catch on to the fact that we were no longer talking about Elizabeth and Mr. Darcy.

"I'd say you hit the nail on the head, Grace. Without the tension. Without the misunderstanding. Without our need as readers for them to get their shi—stuff together," the teacher said with a laugh, "our story would not be the classic it is today."

CHAPTER 27

Seren

"So, where're we going?" Grace asked.

I glanced over at her in the passenger seat of my car. My dashboard lights cast a soft white glow around her, and the angelic vision wasn't lost on me. *I hear ya, Dad.* "I told you. It's a surprise."

She smiled and I could sense she enjoyed surprises. "Can I guess?"

"You can guess, but I'm not telling you."

"That's no fun."

"Never said it was gonna be fun," I said, lying through my teeth. She was gonna fucking love my surprise.

We hit the town line and turned onto the highway. She glanced over at me. "Mini golf?"

I kept my eyes on the road. "Don't waste your time trying to guess. I'm not telling."

"Well, just to be clear, is this a date?"

My eyes cut to hers, kind of enjoying that I kept her on her toes. "Do you want it to be a date?"

She pretended to consider the notion as the sign for our exit appeared ahead. I hit the blinker and took it. "Woodland? *Hmmmm.* I wonder what's in Woodland," she mused.

"I guess you'll just have to wait to see," I said as I drove through the quaint town's streets.

"You know, I don't even have your phone number."

I laughed. "We live in the same house."

"Yeah, but what happens if I want to tell you something late at night?"

"I give you full permission to come up to my room. Preferably in my bed with no clothes on."

"Ugh. You're such a guy."

I laughed. "Fine." I rattled off my number and she programmed it into her phone.

"You never told me when you leave for school? Don't football players go early?" she said.

"Yeah. I'm heading south in early July. How about you?"

"I applied for a summer internship. I'm just waiting to hear if I get it."

"Doing what?"

"I'd be at the Tampa Marine Life Rescue Center."

"Will you actually be rescuing animals?"

"Not at first. I'll just be answering rescue calls and stuff. But after training, I'll be able to assist the marine biologists when they rescue dolphins, seals, and sea turtles."

"Sounds cool."

She glanced out the window and her voice became unsure. "If I get it."

"You will."

"You don't know that."

"I know you. And you deserve it."

She gasped, and I knew she'd spotted the sign on the old theater marquee. "You're joking?" she said.

"Nope. My buddy works here and he set us up."

"Which version?" she asked, all wide-eyed and excited.

"Kiera Knightly."

"*Yes,*" she said.

I rolled my eyes.

"You don't like that version?"

I shrugged. "Just because I understand the novel doesn't mean I've seen the movie."

Her mouth formed an O. "You've never seen it?"

I shook my head as I parked in the small parking lot on the side of the building.

"You're gonna love it," she said, opening her door before I even switched off the engine.

I wasn't sure I'd love it. But I wouldn't mind spending two and half hours alone with her in a dark theater. I opened my door and stepped out. Grace was already at my side, slipping her hand into mine. "Best first date ever," she said.

I laughed. "It hasn't even started yet."

"It couldn't get any better," she assured me.

Oh no? If that was a challenge, I was most definitely up for it.

CHAPTER 28

Grace

My phone pinged with birthday wishes from people back home. I reveled in the messages knowing no one in Windham would be wishing me a happy anything. Except maybe Seren, who knew my birthday was today. But he wasn't waiting in the driveway and he wasn't in English class.

My phone vibrated in my pocket during third period. I slipped it out and finally received a text from Seren. **Happy Birthday, Grace. Meet me in the treehouse tonight at eight.**

I didn't even try to conceal the smile that slipped across my lips as my finger lingered over the thumbs-up emoji. Was that too informal given Seren had reserved an *entire* movie theater for us to see *Pride and Prejudice*? I honestly nearly died when I saw the marquee. For all his faults, Seren was a thoughtful guy who didn't half-ass anything. And, despite what I expected, he behaved himself during the movie, only trying to make out during Mr. Collins' scenes. He knew better than to interrupt any scene with Mr. Darcy and Elizabeth. Still, I settled for a thumbs-up response.

During lunch, I replied to all the other texts while I ate in my car.

Any new developments with psycho bitch? Holly asked.
None. Thankfully.

I'll be at your school in an hour flat to beat her ass. Holly fired back. **Just say the word.**

I laughed.

Do I need to beat a bitch's ass today? Laney texted.

I laughed and replied. **Not so far. But laying low so my bday isn't ruined.**

Laney texted back with a kiss-blowing emoji. **Miss you.**

Miss you more. I replied.

I hurried back into school. I walked into gym class for my last class, so happy to be almost done for the day. I'd avoided the locker room since the video, opting to take the zero like the rest of the girls who didn't change for gym class. I was already admitted to Tampa. A lower gym grade wasn't going to affect that.

I sat down on the outdoor bleachers while people played flag football or walked laps around the track. I skimmed my email, checking to see if there was any word on the internship. But like every other day, there was nothing yet.

"I seriously thought it would be more entertaining to watch the bitch wither away and die," Kiki said as she and her friend walked by me.

I kept my eyes down, knowing she wanted me to hear her.

"What? No bodyguards to talk for you?" Kiki asked, stopping in front of me.

I lifted my eyes, all the while telling myself not to get

into it with her. This was my day, and she was not going to ruin it.

"Where'd you find those two gutter dwellers?" she continued while her friend snickered beside her.

"I'm sorry, did you say something?"

"You heard me."

"Nope. Not a word."

Her eyes flared. "Too bad getting rid of you isn't as easy as getting you here."

All coherent thoughts ground to a halt. My face must've shown it.

She arched her brow. "Oh, you didn't know? Yeah. I made the call to Coopersville. And your principal was so appreciative of the information."

Every part of my body trembled. A mixture of anger, shock, and sadness rushed through me. How could one person be so vindictive? So evil?

"I thought it would be more fun watching you flounder. Turns out, it isn't. So, what to do with the bitch who suddenly thinks *she's* a Grayson?" she mused.

"Are you trying to threaten me?"

"Stop whatever it is you're doing with Seren, or I will do so much worse than have you kicked out of a school." She turned away and her minion followed her.

My heartbeat thrashed in my chest as my mind whirled. *She* had me sent to Windham Prep. Not Seren. Not someone from back home. Kiki. *She* wanted to toy with me and embarrass me. It was all a game to her. All a messed up disturbing game.

Holly had it right. She *was* a psycho bitch.

* * *

I returned from the Grayson's kitchen a little after seven. A sudden flurry of excitement replaced the anger I'd been feeling since learning the truth about my premature exit from Coopersville High.

After a quick shower, I slipped on some jeans, a cute navy top with peepholes down the sleeves, and some nude flats. I snuck out of the apartment while my mother had dozed off in her bed, leaving a note that I headed out for a walk.

I hurried across the lawn and down the walking path, passing the pool and pool house. I turned on my phone flashlight when I was far enough away from the manor so no one would see. As I neared the edge of the property, I could see a light inside the treehouse. My stomach dipped with anticipation. I reached the foot of the tree and dragged in a deep breath. I braced my hands on the plank steps and climbed through the open trap door. Bright red balloons filled the ceiling with twisty silver ribbons twirling down from them. Two lanterns placed on the benches cast a soft glow over the space.

Seren stood there in low-hung jeans and a black T-shirt that clung to him like a second skin. "You know I had to outdo your friends, right?" he said, clearly meaning the number of balloons he'd managed to get into the treehouse.

I laughed, feeling special despite his need to outdo Holly and Laney. I noticed a small table set up with a black tablecloth and two chairs. "It looks amazing in here."

He said nothing, though his small grin displayed his obvious pride in what he'd accomplished.

"How are you feeling?" I asked.

His eyes narrowed. "Fine. Why?"

"You weren't in school."

He smirked. "I had stuff to do."

Stuff?

He chuckled and I knew I'd never get used to seeing him happy. He held out his hand and I moved forward, taking it. He wrapped his arms around me, holding me to him in an embrace that felt so safe. But I wondered if he'd been telling the truth when he said I'd be legal. Did he expect more than I was willing to give the person who I despised only a week before. "Happy birthday, Grace."

"Thank you."

He released me and stepped back. "Are you hungry?"

"Did you cook?" I asked.

"Don't be crazy. Chef would hurt me if I tried to make anything in his kitchen."

I laughed, trying to picture Seren cooking anything.

He moved to one of the benches. He reached inside a brown bag, pulling out two carryout boxes and placing them on the table. "Have a seat."

I sat down and he did the same. I still couldn't get used to this thoughtful version of Seren when he was so tough with everyone else.

He opened the cover of my box. "I hope you like spaghetti."

I smiled. "It's perfect."

"I figured who doesn't like spaghetti."

I laughed, knowing not everyone got to see the lighter side of him. I was grateful I did. I twirled my spaghetti around my fork and took a bite.

"Did I miss anything in school?"

"Oh, like a run-in with Kiki?" I said with my mouth full.

He groaned. "What'd she do?"

I finished chewing. "She's the reason I ended up at Windham Prep."

His eyes widened. "What?"

"She's the one who called my school."

He scrubbed his hands up and down his face. "I thought I was the only one crazy enough to do something like that."

"Nope. You've got competition," I said.

"I'm not gonna say I'm not happy you're at Windham Prep. I'm just sorry you got ripped away from your friends because of Kiki."

Once we finished eating, Seren cleaned up, putting all our garbage in the bag. He returned to the table and sat down, holding a small box with a red velvet bow out to me.

"I don't need a gift," I said, uncomfortable with the notion that he'd bought me a gift.

He pushed it toward me. "You'll insult me."

I sighed and took it from him. His eyes focused on the box, clearly eager for me to open it. My heartbeat raced as I untied the bow and lifted the cover off the box. A black velvet ring box sat nestled inside gold tissue paper. I glanced up at him.

"Go on," he urged.

I pulled the ring box out and placed the wrapping on the floor at my side. I slowly lifted the cover and I gasped. Tucked inside its spot in the box was a ring very much like the one my father had given me. The one that read *My Girl* inside that I valued more than any other object on this planet. But this ring was different. This one was covered in tiny diamonds. "Seren?" I said both awed and angry he'd done something this big.

"Take it out," he insisted.

"This is too much," I said.

"You're hurting my feelings," he said, his voice low.

I removed the ring from the box, examining the gorgeous piece of jewelry. Diamonds wrapped around it, twinkling in the soft light. It was exactly like my dad's ring, only flashier.

"You can wear it with your other ring," he said. "But look inside first."

I tilted the ring so I could see inside. Just like in my father's ring, there was engraving inside. It was the same scrolling font, but this engraving read *And Mine*.

I glanced at Seren. I could see the worry in his eyes. He was scared I wouldn't like the gift. Or, the engraving. "Is that how you see me?" I asked, taken aback by what it said.

His lips slid into a small smirk causing dimples to dig in. "As my girl?"

I nodded.

"Yes," he said.

I was quiet as I stared at the ring in my hand for a long time. It wasn't that I didn't love the ring. It was all just …so much. I looked back at Seren. The anxiousness in his eyes was like a rush of adrenaline. He was watching my expression and awaiting my next move. The ring was beautiful, no doubt. But what would I be saying if I wore it? Because I really wanted to wear it. Not giving myself any more time to wimp out, I slipped the ring onto my finger, fitting it right up against my father's ring.

"Let me see," he said, excitement coloring his tone.

I held out my hand so he could see his ring with my dad's. "It fits perfectly."

"It should. I used your other ring to be sure I had the right size." Suddenly, guilt crossed his features realizing we hadn't discussed that indiscretion yet. "I'm sorry. I took it for one reason and realized I needed it for another."

"It went missing right when I got here. How could you have known?"

"I *knew*, Grace." He stood up and moved to my side of the table, squatting beside me and taking my hand with the rings on it. "I may do a lot of fucked up stuff, but there's always a reason. Even if on the surface I look like a crazy bastard, just know there's always more to it."

"How am I supposed to know that?"

He shrugged. "We can have a code word."

I laughed. "A code word?"

"Yeah, like a safe word but not for sex. For my irrational decisions."

Humoring him, I asked. "So, what should our word be?"

"You choose," he offered.

I thought for a moment before settling on one. "Dolphins."

He nodded. "I like it."

"So, just to be clear. If you say dolphins, it's you being irrational because something else is going on that I don't realize at that moment?"

"Yes," he confirmed matter-of-factly.

"And, you think this will help us moving forward?"

"Yes." He sounded so certain, like having a word to decipher when his craziness was warranted would make things better.

Feeling cautious yet optimistic—more so than I'd been in a long time when it came to Seren, I agreed. "Okay."

He smiled, and my insides turned to mush knowing I was the sole cause of it. "Happy Birthday, Grace. Can I give you your cake now?"

"I don't need a cake," I said.

He stood up and pulled me to my feet, wrapping his arms around my hips and holding me to him. "What do you need?"

I draped my arms over his shoulders and pretended to consider the question. "Well—"

His lips were on mine before I could finish. His tongue didn't ask for permission, entering without warning. Our tongues melded with one another, a perfect fit—just like my new ring. Seren pulled back much too soon wearing a scheming smirk. "You're legal now."

"And, yours, it would seem," I said, holding up my hand so he knew I meant the inscription in the ring.

His brows shot up.

"Not tonight, lover boy."

He laughed and kissed me some more. "Go to the prom with me."

"*You* want to go to the prom?" I asked, unable to picture him doing anything school-related besides football.

"With you, if you say yes."

"It's in four days," I said, leery of the timetable.

"So?"

Did I even want to go to a dance surrounded by people I didn't like? "I don't have a dress."

"I can help with that," he said.

I cocked my head, knowing there was more to his sudden urge to go to the prom with me. "Why do you really want to go?"

He smirked. "Because the hottest guy should always go with the hottest girl."

"Smooth," I said, not buying it. "Now tell me the truth."

"Well, I think we should probably wait until prom night to have sex. But, if you want to skip prom altogether, then I'm all for it. I just figured actually going was part of the whole lead up to sex."

Laughter burst out of me. "You're kidding, right?"

He feigned hurt. "Why would I be kidding? Four days is a long time to wait."

"You're crazy."

"Never claimed not to be."

I shook my head, never surprised by anything Seren said or did.

"But seriously. Don't tell me you haven't thought about it?" he said.

"Prom?"

He leveled me with his eyes, shaking his head slowly. He had smoldering down to a science.

"Nope," I said.

His knowing smirk told me he knew I was lying. "So, you're telling me you've never thought about me naked?"

"Never."

He lifted his brows, seemingly surprised by my honesty. "Me on top of you?"

"Sorry."

His voice deepened. "Inside of you?"

I swallowed hard. He was a lot better at this game than I was.

He smiled. "I knew it."

"We were talking about prom," I said, redirecting our conversation. "And I know why you really want to go."

"I just told you," he said.

"You want to rub us in Kiki's face," I said.

"*Everyone's* face," he amended.

"Why?"

"Because there's nothing sweeter than making followers look pathetic for following. They didn't like you because they thought *I* didn't like you. How are they gonna feel when they see I *more* than like you?"

My belly dipped at his assertion.

He grew silent for a minute. "You deserve to have something good come out of moving to Windham."

"Something good did come from me moving here," I assured him.

His brows shot up.

"Sawyer," I explained. "I love that kid so much."

A smile spread across Seren's face. He knew—even after he'd given me the perfect night—I wouldn't stroke his ego.

He had enough people doing that.

CHAPTER 29

Grace

"Would you mind bringing this into the dining room for me?" Chef asked me the next night, handing me a serving platter filled with calamari.

"You sure you trust me not to drop it?" I teased as I pulled off my rubber gloves and took it from him.

"If Janette were here and I didn't have food on the stove, I wouldn't let you anywhere *near* that dining room."

I laughed. "Thanks for the reassurance." I used my butt to push the swinging door open and stepped into the dining room. The entire Grayson family was seated at the table, including Martine, and it was awkwardly quiet.

"What are you doing?" Seren jumped up and took the platter from my hands.

"Chef asked me to bring this out," I explained, realizing all eyes were on us.

"I don't want you serving us," he growled.

"Seren," Maureen said. "She works here."

"But she is *not* going to serve us," he said, his words meant for them as well as me.

"You're embarrassing me," I whispered, wondering where his anger stemmed from. Was it the charade of a family that pissed him off or the sight of me serving them the real cause?

"Stop being so damn angry, Seren," Maureen hissed. "It's unbecoming."

An unexpected bout of defensiveness washed over me. "Seren's not angry," I assured Maureen. "He's thoughtful, funny, and caring."

Everyone stared wide-eyed at me. Even Seren, who had no idea what to say.

"For what it's worth," I mumbled, before turning and hurrying back into the kitchen. I rushed to the sink and pulled on my rubber gloves knowing I just stepped out of line.

"What did you drop this time?" Chef asked.

"Just a bomb."

"God help us," Chef muttered.

As I picked up my scrub brush, the kitchen door swung open. I glanced over my shoulder. Seren stormed toward me. Something I hadn't seen before clouded his eyes. He stopped in front of me and cupped my cheeks, slamming his mouth down to mine. His tongue plunged into my mouth and he didn't care that Chef stood five feet away at the stovetop or that his family could walk in at any time. He was going to kiss me now and he was going to kiss me the way he wanted.

Chef eventually cleared his throat.

I pulled back, flushed and embarrassed. "Ummmm."

"You don't need to stand up for me," Seren said.

"If I don't, who will?" I asked.

His eyes riveted between mine like he couldn't fathom me thinking I needed to protect him. "Thank you."

I smiled.

He winked and walked back into the dining room leaving my heart racing in my chest.

* * *

As I sat on my bed painting my toenails, there was a knock on my bedroom door. Had my mother heard what I'd done in the dining room? I winced. "Come in."

The door opened and my mom stood there holding hangers filled with garment bags.

I swallowed hard as I twisted the top back onto my nail polish bottle. "I can explain."

"Explain why a delivery man just showed up with expensive clothes for my eighteen-year-old daughter? I know how much you make, and it is *not* enough to afford anything from Greta's Boutique."

I stood up, careful of my wet toenails, and took the garment bags from her. "I got asked to the prom." I lay the bags down on my bed.

"And?" she asked.

"That's it. I got asked to the prom and my date offered to get my dress since it's in three days."

She looked afraid to ask. "Who's your date?"

"Seren," I said, knowing it was best to just put it out there.

The color drained from her face. "No."

"Mom. We talked about this. You need to let me make up my own mind about people."

"Yes, people. Not *him*."

"He's not what you think."

She crossed her arms. "And how would you know what I think?"

"You think he's an angry guy who has mommy issues."

She scoffed. "That doesn't even come close."

"I know he thinks his mother is responsible for his father's death."

She huffed as if that wasn't news to her, but she didn't like hearing it.

"I know no one believes him," I continued, "which would make any person act out."

"Acting out is one thing. His behavior has been deplorable."

"He's a teenager. What do you expect? We don't all make the best decisions. He deserves a little leniency."

"He's had leniency his entire life. And look how he turned out."

"How? He's got a full ride to Alabama to play football. He's passing all of his classes. And he understands *Pride and Prejudice* which is completely over most guys' heads."

"Grace."

"Mom."

"He's not like you and me."

"Because of circumstance. Look at his mother. She remarried right after his father died. How did that look to you?"

She said nothing, just stared at me with those concerned eyes I knew all too well. It was the look she gave me when we'd sit at my father's bedside. When she wanted to make it clear that he wouldn't recover without admitting it. When she watched me cry and didn't know what to say because 'he's gonna be okay' would have been a lie.

"I'm leaving for college in three months—"

"Hopefully sooner if you get the internship," she said.

"Oh? Now you want me to leave?" I asked, surprised by the news.

"I want you far away from these Grayson Boys," she admitted.

I held up my index finger. "It's one dance."

Her eyes narrowed, zeroing in on my hand. "What's that?"

I dropped my hand knowing full well what she was referring to. "What?"

"On your finger."

I glanced down at my hand. "Oh, this? Just a ring."

"Where'd. You. Get. It?" she asked through clenched teeth.

I cocked my head. "Do you really want to know?"

She dropped down onto my desk chair, looking more exhausted than I'd seen her since my father died. "How did this happen?"

"Nothing happened. It was a gift. And now I want to go to a dance. It's that simple."

"I'm scared for you."

I knelt in front of her, taking her hands in mine. "There's nothing to be scared about."

"So you think. But I've seen this same scene play out before."

"I'm not Maureen. I'm not going to marry Seren and forget about the little people."

"That's not what I'm scared of," she said.

"I told you. He's not who you think. Come on," I said, trying to lighten the mood. "Help me pick out a dress."

She didn't look convinced or excited, but her eyes moved to the bags on my bed for a long time before she responded. "Well…let's see them."

Relief swept over me. I knew she didn't like the idea of me going with Seren—or him giving me a ring, but she at least wanted to help me look nice.

I stood up and unzipped the first bag. A gorgeous deep green, floor-length, strapless dress lay inside. Sparkles adorn the bodice.

"Oh my," my mother said.

Yes. Oh my, indeed.

CHAPTER 30

Grace

Seren stood in the driveway, waiting for me the next morning. "Hey."

"Hey," I said, as he moved toward the garage.

"Come on. I'm driving you today."

I didn't hesitate, hurrying to the passenger side of his Land Rover and slipping into the passenger seat.

"Did you like any of the dresses?" he asked once we were on the road.

"God, *yes.* They were all gorgeous."

"Which one did you choose?" he asked.

"It's a surprise."

He laughed, the raspy sound filling the car. "Well, I can't wait to see."

"Are you picking me up in the basement or should I meet you in the driveway?"

"Will your mom wanna take pictures?"

I swallowed, not sure if she'd actually want to *see* the two of us together. The idea of it was bad enough.

"What?" he asked, sensing my apprehension.

I shook my head. "Nothing. I'll have to ask her."

"She doesn't want you going with me, does she?"

"It doesn't matter. It's my decision."

He scoffed his eyes remaining on the road. "She's always had my mother's back. And the kicker? My mother treats her like shit."

I said nothing because it was the truth.

"If someone were that loyal to me," he said. "I'd treat them like fucking gold."

I reached over and slipped my fingers into his. "You've got me."

"I do, don't I?"

I smiled. "And, I already feel like I'm getting the gold treatment."

He chuckled and squeezed my hand.

* * *

After school, Seren waited at his car. I couldn't help admiring the way he leaned against it, so cool and unfazed by anyone. "Waiting for someone?"

He smiled once I stepped in front of him. "Yeah. The new girl who came in and said to hell with everyone in this place."

"She sounds pretty rad."

He laughed as he slipped my backpack off my back and opened my door for me. "I've got somewhere I wanna take you."

My brows furrowed. "Where?"

"Can't you just accept my need to surprise you?"

I laughed. "Fine."

I hopped inside and relaxed into the leather seat, loving the smell of Seren all around me.

We drove for about half an hour, but he never let on where we were going. He was getting good at surprising me, and I'd be lying if I said I didn't enjoy getting the Seren-treatment.

My phone pinged. I checked the screen. It was a text from Roger, a guy I'd grown up with. **Hey, Grace. Any chance you wanna go to prom with me?**

I winced.

"What?" Seren asked, his eyes jumping between me and the road.

"It's just some guy from Coopersville," I said, downplaying it so he didn't overreact. "He wants me to go to the prom with him."

"Do you wanna go with him?" Seren asked.

I shrugged. "I wouldn't mind being with my friends, but…"

"But what?"

I shook my head. "I'm just gonna tell him I can't."

"Go, if you want," Seren said, his words holding no conviction whatsoever.

"I think I have plans that night," I said.

His eyes cut to mine. "Doing what?"

"Hanging out with you."

He smiled, and there wasn't anything better than a Seren Grayson smile. "Great fucking answer."

I laughed before sending off a thank-you-but-I-can't text to Roger who sent a quick response. **No worries**.

When I looked up, I realized where Seren was taking me. My eyes shot to him. His eyes held a mix of indecision, and I understood why. His surprise could bring me sad memories or help me create new memories with him. I'd asked Seren to show me the real him. I'd asked him to stop screwing up. But nothing prepared me for *this* thoughtful surprise. "One of these days, Seren Grayson," I said. "One of these days I'm gonna tell everyone your secret."

His face sobered. "What secret?"

"The one about you being the most thoughtful guy I know."

"I'm only this way with you."

"*Exactly*. No one else gets to see it. And it's such a shame."

"I don't care about anyone else. I only care about you."

Sincerity coming from Seren seriously floored me.

He turned into the parking lot—the *aquarium* parking lot. I pulled in a deep breath as he parked and killed the engine. He glanced over at me. "Are you okay with this?"

I nodded.

We stepped out of the car and he met me at the front, linking our fingers as we walked to the aquarium entrance. He showed the cashier our tickets on his phone and we stepped inside.

Nostalgia swept over me as the sea blue walls and ceiling surrounded us. It had been two years since I'd been there, but it looked the same. Glass exhibits filled the first floor, and I suddenly couldn't wait to explore every inch of the aquarium with Seren.

We wandered over to the penguin exhibit first. The adorable penguins waddled over rock formations before diving into their pond. I paused to watch them speed through the water like little darts, so free under the water.

We continued to the next exhibit, stopping at its glass wall. A beluga whale appeared, swimming toward us as if it knew we were waiting to see it materialize. It took a sharp left turn so it didn't collide with the glass and disappeared. We waited for a few minutes, but it didn't return so we moved to the next exhibit.

My excitement grew.

Two dolphins swam side by side behind the glass wall and I couldn't contain my smile. One of them returned within seconds, making a pass by us before twisting back around and swimming by again. I held my hand up to the glass and, as it made another pass by, it slowed, letting my hand drift over it through the glass until it disappeared. But, it wasn't finished with me yet. It twisted back around and stopped right in front of me, turning so his snout tapped the glass gently as he stared at me. Excitement bubbled inside of me as my eyes cut to Seren.

He was recording the whole thing with his phone. "I've never seen anything like it. It's like it sees you and wants you to communicate with it."

A bout of sadness washed over me. I was happy Seren was there to see it, but I couldn't help thinking that my dad wasn't there to see it.

"Or, it just knows a beautiful girl when it sees one," Seren said, lowering his phone and attempting to make me laugh.

I appreciated him trying to bring levity to the moment because it would have been so easy for me to stay in that sad place.

Once the dolphin swam away, Seren directed me toward a sign for the Dolphin Showcase. "Come on."

My heartbeat hastened in my chest as we entered through the cave-type entrance, stepping into the auditorium filled with rows of empty metal benches and a huge pool in the front. A rush of anticipation swelled in my chest until I saw the showtimes sign. "Looks like the next show isn't for another hour."

I heard a splash and looked to see what had caused it. A male trainer in a wetsuit waded in the water with a dolphin. A female trainer crouched at the side of the pool in a wetsuit. She looked up at us. I was prepared for her to tell us we needed to leave, but she didn't. "Seren?" she asked.

"And Grace," Seren said.

She smiled. "Come on over."

My eyes cut to Seren who tugged on my hand, moving us closer. *What had he done?*

"I'm Jim and this is Lori," the trainer in the water said to me. "We hear you're gonna be a marine biologist."

I nodded.

"And you want to work with dolphins," Lori added.

"I'd like to work with their rescue and rehabilitation."

She smiled. "Well, come around." She motioned to the area beyond the railing where she kneeled at the side of the water. I joined her. "You don't mind getting wet, do you?" she asked.

"Not at all." I kneeled beside her, my knees becoming damp from the small puddles on the tiled floor.

"This is Peekoo," Jim explained as he held his hands beneath the dolphin who stayed in front of him. "She was rescued from the waters off the coast of Florida. We found her tied up in rope from a fishing trap which injured her fin right here." He moved his hand gently over a spot on her fin that had been slightly distorted.

"Put your hand like this," Lori said as she placed her hand on the top of the water—barely touching it. I did. Jim moved his hands from Peekoo's belly and she swam to us, gliding beneath our palms. Her skin felt like wet rubber and goosebumps scampered up my arms. I laughed, feeling so alive at that moment. Peekoo swam in a circle and returned, doing the same move under our hands again.

Jim made a swirling motion in the water with his hand.

Peekoo rolled onto her back and glided beneath our hands on her back while a clicking sound emanated from her.

Laughter tumbled out of me again as she stopped in front of me, letting me move my hand over her belly as Jim held his hand beneath her, making sure she stayed. I looked into her eyes and tears pricked my own. My dad was right. I needed to work with these beautiful creatures. I bet he knew it would help ease my pain once he was gone.

I glanced up at Seren. He gazed down at me with his arms crossed wearing a satisfied smile. He had every reason to be pleased with himself. He'd done something selfless. Something he knew would make me happy. Something that would show me the *real* him. He wasn't the heartless person he wanted people to think he was. There was so much more to him, and I was really starting to like that person.

* * *

"How did you ever manage that?" I asked Seren as we walked back to the car after spending over an hour in the Dolphin Showcase with the trainers.

"Let's just say they appreciated the donation from the Grayson family."

"*Seren*. You didn't have to do that."

He stopped in the middle of the parking lot and wrapped his arms around me. "I wanted to."

I stared into his beautiful green eyes, unable to articulate all the things I wanted to say about his generous gift. I settled for the easy one. "Thank you."

"I wish you could've seen your face," he said. "I get what you said about being able to read them. That dolphin adored you."

"Stop it," I said, assuming he was teasing me.

"I'm serious, Grace. I saw what your dad saw. Working with dolphins is where you belong."

I pushed myself to my tippy toes and pressed my lips to Seren's, trying to convey what I knew my words couldn't. He had no idea how much I needed to hear that—or how much I appreciated him taking me there.

He pulled back. "Where would you like to go tomorrow?"

I laughed. "Oh, now I see. You had ulterior motives."

He laughed. "Always."

CHAPTER 31

Grace

After acing a quiz in chemistry class, I headed upstairs toward English class excited to see Seren. As I neared the room, a blockade of students obstructed my way. Something was happening on the other side of the congestion. People held their phones up, recording whatever it was. A few girls screamed. Then, a couple of male teachers ran through, parting the crowd. They quickly pulled apart the two guys who'd been fighting, holding their arms behind their backs so they couldn't continue—*and* the teachers wouldn't get punched. I didn't recognize the first guy, but he looked like he'd taken the brunt of the attack. His shirt was torn and hanging wide-open and blood gushed down from his nose. The other teacher struggled to calm down the other guy who was trying to break free from the teacher's grasp. He spun him around. That's when I saw it was Seren.

Shit.

Blood covered his teeth and dripped from his mouth. His shirt was also torn and hanging off his body. The teacher directed Seren in the opposite direction, but Seren yanked free from the teacher's grasp, walking on his own accord in the opposite direction of where I stood. I watched until he was swallowed up by the crowd, and I couldn't see him anymore.

I hurried into English class and pulled out my phone, quickly texting him. **R u ok? What happened?** I stared down at my screen, waiting for him to respond.

"Thomas got his ass kicked," a guy somewhere behind me said.

I spun in my seat, hoping to hear more.

"I've never seen Grayson that angry," another added. "Not even on the football field."

"What caused it?" a girl asked.

"No idea," another said. "He just walked up to Thomas and kicked the shit out of him."

"They're both getting suspended," a girl nearby said.

"All right, ladies and gentlemen," our English teacher said. "Now that the melee has subsided, let's discuss our own battle. The battle of wits in our novel. Darcy and Elizabeth have been at odds for so long, it seems they both don't know what to do when faced with the realization that their battle has ended. Do they live happily ever after or will circumstances tear them apart?"

Great question.

I ate lunch by my car, waiting for Seren to appear or at least text me back, but he did neither. I looked for Sawyer or Saint in the hallways. But saw neither. Had they been involved in his fight somehow too?

I made it to last period gym class and sat on the outdoor bleachers instead of changing and participating. A text from Seren finally popped up on my screen. **Had to duck out early, Dolphin.**

Disappointment filled me, but his use of the word *dolphin* told me there was more to what happened today, and he must've had a good reason for fighting that guy.

"So unfortunate," Kiki said.

I glanced up from my phone, knowing—as much as I wanted to—I couldn't ignore her.

"I assume you and Seren planned on going to the prom together," she said, her lips in a tight line like it pained her to say it.

I narrowed my eyes, wondering where she was going with this.

"Sorry to have to break it to you," she said with a devious smile, "but it looks like you won't be going now. Fights equal suspension. And suspension means no prom. Too bad. I'm sure it would have been a magical evening for a poor girl like you."

Humorless laughter escaped me as the truth hit me. "Of course. You caused the fight."

"Sometimes it's just too easy," she said with a satisfied smile.

My blood boiled. I could feel myself itching to do something rash—like attack her. But that wasn't me. That wasn't how a sane person reacted. "Well, then I guess you got what you wanted."

"When I have Seren back, I'll have what I wanted." She spun away from me and walked off.

I knew I wasn't in Coopersville anymore.

I learned that the first day at Windham Prep.

But each day this horror show became more and more unbelievable. The kids here were crazy. And the lengths they'd go to get what they wanted were insane.

CHAPTER 32

Seren

"Why, Seren?" my mother pleaded from beside me in the backseat of her car.

I glanced to the front seat, making sure her driver wore his earbuds and his eyes were on the road. "He was running his mouth," I said without looking at her.

"Do I need to get you back in counseling?" she asked as if she actually gave a damn about me.

"Nope. Alcohol works just fine."

She groaned and, in the afternoon sunlight, her makeup couldn't conceal the dark circles beneath her eyes. "Tell me what I need to do."

"Nothing. You've done enough. I'm just biding my time until I'm away from this Godforsaken town and have my own life in Alabama."

She crossed her arms and stared out the window. "You act like your childhood here was so terrible."

"Only after dad died."

"I tried the best I could. But that wasn't good enough for you."

I said nothing.

She turned back to look at me. "I love you, Seren."

I scoffed.

"Laugh if you'd like, but it's the truth. I love you, and I love your brothers. And I loved your father."

I scoffed again, unable to stop myself.

"But I can only say that so much. And you'll either believe me or you won't."

"Fine. I won't."

She shook her head. "Where did I go wrong with you?"

"Would you like the list?"

"That's not fair," she admonished.

"Neither is this life."

"I'm calling Doctor Evans," she said.

"You can call her all you want. Doesn't mean I have to talk to her."

She buried her face in her hands and began to cry. "I didn't ask for this. I didn't ask for my husband to die and leave me with three growing boys. I didn't ask to have my firstborn despise me. I didn't ask to feel sick most days because of his hatred."

"Oh, so now you're blaming *me* for not feeling well."

She dropped her hands. Black mascara tears rolled down her cheeks. "I'm under a lot of stress. And, now, you're fighting in school and getting suspended. Maybe it's better that you leave. We'll both be happier and healthier."

"And there it is."

"There what is?"

"The truth. Was that so hard, Mother?"

"Oh, don't put this on me. I've tried with you, Seren. I've tried until I didn't know what else to do. Now, I'm bowing out. Go. Leave for Alabama as soon as you graduate. I'll pay for a place down there until you can move into the dorm. I want you to be happy. And, if leaving here will do that, then so be it."

Silence filled the car as her driver pulled up the driveway and stopped at the front door.

My mother opened her door and stepped out. "Your father would've despised the person you've become." She slammed the door behind her.

I stayed in the car, digesting all she'd said. She loved me, but she was letting me go. I'd heard that saying before. If you let something go it would come back to you if it was yours to begin with. Hopefully, she didn't wait too long for a return that was never going to happen.

Grace

I pulled through the gates of the manor after school, hoping Seren would be outside. But the driveway was empty. Did he know Kiki was somehow behind the fight?

I switched off the engine and made my way down to the apartment. If ever there was a good time for Seren to have broken in, now would have been it. But the apartment was empty. I still hadn't heard from him when I reached the kitchen for my shift. Chef was busy cooking so I moved to the sink and pulled on my rubber gloves.

"You have the night off tomorrow, right?" Chef said.

"Oh…I…" Would I still need the night off? Had Kiki been right about Seren not being able to go to the prom? "Yeah," I said, never one to take Kiki at her word. She was a snake. As I began scrubbing the stack of pans in the sink, I listened for voices in the dining room as Janette moved between the kitchen and dining room with trays of food. Though I strained to hear, there was nothing. The dining room was eerily quiet.

Janette stepped back into the kitchen, loading up her tray with shrimp atop lettuce leaves.

"It's quiet in there," I said.

She shrugged, never one to say much.

"Is Sawyer in there?" I asked, knowing better than to ask about Seren in front of Chef.

She glanced to me, her eyes narrowed curiously.

"I needed to ask him something about school," I said offhandedly.

She nodded. "Just him and his mother."

"Thanks," I said, wondering where Seren was. I knew he and Maureen had a strained relationship—with him accusing her of being a murderer and all. Maybe she'd sent him away. Maybe she realized she couldn't control him.

Chef glanced over his shoulder at me with a raised brow.

I twisted back around and continued scrubbing my pans.

It wasn't until I was sound asleep in bed that night that my phone buzzed. I reached out from underneath my comforter, feeling around for it on the nightstand. I squinted at the screen as the light blinded me in the dark room. **Meet me in the driveway tomorrow night at 8. Alone. Can't wait to see u in your dress.**

A rush of excitement moved through me. I hadn't realized how disappointed I'd been thinking it wasn't going to happen. I sent off a heart emoji and **R u ok?**

I waited, but he didn't respond.

I studied his text. Alone? I wondered what that was about. At least, since my mom wasn't thrilled I was going with him, it wouldn't be a big deal for her not to get a picture of us. I fell back asleep wondering why he hadn't mentioned seeing me in the morning or at school.

CHAPTER 33

Grace

I stared in my bedroom mirror, applying some blush to my cheeks.

"Girl, you look gorgeous," Holly said from our Facetime call. She and Laney were grinning like fools.

"Turn so I can see the back of your hair," Laney said.

I twisted so they could see the loose curls around my head. I'd clipped rhinestones in random spots so they'd sparkle when they caught the light.

"It looks so *good*," they cooed.

I laughed.

"Did you find out anything about the fight?" Holly asked.

I shook my head. "He wasn't in school and neither were Sawyer or Saint as far as I could tell."

"But gossip had to be spreading," Laney ascertained.

I shrugged. "Most girls left early to get their hair and makeup done, so my classes were pretty empty. Everyone was pretty consumed with the prom."

There was a knock on my bedroom door.

"Come in." I glanced over my shoulder.

My mom stepped inside, her eyes taking me in. "You look beautiful."

I smiled before looking back at Holly and Laney on my phone. "Gotta go."

"Have *fuuuuun*," they said before I ended the call and stood up.

"Turn around," my mom said.

I did a little twirl, having opted for the flowy pink dress with the rhinestone bodice and open back. I'd known it was the dress the moment I slipped it on. I hoped Seren liked my choice.

"Breathtaking," she said.

"I know. It must've cost a fortune."

"Not the dress, Grace. *You.*"

I tilted my head to the side, appreciating her compliment when I knew she didn't want me going with Seren. "Thank you."

She walked over and hugged me, careful not to wrinkle my dress or mess up my hair. "I love you."

I laughed. "I'm going to the prom not getting married."

She stepped back with tears in her eyes. "I know. It's just sometimes I forget how quickly you're growing up."

I glanced at the time on my phone. Seven fifty-eight. I grabbed my rhinestone clutch and tucked my phone and lip gloss inside. "Well, this is it."

She gave me one last look and smiled. "Have fun. Just not too much fun."

I laughed. "Don't wait up."

"*Grace*," she warned.

"I'll text if I'm gonna be late. But remember. You can trust me."

"It's not *you* that I'm worried about."

"Love you," I said, twisting away from her and hurrying out of the apartment.

I climbed the steps, careful not to misstep in my sparkly high heels. I pulled in a deep breath before opening the door. I stepped outside and froze when I hit the driveway. Seren stood there with a huge bouquet of flowers in his hand. His lips pulled into a smile as I drank in his dark suit and the black tie that brought out his gorgeous green eyes.

Seren

Holy fuck.

I was staring and I didn't even care. I hadn't expected to lose all track of space and time, but Grace all dressed up sucked the air right out of my lungs.

"Hi," she said, moving toward me. She lifted her hand to my cheek, her thumb brushing gently over the bruise under my left eye. "Are you okay?"

"I'm fine." I couldn't say the same for the douchebag who deserved getting his face beat in. I lifted the flowers. "These are for you."

She took them from my hand and brought them to her nose. "Thank you. They're beautiful."

"You're beautiful," I said, causing a slight blush to creep into her cheeks. It might've sounded like a line, but it was the fucking truth.

"Can I get a picture?"

We both turned to find Sawyer standing in the doorway, his big dopey grin stretching from ear to ear.

"Sure," Grace said before I could tell him to fuck off.

He took the flowers from her hand and placed them on the nearby bench as Grace slipped her arm around my waist and leaned against me. Another girl would've pressed herself to my side and given one of those #CouplesGoals poses. But Grace just wasn't that type of girl.

"Smile," Sawyer prompted as he clicked more than one picture.

I wanted to tell him to knock it off, but I couldn't bring myself to let Grace move away from me, especially when her sweet fruity scent had wrapped itself around me, holding me prisoner.

"Okay," I finally said, trying to keep the growl from my voice.

Sawyer lowered his phone.

"Send me the pictures," I said.

He smiled, and I knew it was because as much as I hated my picture being taken, I wanted the pictures of me and Grace. *Yes, little brother. I have a soul after all.*

"Have fun," Sawyer called as he walked back inside.

I looked at Grace. "You ready?"

She nodded, her eyes all hopeful and excited.

I hoped she wasn't disappointed with our change in plans. I slipped my hand into hers and walked her down the path toward the back lawn. I noticed her glance over her shoulder, wondering why we weren't leaving yet. But in true Grace fashion, she didn't ask.

"You weren't in school today," she said.

"I got suspended for the fight."

"I kinda heard that," she said. "Why *did* you fight that guy?"

"He posted the video of you. I told him to take it down and delete it. He refused, so I lost my shit."

"You didn't have to do that for me."

"Of course I did," I said. "What else did you hear?" I asked.

"Well…just that you weren't gonna be able to go to the prom."

"True story," I said as we approached the edge of the property. She had to know by now where we were headed. "I'm sorry I couldn't give you a real prom. But I'm hoping this will suffice."

She stopped, her hand squeezing mine in a vice grip as her eyes widened.

CHAPTER 34

Grace

Speechless didn't even come close to how I felt. Strands of big bulb lights were strung from the top of the treehouse down to the trees all the way around forming a big top, circus-like tent made up solely of lights. *Thousands* of lights. Soft music played from speakers inside the treehouse. I looked to Seren. "You did all of this for me?"

"Well, yeah. *I* didn't need a prom."

"It's beautiful," I said, taking in the transformed area that was so much better than any prom would've been. "Oh, we are so posting pictures of this."

"Why?"

"Because Kiki is gonna be so pissed."

He pulled me to him, wrapping his arms around me so all I could do was look up into his eyes. "I don't give a fuck what anyone thinks but you." His lips were on mine before I could respond. His tongue pushed between my lips, and our tongues tangled in a delicious dance.

I pulled out of the kiss first, knowing if our night started this hot and heavy, we weren't getting through a single dance. "So, what do we do at a Seren prom?"

"You sure you want to know?"

I laughed. "Keep it clean."

He balked. "With you looking this hot, not a chance."

Heat pulsed in my cheeks, spreading to the rest of my body.

He took my hand and led me to the area beneath the treehouse. He spun me around slowly before slipping his arm around my waist and swaying us to the slow music. My heartbeat sped up as he buried his nose in my hair. I'd never been so turned on by another human being in my life. But Seren brought that out of me. And we were all alone out there. And there was music and lights and this take-me-right-now-or-I'll-die-feeling pulsing through my body.

"Why do you like me?" Seren asked as we danced.

"Why do you like *me*?"

"You didn't answer my question," he said, and I knew he was purposely avoiding looking at me when he asked.

It was a tough question to answer. He was such a mystery. But at the same time such an open book when it came to me. "You trust me," I offered.

Silence passed between us as we continued to dance beneath the lights.

"Is that it?" he asked, disappointment evident in his tone.

"You gave me my own prom," I said.

"Because I got suspended," he countered.

"You're passionate about what you believe in," I said, knowing his analysis of *Pride and Prejudice* touched the surface of his passion for what he knew to be right. Just like his allegations about his mother. Though crazy, he wholeheartedly believed them and would convince you he was right. And, knowing he wanted full honesty from me—since he had the nerve to ask the question in the first place—I admitted, "You make me feel things I've never felt before."

"Like?" he pried.

"Like…extreme rage."

His head hitched back, his eyes meeting mine.

"But then extreme happiness, too."

He smiled, and I liked knowing my words caused that reaction in him.

"Why do you like *me*?" I asked again, not letting him off the hook so easily.

He didn't hesitate. "Because when I'm with you, I don't feel so broken."

I swear to God part of my heart shattered into tiny pieces at his words. Not because they hurt, but because they were the truth. He felt broken because he was angry. Because no one believed him. Because no one else understood him.

"When you're around," he continued. "People's expectations of me and my own anger just drop away."

If I could've fallen into a pile of useless goo, I would've. His words broke me—in the best possible way.

We finished dancing to the song and when a new one began, Seren took my hand. "Come on," he said, his head ticking toward the tree steps. I slipped off my heels and handed them to Seren who held them as I tried to navigate the plank steps in a dress. I glanced down at him standing behind me. "Don't look up my dress."

He chuckled. "Try and stop me."

I rolled my eyes and climbed the rest of the way up. I froze once I stood inside, my eyes taking in the pillows covering the floor. Flickering candles were placed all around the bench seats giving off a beautiful soft white glow. I glanced over at Seren who stepped up beside me. A small smile pulled up one side of his mouth. He knew what I was thinking. "This is…"

"For you," he said.

I faced him, my head tipping to one side. "Thank you."

"You should have been in Coopersville. You should have had your own prom. I hope this is enough."

Balloons and a ring on my birthday. A private movie showing. A chance to interact with dolphins. A prom just for me. Was I becoming Maureen? Was I being swept up in this fairy tale Seren was creating for me? If I was, I never wanted it to end. "It's more than enough."

He wrapped me in his arms and kissed the top of my head. We stood like that for a long time. I waited for him to say something, but he didn't. Was he waiting on me? Was he confused about how to proceed? Had he not thought that far ahead?

Another song began and Seren began to move us slowly to the music. I didn't want to feel as safe in his arms as I did. I didn't want to believe that this was supposed to happen. I didn't want to think that the two of us—from such different worlds—just fit. But we did.

Seren pulled back just enough to see my face, but he said nothing as his eyes drifted over my features.

"What?" I asked.

He shook his head. "I'm just happy I get you all to myself. I never would've made it through the whole night with you looking so beautiful in a room full of jealous guys."

"And jealous girls," I added. "They would've been shooting me death glares all night with you looking this hot."

He chuckled.

"Don't stop."

His brows inverted.

"Laughing. I love when you laugh."

"*You* make me laugh."

I gestured with my hand as if to bow.

His face sobered and his lips puckered in contemplation. "It sucks that I'm leaving for Alabama soon."

"To be college football's best quarterback," I added.

I expected him to smile and say something smug, but he didn't. "I was so excited to go. You know, to get the hell away from this place. But now, this place is looking a lot better."

"I'm leaving right after you, you know?"

"Can I talk you into going to Alabama instead?" he asked.

I swallowed hard as butterflies fluttered in my belly. I lifted a hand to his cheek, gently letting my fingertips trail over his freshly shaven cheek and jawline. "You've got a big football career ahead of you."

"So?"

"So, I'll just be a state away. That's all."

His mouth turned down as if he expected me to say I'd drop all of my plans to follow him and his dreams. He had to know I wasn't that girl.

I lifted my other hand, now cupping both of his cheeks. "Looks like we're just gonna have to make the most of our time together now." I urged his mouth down to mine and met his lips in a slow kiss. I was in charge, taking my time and exploring his mouth as if it was the very first time. He let me lead, a willing recipient as I teased his bottom lip between mine before moving to his top lip. I wanted to go all-in, but the torture of going slowly—of savoring each second—was causing my heart to race and my body to hum. I slipped my tongue between his lips, moving in a slow tangle with his. He played along, his hands gliding down my lower back, gently coasting over my ass until he scooped me up in his arms.

I giggled against his mouth and wrapped my arms around his neck. My flowy dress allowed me to easily wrap my legs around his waist. Maybe not the most lady-like move, but we were alone, and I really liked knowing that we were.

Seren moved us toward the huge heap of pillows in the corner of the treehouse. He sat down on them with me straddling his lap. His hands lifted to my face and, as if a magnetic pull controlled us, our lips collided in an intense explosion of want, need, and excitement. I fumbled for the buttons on his shirt. Seren stopped kissing me, grabbing my wrists and holding them where they were. "Grace?"

"Seren?"

"What are you doing?"

"You know what I'm doing," I said, my chest rising and falling at an alarming rate.

"But do you *really* know what you're doing?" he asked, his voice low and gravelly.

"God, I hope not."

He shook his head, amused. But the amusement quickly faded from his face. His eyes became serious and focused solely on mine. "I do not expect anything tonight."

"Where's the fun in that?" I asked.

His brows shot up. "You're looking for fun?"

"I'm looking for something," I said, unsure where my candor had come from.

His lips slid into a cocky grin. "Well, I can definitely give you something."

My belly dipped as he slipped off his jacket and tossed it aside. He loosened the knot of his tie, ready to remove it when my hand shot out and stopped him. "Leave it on."

A flash of intrigue crossed his eyes.

I watched as he unbuttoned the buttons down the front of his shirt, each revealing more and more of his chest. Once they were undone, I pushed his shirt wide open. I couldn't stop myself from admiring the perfection that lay underneath as I pulled off his first sleeve then the other, leaving the black tie around his neck.

"Your turn," he said with a grin.

I swiveled on his lap, offering the back of my neck where my dress was clasped. He undid the first of the three clasps as I held the front of my dress to my chest, knowing as soon as all three were unfastened, the dress would fall away from me. His fingers brushed the back of my neck, and a shiver scampered down my spine as he unclasped the second one. My pulse spiked as he unfastened the last clasp. I turned back to him, my arms crisscrossing my chest to hold the dress to me.

His eyes were on mine, eager for me to undress, but I wasn't that bold. I grabbed his tie and pulled him forward, pressing my lips to his as I wrapped my arms around him. Thankfully, my dress was held up by our bodies. I couldn't get close enough and could feel his want for me between my thighs as he kissed me like he needed me to breathe. His hand slipped under my dress, and he squeezed my ass as we continued kissing. I shifted my hips, rocking back and forth over his erection. He groaned against my mouth which only urged me on.

He eventually tore his lips from mine and buried them in the crook of my neck, peppering my skin with open-mouthed kisses that made me dizzy. "Jesus, Grace."

There wasn't a doubt in my mind that no one would ever make me feel the way Seren was making me feel in that moment. He wanted me. All of me. And I wanted to give him that. "Do you have a condom?" I asked, though as soon as the words left my lips, a vision of the huge box under his bathroom sink flashed in my mind. I shook off the thought, knowing it would only cause me to push him away. And, the Seren *I* knew was not the one I first met.

He reached in his back pocket and pulled one out, tossing it beside us. Of course, he came prepared. He seemed to plan each of his moves carefully. That's why he was so baffled by me. He hadn't planned on me.

Seren grasped my shoulders, gently guiding me off his lap. I held my dress up to keep it from falling down as I watched Seren stand. My breathing was labored and my eyes hooded as I watched him close the trap door to the treehouse and twist the lock. I hadn't even realized it had a lock. He slipped off his black shoes before turning back around. He unbuttoned his pants and lowered the zipper as he watched me watching him. He pushed down his pants and black boxer briefs and stepped out of them. He had so much more resolve than me because my eyes went right to his erection, standing tall against his stomach. My eyes flashed up to his. He wore a smirk, clearly not minding me staring. He reached down and grabbed himself, pumping his hand a few times. The ache between my thighs came hard and fast. I let my dress fall away from my chest, pushing it down the rest of the way until I wore nothing but my pink thong. Seren's breath caught in his throat before he moved toward me, easing me back on the pillows as his body covered mine. His thumb brushed over my cheek as his eyes riveted between mine. "I've got you, Grace."

I swallowed hard. "I know."

He leaned down and captured my lips. One of his hands slipped between my legs. I sucked in a sharp breath when he pushed aside my thong and his fingers slid across my wetness, gliding back and forth. *Oh, God.* My head dropped backward as my eyes snapped shut. His lips abandoned my lips, sucking his way down the front of my neck. At the same time, his fingers plunged inside me, moving in and out in a slow rhythm. Tingles built with each brush of my clit. I began to pant, but I was too overwhelmed with sensations to be embarrassed. I was there for it. I was so there for it. Before I realized what he was doing, he'd removed his fingers and my thong. My eyes popped open.

"You ready?" he asked, his face lingering over mine.

I nodded.

He smirked before pressing a quick kiss to my lips. He reached for the condom, tearing open the packet and rolling it on. I watched as he aligned his erection between my legs. I held my breath, ready for him. *So* ready for him. He pushed once, twice, and then he slipped right inside. We both groaned, ready to spiral down the same path together.

"You feel so fucking good, Grace."

I tried to smile, but so many emotions were washing over me with Seren looking so hot on top of me and feeling so amazing inside of me. Every part of his body was strong and in charge. And right then, I was getting all of him.

I slipped my hands around his hips, gliding them over the rock-hard muscles in his back. I trailed my fingertips down, sliding them over the dip in his back and then his ass, grasping him there as he thrust in and out of me. He wasn't moving fast. He'd set his rhythm and didn't waver from it. So Seren-like. So planned out. So focused.

I lifted my hips, craving the feel of him moving against my clit. He sensed my need and adjusted his hips, hitting it every time. White spots formed behind my closed eyes. Heat began to build between my thighs. My panting became heavy. My whimpers became pained. I wanted to hold on and let go all at the same time.

"I've got you, Grace."

I opened my eyes to find his eyes focused on mine. His cheeks were flushed and sweat clung to his forehead. God, he was a vision.

"I want to see you come, Grace," he panted as his thrusts became harder. "It's all I can think about."

My belly dipped. I kept my gaze on his as I let the sensations spiraling inside me coil so tightly that all I could do was let go. Everything inside me released and tingles shot out from between my thighs to every part of my body. "Oh. My. God," I panted, never having endured something so all-consuming in my entire life.

Seren didn't stop even when the waves that washed over me subsided. He linked his arms under my bent knees, urging them to his sides. "Holy fuck," he said through clenched teeth, gliding in faster and harder. I held on to his hips, watching his face contort from what looked like pain to what I knew to be pleasure. He thrust a few more times before groaning, then stilling inside me. He unlinked his arms from my knees and lowered himself on top of me, dropping his head to the side of my neck and remaining like that for a long time. Our labored breathing and racing hearts mirrored each other as we lay together in silence.

I hadn't planned on having sex with him. It was definitely very soon. But I knew I had strong feelings for Seren. He made me feel special and he trusted me with everything sacred to him—even though I knew it was difficult for him to let people in.

"Thank you, Grace," he said, finally breaking the silence.

"For what?"

"For trusting me."

Ripples rolled through my belly. How was it that I was the only one who got to see this side of him? "I would definitely go to a Seren prom again."

He laughed, finally lifting his head and resting his chin so he could look at me. "Is that so?"

I nodded.

"Would it freak you out if I told you I loved you?" he asked.

My eyes widened.

"I'll take that as a yes," he said. And, though he tried to conceal his disappointment, it was there.

"It wouldn't freak me out," I admitted, needing him to know he could feel however he wanted to feel.

A small smile formed in the corners of his lips. "Good to know." He lowered his head, resting his cheek on my chest. There was no way to conceal my heartbeat knocking around inside me because Seren Grayson just told me he loved me in the only way he knew how to.

CHAPTER 35

Grace

The seniors were called to the auditorium on the last day of school to watch a senior slideshow (I wasn't in it), sign yearbooks (I didn't buy one), and pick up graduation caps and gowns. Seren waited for me outside the gym.

"You made it," he said as we began walking to the auditorium.

"Did I?"

"You've just gotta cross the stage this weekend and your time here will be over," he assured me.

"It hasn't been all bad," I said, bumping him with my shoulder.

"Oh, that's right because of Sawyer."

I laughed and so did he.

"If it isn't the happy little couple," Kiki said, stepping in front of us and blocking our path. "Let me guess. He knocked you up."

My eyes widened. "What?"

"It's the only reason I can fathom he'd choose you over me." She looked at Seren. "Is that it?"

"You want the truth?" he asked her, a scary look crossing his features and causing me to tense beside him.

"Yes," she said, tipping her chin in an attempt to even the one-foot disparity in their heights.

"You're a bitch," he said.

She laughed. "Well, obviously. That's no secret."

"Yeah, but Grace isn't," Seren continued. "She's kind and funny, and the girl I fell in love with."

As tense as I was, hearing him admit that to Kiki had my stomach flipping over itself.

"You don't want kind, Seren," Kiki snarled. "You want angry and you want cruel. You thrive on it."

"You're angry, Kiki. *So* fucking angry," he continued. "We were never gonna work."

"Of course we were," she snapped. "We're the king and queen of this place. These people adore us."

I glanced over my shoulder and noticed someone capturing the interaction on their phone. I quickly looked back to Kiki. "You *think* they adore you, Kiki," I said. "The truth is, no one can stand you."

"Shut up, bitch," she snapped. "These people follow us and fall at our feet like the followers they are—the ones we *trained* them to be. They're nothing without Seren and me." She looked back to Seren. "We own this place. Just like we'll own the whole fucking town one day, and these people won't even make the guest list for the parties we'll throw."

"I love Grace." Seren shrugged. "It's that simple."

Anger swept over Kiki's face. She wasn't getting her way, and she was coming unhinged before our eyes. She hauled off and slapped Seren across the face.

Before he could react, I grabbed Kiki's arm and flew into her face. She may have been a bitch, but I was pissed. "Don't *ever* touch him again. Got it, bitch?"

"Grace," Seren said, his hand gently grasping my arm and urging me away from Kiki.

"Or what?" Kiki sneered at me. "You'll try to fight me like your sewer rats from Coopersville?"

Seren was behind me and now had his hand on my arm. "She's not worth it."

I looked her dead in her eyes. "You're right. She'll get what she's got coming." I spun away from her and slipped my hand into Seren's as we made our way toward the auditorium. "Did she hurt you?" I asked him.

"She can't hurt me. And you don't have to stand up for me," Seren said, though the pride in his eyes told me he appreciated me having his back again. He squeezed my hand and I knew—at least for the time being—all was right in the world.

CHAPTER 36

Graduation Day
Grace

The sun shone down on the football field as I crossed the stage in my navy cap and gown. I smiled as I accepted my diploma from the principal then held it up toward the audience. My mom and Sawyer snapped photos from their seats amongst the families in the bleachers. I glanced at the sea of navy graduates seated down on the field. Seren, looking so damn hot in his cap and gown, clapped from his seat with a smirk on his face.

That boy would be the death of me.

I stepped off the stage and filed back to my seat. My legs bounced anxiously beneath me. Seren, seated three rows in front of me, had already received his diploma, but he wasn't the one I was waiting to see.

"Marissa Winslow," the announcer called.

The audience applauded as she crossed the stage.

"Trent Young," the announcer continued.

The audience grew louder when Trent did a backflip before accepting his diploma.

"And, our final graduate of this year's graduating class, Kiki Ziegler!" the announcer shouted with enthusiasm.

Before the audience could even applaud, the speakers crackled and Kiki's voice blasted out. "I'm the queen of this place. These people adore me."

Kiki stopped at center stage and looked around confused by where her voice was coming from.

"These people follow me and fall at my feet like the followers they are—the ones I *trained* them to be," her voice continued echoing throughout the stadium.

The graduates looked around, their narrowed eyes conveying their disgust at Kiki's words. Because there was no denying it *was* Kiki's voice. And thanks to a little creative editing, every nasty thing she'd said was included.

"Shut it off!" the principal demanded whoever would listen.

"These sewer rats are nothing without me," Kiki's voice continued. "I own this place. Just like I'll own the whole fucking town one day."

Boos erupted from the graduates. Some stood and yelled at her while others shouted obscenities. Kiki, looking like a deer in headlights, rushed off the stage without her diploma.

Cheers erupted.

I glanced at Seren who was looking over his shoulder at me. I shrugged. He laughed, realizing that there was no way I was letting Kiki win. She'd done all the terrible things I'd once believed Seren had done to me—and then some. She deserved a little retribution. And if that meant letting people know the real Kiki, then I felt as though it was my duty as the "poor girl" in town to give that to them.

One of my classmates jumped to his feet, and the rest of us followed suit, throwing our caps in the air and leaving Kiki a distant memory.

Seren found me after the ceremony. "Well, that was interesting."

I laughed, quickly changing the subject before my mom caught on to what he was talking about. "Congrats! We made it."

He chuckled before looking at my mom. "Would you like me to take some photos of you and Grace?"

"That would be really nice," my mom said, seemingly surprised Seren would offer to do such a thing.

"Thanks," I said as I handed him my phone.

My mom and I smiled with our arms wrapped around each other's waists as Seren snapped a bunch of photos.

"Let me get a couple of you kids," my mom offered as she stepped away from me and took my phone from Seren.

I nearly fell over, knowing it was the last thing she probably wanted to be doing. Seren moved beside me, smiling down at me. I returned his smile as I wrapped my arm around his waist and he wrapped his around my shoulders—keeping it PG for my mom's benefit.

"Smile," my mom said.

We did and she snapped a few photos of us. I really hoped she knew what she was doing and didn't cut off half his head. Scratch that. She knew *exactly* what she was doing and likely cut off half his head.

"That's good," I said as I stepped away from Seren and retrieved my phone from her.

Seren's family appeared, ready to take their own photos.

"Congratulations, Grace," Maureen said. She looked like she was trying to look put together, but her makeup was overdone and her words were weak.

"Thank you," I said.

She smiled at my mom but said nothing.

"Would you like to join us at the country club?" Martine offered, his eyes moving between my mom and me.

"Oh, thank you. But my mom already has reservations for us," I said, saving us all the awkwardness of sharing a meal.

"Too bad," Maureen said, though I couldn't tell if she was being sincere or not.

Sawyer gave me a quick hug while Saint gave a vague nod.

"I'll see you later," Seren said to me before moving his family away from us.

I breathed a sigh of relief once they were gone. All of us sharing a meal would have been way too weird.

* * *

My mom and I returned from lunch, parking beside the manor's garage as usual. No one was around. Seren must've still been out celebrating with his family. Maureen had wanted to throw an elaborate party for him, but he nixed that idea opting for a luncheon, which I knew still killed him to accept.

I changed and slipped on some cutoffs, a black Savage Beasts T-shirt, and black Chucks. I'd gotten Seren a graduation gift, knowing he'd been so thoughtful when it came to gifts for me. Since the Graysons weren't home yet, I'd dash up to his room, leave it there, and sneak out without anyone knowing I'd been there.

I grabbed the small box wrapped in graduation caps wrapping paper and called to my mom. "I'll be back in a little bit."

"Okay," she called from her room.

I climbed the stairs to the main floor and hurried toward the kitchen entrance. I stopped short when I found Martine standing at the center island pouring a small tube of something into a teacup. He must've heard my sneakers squeak to a stop because his eyes cut to me, and he quickly tucked the tube into his pocket. "Oh, hi, Grace."

"Hi."

"Did you have fun today?" he asked, his voice nervous and his hand shaky.

I nodded, my eyes focused on his pocket and my mind whirling back to chemistry class.

"Thallium in this form is dangerous, but what if ingested? In its powder form, it used to be used in rat poison until it was outlawed…"

"Can you be arrested for having it?" a girl in the front asked.

He laughed. "Only if I try to poison someone with it."

"Did you bring your own sweetener?" I asked Martine, my heart suddenly beating out of my chest.

"Oh, yes," Martine said. "I have it imported from Italy for *mi amore*."

I nodded, but every fiber of my being told me that I already knew the truth. Seren had been wrong about his mom. "That's very nice of you," I said, trying to keep my voice steady.

"Happy wife," he grinned, referencing the earlier conversation we'd had.

"Is Seren in his room?" I asked, needing to get away from him as quickly as possible.

"Oh, probably. Why don't you run up and check?"

"I will. See you later." I hurried out of the kitchen and toward the staircase, taking two steps at a time. I needed to tell Seren what I saw. If anyone was going to believe me, it was him. I reached his room and tapped on his door. When he didn't respond, I opened it. He wasn't there. I hurried to his bathroom, but he wasn't in there either. I pulled out my phone and texted him. **Where r u? Need to talk.**

I sat on the edge of his bed and stared at my phone, desperate for him to respond. My legs bounced beneath me; I'd stumbled upon something big. I knew I hadn't imagined it. Martine was putting something in Maureen's tea. Something that shouldn't have been there. Sweetener my ass.

I typed Thallium poisoning in my search bar. I knew there were other ways to poison someone, but since my teacher mentioned it, I started there. According to one article, people who ingested it over a short time reported issues with their lungs, heart, liver, or kidneys. It also contributed to hair loss and vomiting. It could cause death, but the effects of long-term ingestion were inconclusive.

Could that be the cause of Maureen's withering appearance? *And* Seren's father's "heart attack?"

There were tests for Thallium levels in urine or blood, but it was difficult to detect if not tested right after ingestion. This would explain why an autopsy wasn't done on Seren's dad. Martine would have been discovered. But why get rid of him? If it was for Maureen, why was he slipping something in *her* drink?

I thought back to the day I'd heard him yelling in his office. He'd said he needed more time. More time to murder Maureen? This was all so insane. But what if it wasn't?

If we could just get that tube to see if it could be tested for whatever was inside, we'd have proof.

"Grace?"

I glanced up from my phone. Martine stood in Seren's doorway. Alarm bells wailed in my head. "I have great news for you," he said. "Would you mind following me up to my office?"

Shit. Shit. Shit. "I'm waiting for Seren," I said, hoping he let me be.

"Oh, silly me. Did I say he might be up here? Maureen got him and his brothers tickets for New England's preseason training session. She surprised him at lunch."

My stomach dropped.

He wasn't coming home.

"Oh, you know what?" I stood up. "I just remembered I need to help my mom with something." I moved to the door, but Martine blocked my way.

"Please," he said. "Come with me."

I wanted to run. I wanted to scream. But if I had totally blown all of this out of proportion, I'd look like a raving lunatic. Maybe this was a simple misunderstanding. Maybe this was nothing. "Okay," I said, knowing I was going to regret this decision because everything inside me told me this *wasn't* a misunderstanding.

Martine held out his arm, allowing me to pass to the stairway first. We climbed the stairs in silence to the third floor. Each step brought me closer to God-only-knew-what. The third-floor hallway still carried that dark coldness that the second floor did not. As we reached his office, Martine opened the door and again allowed me to enter first. I stepped inside with my heart in my throat. I glanced around at the dark-paneled wood walls that looked similar to those in the hallways. A huge bookshelf covered one wall and his desk sat prominently in front of the other. He rounded his desk and sat in the high-back leather swivel chair behind it. "Have a seat."

On the wall behind his desk hung a big flat screen. He switched it on. His computer screen was mirrored on it. He clicked a few buttons and rows of boxes filled the screen, all of them live camera feeds from different rooms in the house. Some of them switched between hallways. But every room was there. He pointed to the right bottom corner. "I can even see in your room," he said with delight.

A cold chill raced up the back of my neck. He'd been watching me?

"I know everything that goes on in the manor. And outside of it." He clicked a few buttons and the inside of the treehouse appeared on the screen. He clicked a few more buttons and then there was the image of Seren and me having sex.

I jumped to my feet on wobbly legs. "Shut it off!" I needed to get out of there. And I needed to get out of there fast.

"Sit down, Grace," he clipped, leaving the video on with the volume up so Seren's grunts and my whimpers echoed throughout the room.

Tears stung my eyes. "I want to leave."

"That's why I brought you up here. Remember our conversation about that internship at the Tampa Marine Life Rescue Center?"

I lowered myself back into the chair and closed my eyes so I wouldn't have to look at the screen.

"They appreciated the very generous donation I made and were all too happy to have you in their internship program. But, you must leave tonight."

"Tonight?"

"You were a last-minute addition," he said.

"I don't understand."

"What's to understand? You wanted in and I got you in. Now you must go."

My mind was reeling. It was as if a tornado had swooped me up and was now placing me back down and I couldn't make sense of where I was or what was going on. He was trying to get rid of me because he knew that I knew his plan. He was blackmailing me.

Martine switched off the video and played another: my mom and me in my room discussing Seren. 'You think he's an angry guy who has mommy issues,' I said in the video. My mom scoffed. 'That doesn't even come close.' I responded quickly. 'I know he thinks his mother is responsible for his father's death.' My mother huffed. So, I continued. 'I know no one believes him,' I continued, 'which would make any person act out.'

Martine paused the video there. "My stepson certainly acts out. Maybe he even killed his own father. Or, maybe his mother did. I guess you never really know a person. But I'd be willing to bet that if the police ever decide to show up here, your mother would come under major scrutiny. You know, distraught that her best friend treated her like garbage after all those years of servitude. She has access to every room in this place. She could easily have poisoned Maureen—or her husband."

Rage festered inside of me. My head spun with confusion. Who could I tell? Who would believe me? What could I do to stop him?

"I would hate for any sweetener to end up in the wrong cup," he mused.

I didn't know what to do. How could I be sure he wouldn't hurt anyone? If no one believed Seren, why would they believe me?

"You will leave on the eight-forty flight I have booked for you," Martine said. "My driver will take you. He has all the information you need to get settled in Tampa. You will speak to no one. I have cameras and microphones on every part of this property. I have tracking on everyone's phones and access to all conversations and texts, including your mother's and Seren's. You will not try to contact him. You may contact your mother, but if you do, I will be monitoring every word you say. If I think you're trying to tell her anything, she will have an unfortunate accident. If you contact the police, she's dead and I will pin it on Seren. You will lose them both. Do you understand me?"

It was as if the air had been punched out of my lungs. I was lightheaded and devastated. I was stuck with no one to turn to. No one to help me. "And if I stay away?"

"Everyone will be just fine," he assured me with a shifty grin.

"Including Maureen?"

"Oh, my sweet *amore*. All she has to do is sign the business over to me and she will be fine. But she wants Seren to have it. So, we will see. The ball's in her court, as they say."

"Make Seren a deal," I pleaded. "Buy him out. There has to be something you can say to convince him. Let *me*. I'll get him to give you the entire business. He doesn't want it anyway. He just wants to play football."

"You think you're that convincing?" he scoffed. "You spread your legs in a matter of weeks. You're lucky he's paid you this much attention. He fucks them all and leaves them. I'm doing you a favor getting you away from him." He glanced down at his expensive watch. "By my calculations, you're already on your way out."

My stomach churned, not only because of what he'd said but because he'd disregarded my pleas. If Seren knew what was on the line, he'd hand over the company. But, then again, he'd know who killed his father. So, Martine would never pressure him and risk showing his hand. "I'll go."

He smiled. "I knew you'd see things my way."

"I need your word that you won't hurt anyone."

"I'm the one running the show, sweetheart. Not you."

I stood on unsteady legs.

"And just remember. I'll be watching you," he warned with a sick smile on his face.

CHAPTER 37

Grace

I moved as quickly as I could from the third floor to the basement, trying not to break down until I'd reached my room. And even then, I reined in my tears because I knew Martine was watching.

"Grace?" my mother called.

I froze when she poked her head into my room.

"What are you doing?"

"I just got some great news," I said, trying to pull it together. "I got the internship."

Her mouth opened. "That's amazing."

I tried to smile. "I leave tonight."

She gasped. "Tonight?"

Tears glazed my eyes. "Yes, isn't that great?"

"Oh...I...I wasn't ready. You just graduated."

"It's a great opportunity," I said, moving to my closet and pulling my suitcase down from the top shelf, avoiding eye contact so I didn't make her suspicious. "And, you know how much I've wanted this." I placed the suitcase down on my bed and opened it.

My mother went to my dresser and started taking out the clothes inside, packing them in my suitcase for me. "It's gonna be quiet around here without you."

A perpetual ringing pierced my ears as I went to the closet and pulled some hoodies and jeans off their hangers. I folded the clothes and placed them into my suitcase.

"I got so used to being with you every day. It's been nice." I was happy she walked into the bathroom because tears trailed down my cheeks.

Pull it together, Grace. I wiped away the tears and began packing my shoes.

"I missed out on a lot of your childhood working here," she admitted when she walked back out with an armful of my toiletries.

"But at least we had this time," I said, on the verge of breaking down.

"Is Seren taking you to the airport or do you need me to?"

Her question knocked me off balance. *Seren?* I wouldn't even get to see him before I left. And even if I did, I risked Martine misconstruing whatever I said to him. It was a lose-lose situation, and my heart was breaking with each moment that passed.

"No. I have a car taking me," I said, hoping she didn't ask any questions.

She didn't, but only because she too was trying to hold it together.

"I'm gonna carry this up to the door and come back down to pack my backpack."

"I can send anything you forget," my mom offered. "Do you know where you're staying?"

My chest tightened, and a knot swelled in my throat making it difficult to swallow. The truth was, I had no idea. Martine said his driver would give me the information. "I get all that info when I arrive," I said before heading out of the apartment and dragging the suitcase up to the doorway.

That's when it hit me. What if Martine planned to have me killed? What if this whole sending me to Tampa story was to get me alone so he could kill me? It wasn't like he hadn't been behind Mr. Grayson's death. Would my life be over the second I got into the car? It wasn't like I even had a choice. Stay and everything was pinned on Seren or my mother. Go and keep everyone safe.

I went back down to my room with a growing pit in my stomach. Every part of my body trembled. I dropped down onto the edge of my bed and prayed to God I was taken to the airport and not the middle of the woods to be executed.

My mom stepped into my doorway. "You okay?"

I jumped, trying to regain some semblance of composure. "Just a little nervous. This is a big thing I'm doing."

"You're gonna do great," she assured me.

"I'll call you the second I land in Tampa," I said, deciding to use the fact that Martine would be listening to my advantage. "Martine arranged a ride for me to the airport. Wasn't that so kind of him?" I said to my mom, hoping she didn't say anything bad about him.

"He's such a nice man," she responded.

I breathed a sigh of relief. Now, he knew two things: my mom trusted him and she knew who arranged my travel. If I didn't land in Tampa, he'd be the number one suspect.

I stood up, feeling a lot more at peace as I opened drawers and stuffed anything I thought I'd need into my backpack. I went to the closet, noting stacks of sweaters remained at the top and two items hung from hangers: my prom dress—my beautiful prom dress that Seren had bought for me—and my dad's blue sweater. I slipped the sweater off the hanger and brought it to my nose. His scent had begun to fade, but it still lingered enough that I could still smell him. I folded the sweater and slipped it into my backpack.

"You ready?" my mom asked.

I nodded, needing to stay strong. "Can we say goodbye right here? I think I may cry if you walk me outside."

She moved to me and wrapped her arms around me. "I'm gonna cry right here and there's nothing you can do to stop me."

Tears trailed down my own cheeks and onto her shoulder. "I love you."

"Oh, Grace. I love you too."

"Call me every day and fill me in on everything here," I said.

"You bet I will."

I stepped out of her arms, and we both wiped away at our damp cheeks.

"All right," I said, knowing I needed to go. I grabbed my backpack and slipped it on. I gave my mom and my room one last look, making sure I committed both to memory since I had no idea when I'd be back—*if* I'd be back. I forced one last smile for my mom's benefit then turned away and left the apartment. I climbed the stairs and grabbed the handle on my suitcase, pulling it outside with me.

"Hey."

I froze.

Seren stood in the driveway. His eyes moved to my suitcase. "Goin' somewhere?"

I nodded, but words escaped me. I was too scared to say the wrong thing. Too scared I'd break down. I glanced around, trying to find the exterior cameras that I now knew were out there, but they were impossible to detect. I wondered if Seren knew they were everywhere.

"Are you gonna make me guess?" he asked.

I shook my head, but words still wouldn't come out of my mouth.

"Grace? What's going on?"

I pulled in a deep breath and forced myself to answer. "I just found out I got the summer internship in Tampa."

"That's great," he said.

"And I leave tonight."

He frowned, seemingly hating the news as much as I did. "Oh."

I nodded.

"Were you just gonna leave without saying goodbye?" he asked.

"I thought it might be easier that way."

"Easier?" Anger grabbed hold of his features. "Easier for who? *You?*"

"Come on, Seren. You knew we were both leaving soon." It killed me to say that. Killed me to lie to him like that. But what was the alternative?

"So, this is how you planned to end it?" he asked, his voice growing louder. "Just leave without saying a damn thing?"

"I didn't want you overreacting like this," I said, needing to blame it on something.

"*I'm* overreacting? Well, you're not fucking reacting at all! What the fuck, Grace?"

"You know I want to go work with *dolphins*," I said, hoping he caught on to my choice of words.

"So, what? Am I selfish now? I'm trying to keep you from your dream because I don't want you to leave?" he said, totally missing my point.

"No, I meant, you know working with *dolphins* has been my dream just like football has been yours. We can't hold our dreams against each other."

"I may be a lot of things, Grace, but at least I'm not a coward."

"What's that supposed to mean?" I asked, my bottom lip beginning to quiver because he was getting angry and hurtful. And, though I knew what I was doing was necessary, I hated that it was bringing out *this* version of him.

He glared at me with the same coldness I hadn't seen from him since when I first arrived. "I was wrong about you. You're nothing like Kiki or the other girls at Windham Prep because at least they don't run. They say what they need to say. Good or bad. You're taking the easy way out."

"There is no easy way out," I said, meaning that more than he would ever know.

"So that's it," he said matter-of-factly. "We're done."

No. Not even close. I love you. I love that you love me. I love that you don't want me to leave. I love that you're mad because it means you care about me. "Yes."

"Well, fuck you."

His words stung, hitting way below the belt. He should've been fighting for me to stay, not letting me go. "That's mature," I said, equally pissed at him for not seeing through my words.

He grabbed the bench by the side of the door and with all his might chucked it with a roar until it sailed across the basketball court. "*That's* mature," he assured me.

"You don't have to make this any harder than it already is," I said.

His lips tightened in disgust. "Doesn't seem like it's hard for you at all."

A black car pulled up, its lights shining on the driveway. Couldn't Seren see the tears in my eyes? Couldn't he see this was breaking my heart? "I've gotta go."

He said nothing, just stared at me as if he didn't even know me.

"I'll send you some pictures of the dolphins," I said, trying one last time to make him hear me.

"Don't bother." He spun away and walked into the house, slamming the door behind him.

Every part of me wanted to break down. Wanted to scream for help. Wanted to run after Seren. But I was stuck. I was alone. And I was terrified. One wrong move and everything could come crumbling down even more than it already was.

The driver stepped out of the car and approached me, grabbing my suitcase. He lifted it into the trunk as I pulled open the back door and slid inside, feeling utterly devastated. My world had imploded. I'd lost everyone I cared about in one fell swoop. And, not only had I lost them, I didn't even know if I'd truly be able to protect them.

Tears fell as soon as I settled into my seat. I glanced up at Seren's second-floor window. But the curtain didn't flutter because he wasn't there.

CHAPTER 38

One Month Later

Seren

"Catch the fucking ball!" I screamed as the receiver missed another easy pass. He was purposely trying to make me look bad. I was up for the starting position which meant his best friend Kenyon would be out of a job if I won the spot.

The offense regrouped and the offensive coordinator called in the play.

"Okay, boys," I said in the huddle. "Red forty black."

We clapped and the guys headed to their positions. I called hike and the ball was snapped to me. Before I could even find my target, the defense was on me, pummeling me into the grass. I slammed my hands down on the ground then jumped up. "What the fuck?"

"Sorry," one of my linemen mumbled.

A few others laughed. These guys stuck together. I respected that. I would've done the same thing for Saint or Sawyer. But this was my future, and I wasn't gonna let these mother fuckers screw it up for me.

"Have my fucking back!" I screamed at all of them.

"Grayson!" Coach called from the sideline.

I looked at him.

"Get over here!"

I huffed my frustration as Kenyon ran back out onto the field and took my spot. I'd been in Alabama for two weeks and just when I thought I'd proven myself, the rest of the team was hell-bent on making me look like shit. I jogged over to Coach.

He pointed to the metal sideline bench. "Sit your ass down!"

I sat, ripping off my helmet and slamming it down beside me. Alabama was hot as hell in the summer, and every part of my body dripped with sweat.

Coach crossed his arms and stared down at me. "Do you want to be here?"

"What?"

"Do you want to be here?" he repeated, annoyed at having to do so.

"Of course."

"Then prove it."

"My ass getting pummeled hasn't proven it time after time?"

"If it's not working, fix it."

"How do you expect me to do that? They want Kenyon as their QB."

"So? Make them want you."

I scoffed. "How do I do that?"

He shrugged. "You better figure it out soon or he's gonna be starting against Tennessee in the season opener."

Kenyon didn't leave the field for the rest of practice and not once was he sacked and not once did the receivers miss any of his passes. Coach knew they were sabotaging it for me. Why was he making *me* fix it?

I stayed on the field long after everyone filed into the locker room. It had always been my dream to play at Alabama. Now I was there. Now I was *actually* on the field where pros like Caden Brooks and Trace Forester played. I glanced around at the thousands of empty seats in the stadium. It was as if I could almost hear the roar of the crowd even though I was the only one around.

My football career was slipping through my fingers just like Grace had.

I needed to fix this.

I needed *this* to work out.

I couldn't fail again.

CHAPTER 39

Grace

"What do you mean?" I asked my mom as I lay on my bed, staring at the flat-screen taking up the entire wall. Oh, yes. Martine had sprung for the expensive condo undoubtedly equipped with mics and cameras, though I hadn't been able to locate them. But since he was psycho, I was sure he'd been keeping an eye on me. Needless to say, it had been a long month of dressing in the shower or my closet in case he was watching. I'd considered leaving but was scared he'd think I was hiding something and would then take it out on my mother or Seren. Yup. Life sucked on so many levels. My internship was the saving grace.

"You just don't sound happy," my mom said.

"I'm happy," I lied as I sat up and moved to my dresser. "I'm just a little homesick." I shuddered at my reflection in the mirror. My once styled hair hung limp and my cheeks were sunken in. Being unable to eat without vomiting would do that to a girl.

"Well, you know you can come home whenever you need to. I'll buy the plane ticket."

My heart wilted. Going back to the manor wouldn't solve anything. "How are you?" I asked, changing the subject.

"Same as yesterday. Good."

"Anything interesting happening at the manor?"

"No, but Sawyer asked about you. He said he texted you but you haven't responded."

I swallowed. "Oh, I forgot." *Another lie.*

"Well, he seemed concerned. So maybe reach out to him."

"Okay." *Another lie.* I knew better than to have contact with any of the Graysons. Sawyer would ask questions I couldn't answer. If I kept my distance, everyone would remain safe.

"Well, I better go," she said.

I hated when she needed to go. I wanted to stop her—to warn her not to drink anything without a sealed cap, but how could I do that without Marine knowing I was trying to warn her? Paranoia was an awful thing. I'd even bought a phone that I only used outside of the condo for fear that Martine was watching or listening. I'd only used it to call Laney and Holly since everyone else's phones were monitored. They begged me to reach out to Seren, offering to do it for me, but they understood the risk if they were discovered.

"Promise me you're okay," my mother said, pulling me from my thoughts.

"I'm great!" *God, I was such a liar.*

"I love you," she said.

"Love you too."

I kept the phone to my ear long after she'd ended the call. I'd never in my life felt so alone.

Seren

I chugged my beer with the rest of the freshmen who'd taken over the back deck at our teammates' off-campus house. The upperclassmen had been trying to order us around all night like we were some lowly fraternity pledges. Fuck that. I was only there because I needed to fix whatever the hell coach told me to fix. And, if I was ever gonna be seen as a leader on this team—with *this* group of guys—I wasn't about to be picking up shit and cleaning toilets. So, plan B. Get wasted.

"They don't make 'em like that in North Dakota," my roommate DJ said.

I followed his eyes. School wasn't even in session yet, but groups of girls had been arriving all night. Their cutoffs and tight-ass midriffs left little to the imagination. These girls weren't like the girls in Windham. They laughed and flirted and didn't seem to think they were better than anyone else. I could get used to Alabama.

I chugged my beer, needing to leave fucking Windham far behind me.

"Go make a move," Blake, our backup kicker, said to him.

"Give me a few, then I'll show you how it's done," DJ said.

I laughed.

"What are you laughing at, Grayson? You blink and they fall at your feet," DJ said.

"It's not his blinking," Blake said. "It's his smirk."

"Oh, the one where only half his mouth turns up in the corner?" DJ asked.

"Yeah, girls love the I'm-thinking-something-dirty-about-you smirk," Blake said.

I flipped them both the bird.

A few girls stared our way. I could tell the moment that our eyes met and they got all giggly that getting one or more of them in my bed would be easy. I just wasn't sure DJ would be happy to get kicked out of our room so early in the season.

I guess time would tell.

CHAPTER 40

Grace

I sat on a bench outside the rescue center during my lunch break. My sleeveless shirt stuck to my body. Florida in the summer was a sauna.

I scanned my newsfeed on my prepaid phone, making sure to check Alabama football news. Had Seren been playing? Would he replace the backup and start as a freshman? I came across some photos taken during practice. Seren threw a football in one photo. He was doing what he wanted to do. And I was doing the same.

I often wondered if we had parted ways the way we should've, would we have made the long-distance thing work? I definitely could have. The number of girls who would've been throwing themselves at him would have definitely tried his resolve. Would he have caved and broken my heart? Or, would he have rejected their advances like I'd seen him do with girls like Kiki? I guess I'd never find out now.

My phone rang in my backpack. I quickly pulled it out, feeling like some type of shady criminal with two phones. *Mom* lit up the screen. "Hey," I said as I lifted it to my ear.

"Hi, honey. Are you busy?"

A sense of dread washed over me. "No, what's wrong?"

She laughed. "Nothing's wrong. I just didn't want to interrupt you if you were busy."

"I just got done with my morning shift."

"I'm so proud of you," she said. "You're doing what you always said you'd do."

"Dad said it too," I reminded her.

"You're right. He did."

"How's everyone there?" I asked.

"The boys seem good. They've got people here every day in the pool," she explained, sounding tired because she was the one who had to pick up after them.

"Sounds fun," I lied.

"Have you talked to Seren?" she asked.

"No," I said, unable to shed the perpetual pit in my stomach whenever I thought of him. "A long-distance relationship just wasn't gonna work for us."

"Everything happens for a reason," she assured me, but I wondered if she really believed that.

"How's Maureen?" I asked.

"She doesn't look good. She seems weaker."

My stomach dropped. I thought Martine would stop if I stayed away. I thought he said no one would get hurt. Was it the residual effect of what he'd been doing to her or was he still trying to hurt her? "That's too bad?" I said, hating that I had the ability to do something to stop this man, but I was too scared to make any move that could jeopardize my mom or Seren. I'd heard of small children being threatened into keeping silent about abuse. But I was a grown woman. I had to be able to fight back. I had to be able to do *something*.

"She used to be so youthful and vivacious when we were kids," my mom mused. "Even here at the manor before her husband passed…"

"I'm sorry."

"Oh, honey. These things happen sometimes. But Martine has been great, bringing in his own doctors to check on her."

Doctors my ass.

The more information I learned from my mom, the sicker I felt. "I really need to get going, Mom."

"Okay. I'll talk to you tomorrow."

"Bye," I said, before ending the phone.

I knew what I needed to do.

I shouldn't have waited so long.

Seren

Showing up at the team party didn't change a damn thing. The guys still dropped easy passes and missed blocks, and I was getting sacked more times than I cared to count. Coach gave us a post-practice speech, then the rest of the team made their way back to the locker room. I walked off the field discouraged and pissed, dropping onto the bench and staring out at the empty stadium.

Maybe I hit my prime in high school. Maybe I should've realized I'd be a small fish in a big pond in Alabama. Maybe I should've gone to a smaller school that would've been glad to have me as their QB. My decision had been clouded by my need to get away from Windham. But now, everything about this experience sucked. Maybe it was all just karma for not accepting my position at Grayson Industries.

"Shouldn't you be in the locker room?"

I looked to my side. Caden Brooks, ex-Alabama quarterback and current pro quarterback for Miami, stood there with a football twirling between his hands. Never one to be speechless, I sat up straight. "Oh, I..."

"You the new starting quarterback?"

I shook my head. "Back up."

"Really? Coach said you were the best prospect they had next to me and Cole Thatcher."

I shrugged. "Things change."

"I've got some time before tonight's fundraiser," he said. "Let me see what you've got."

"I don't mean any disrespect, but my skills aren't the problem. I can hit any target you give me."

He scoffed, likely doubting me.

"I'm serious. The problem's my teammates. They want Kenyon as their QB."

"Go out for a pass," Brooks said, more of an order than anything else.

I stood up, knowing my younger self would've kicked my ass for not accepting a game of catch with Brooks. I jogged down the field and Brooks threw me a perfect spiral which I caught.

"Hit the thirty-yard line," he called to me.

I lined up my fingers on the laces and threw my own perfect spiral, hitting the thirty-yard line like it was nothing.

Brooks nabbed the ball and passed it back to me. "Hit the fifteen."

I did.

"The foul post."

I did.

He grabbed the loose ball and walked toward me. "I wanted you to suck," he said.

My brows furrowed. "Why?"

"Because you're cocky. And you remind me of me when I got the starting position here and didn't know what to do with it. I was never supposed to start."

"Because Thatcher was," I said, knowing the story.

His eyes dropped away and he nodded, seemingly still affected by the devastation of having his teammate drop dead on the field and then having to replace him. "No one knew how to feel about it—especially me."

"How'd you rise above it?" I asked.

He met my eyes. "I knew I had what it took. I knew I just had to be ready to prove to everyone that I deserved to be the leader on the team. I practiced my ass off, and I made sure I was the best player on the field at all times."

"So, you're telling me to practice?" I asked.

"I'm telling you to fight for the job. Kenyon's good. But Coach wants you to start."

"He told you that?" I asked.

"He didn't have to. He brought you here knowing you could lead this team to more championships."

"I won't be doing that from the bench."

"What do you think'll happen if he puts you in against Tennessee?" he asked.

"What do you mean?"

"Do you think your teammates will continue to screw you over?"

My lips twisted as I considered his question. They fucked with me at practice because there were no fans, no competition, no commentators to judge their screw-ups. When the stadium was filled to capacity, they wouldn't risk looking bad. Why hadn't I considered that? I just needed to play *my* game. And if they continued to suck, that was on them. Brooks knew it. And Coach knew it. "I get it."

"Good."

He tossed me the ball. "You got a girl?"

"What?"

"A girlfriend. You got one?"

I shook my head. "Why?"

"Well, there are gonna be girls after you because you're the starting quarterback. Then, there are gonna be girls after you for who you'll be someday. And, then there'll be one girl who could give two shits about you. *That's* the one you want. That's the one you need by your side. She's the one who gets the real you."

"Are you really giving me dating advice?" I asked.

"Dude, I've been where you are. Gold diggers lurk in the corners just waiting to pounce when you least expect it. Go for the one who despises you. I assure you, she's the one you want."

I laughed to myself, knowing that's the one I had until she decided dolphins were more important than us.

When I got back to the dorm after spending a little more time playing catch with Brooks, I lay on my bed with my phone in my hand. He'd gotten into my head. Scratch that, he'd put Grace into my head. I thumbed through the prom photos Sawyer had taken of us. I looked fucking happy. I hadn't smiled like that and meant it since before my father died. She brought the old Seren out of me. The Seren who didn't hate the entire world.

So, what the hell happened?

There was a knock on my door. I rolled off the bed and answered it.

A hot blonde in booty shorts and a tank top stood there. She smiled. "Hey."

"Hi," I said, my eyes taking in her scraps of clothes.

"Can I come in?" she asked with a thick southern drawl.

Curious where this was going, I stepped back and held out my hand toward my room. "Absolutely."

She smiled and passed by me, her swaying hips impossible to ignore as I shut the door.

CHAPTER 41

Grace

The flight from Tampa to Alabama lasted just over an hour and a half. I'd paid cash for my plane ticket and only brought my backpack and the phone I'd purchased. The plane landed just after ten o'clock and I slipped into my Uber. The driver informed me that Seren's school was fifty miles away from the airport. That gave me time to gather my nerves and concoct some type of plan. I pulled a notebook out of my bag and wrote on a piece of paper, knowing I'd need it when I got to Seren's dorm room.

My legs bounced as I watched the passing scenery blur by in the darkness. I couldn't even imagine what Seren's reaction would be to seeing me at his door. Would he turn me away? Would he even be there? I was definitely blindsiding him by showing up—especially with the information I planned to share with him.

After the hour drive from the airport, the driver pulled through the main gates of Seren's campus. "Where to?" he asked.

I swallowed. "I have no idea. The dorms?"

"Which one?"

"I don't know. Do you see any students walking around?"

I could tell by his grunt that he was annoyed by the fact that I didn't know where to go. We both looked around. Because it was nearing midnight—and still summer, there weren't many people around. A guy staring at his phone stood at a bus stop. The driver pulled over to him and I rolled down my window. "Excuse me?" I called to him.

He glanced up from his phone.

"Any idea where the football players live?"

"You can check over there." He pointed in the direction of a multi-level dorm. "I've seen a lot of people coming and going from there lately."

"Thank you," I said, before looking back to the driver. "I guess you can leave me here." I stepped out of the car with my backpack on my shoulders, hoping to God I'd made the right decision in showing up there like this. The night air held no chill but my entire body trembled. As ready as I was to see Seren, I was so not ready.

As the Uber pulled away leaving me standing virtually alone, I pulled in a deep breath and walked toward the dorm where he could potentially live. I reached the front door and pulled on the handle. It was locked. *You've got to be kidding me.* What if no one showed up to open the door? Would I be stuck out there all night?

I went to a nearby bench and sat down. I stared up at the building noting there were quite a few dorm rooms with lights on inside. Was Seren in one of them? I closed my eyes, unable to believe I garnered the nerve to even show up in Alabama. This was such a risk.

The front door of the dorm creaked.

My eyes popped open and I jumped to my feet. "Hold that door!" I called.

The guy stepping outside held it for me.

"Thank you." Before I took another step, I twisted toward him. "Do you know Seren Grayson?"

He looked back at me. "No."

"He's a football player," I said, hoping that rang a bell.

"Football players are on the fifth floor," he said.

I smiled. "Thanks so much." I hurried inside, taking the stairs to the fifth floor as quickly as I could. I was so close now. I stepped into the hallway and heard loud music. I reached in my bag, pulled out the sheet of paper I'd written on in the Uber, and hurried nervously down the hallway. I looked from side to side at closed doors. Thankfully, all of the doors had whiteboards with the names of the residents who lived inside. Room by room there was no sign of Seren's name. I finally reached the end of the hall. The last door on the right had my heart racing. *Seren and DJ.* The door was closed so I dragged in a deep breath, knocked, and held up my sign that read: *Don't Say Anything.*

I could hear shuffling inside. My heart pounded so hard it was all I could hear. The door swung open. I sucked in a sharp breath. A beautiful blonde stood there in booty shorts and a tank top. Vomit roiled up the back of my throat, but I needed to stay strong because I wasn't there for Seren. Him moving on wasn't my business. I was there trying to do the right thing.

"Why can't I say anything?" she asked with a thick southern drawl.

I held up a finger and wrote on the back of the paper: *Is Seren here?* Maybe I was being super paranoid, but I needed to be sure I didn't speak for fear of his room or phone being monitored and picking up my voice.

"You're so cute," the girl said. "Are you trying to pull a *Love Actually?*"

The sight of her in Seren's room had tears pricking my eyes. But I nodded, hoping she got him for me.

"*Awwww.* Seren," she called into the room. "You have a visitor."

It took no more than a couple of seconds for Seren to step into the doorway looking as gorgeous as I remembered in a red T-shirt and low-hung basketball shorts. His eyes widened when he saw me standing there.

I quickly held up my sign.

His eyes narrowed, clearly not understanding my sudden appearance in Alabama *and* my sign.

I pointed to an exit and mouthed the word *Please.*

He looked torn and as if he might not follow me. I could see in his eyes that he hated me, but I'd traveled all that way. The least he could do was hear me out. His lips twisted the way they did when he was unsure about something. "I'll be back in a minute," he called to the girl in his room.

I released the breath I'd been holding then held my finger to my lips.

He huffed, visibly annoyed by my apparent game of charades.

I pointed to the phone in his hand. *Leave it here,* I mouthed.

I could tell he didn't want to leave it, but he tossed it inside anyway.

I took off for the stairs, racing down the five flights until I stood outside the building. I wouldn't talk until we were away from his phone and room. I couldn't risk it now that I'd made it this far. When I heard the door slam, I spun to face him. "I'm so sorry to show up like this."

"What the hell's going on, Grace?" he asked. "And why do you look like that? You're skin and bones."

Tears glazed my eyes. Between seeing him for the first time in a month, finding a girl in his room, and knowing he was right about my appearance, it all became too much. Tears trailed down my cheeks. "I didn't mean for any of this to happen."

"What are you talking about?"

"Martine killed your father."

"What?" Confusion washed over Seren's face as the words must've hit him like an eighteen-wheeler. He'd been wrong about his mother. He'd overlooked the real murderer who was right under his own roof. Now, I showed up after a month of not speaking to him and dropped this bomb. I'd be shocked and confused too.

"And I caught him trying to poison your mother."

Seren's teeth clenched, anger plaguing his eyes. "You *saw* him? And you're just telling me this *now*?"

Nothing he said could make me feel guiltier than I already felt. "He threatened me and made me leave. He was going to pin your father's death on my mom or *you,*" my voice quaked with emotion. "As far as I know, he's got everything bugged, including your room and your phone. He put me up in a condo that I'm sure he's monitoring, though I haven't been able to find anything, and believe me I've tried. I couldn't warn you. I couldn't say *anything*." Tears rained from my eyes, and I knew once the floodgates were opened, there was no stopping the tears.

"Jesus Christ," he said, tunneling his fingers through his hair.

Now that I could finally tell him the truth, all the words and emotions were pouring out of me. "He wants the business. He wants your percent, but your mother won't give it to him."

"So, he's trying to kill her too?" He turned toward the door. "I need to call Saint."

"You can't. He's monitoring everything. I have a prepaid phone. But I couldn't even use it to call you since he's monitoring your phone. It's been hell."

He scrubbed his hands up and down his face. "I can't even believe this."

"I tried to warn you the night I left. I'm working with dolphins, Seren. *Dolphins*."

"Goddamnit!" He began to pace in front of me. "I knew you wouldn't leave like you did."

"He could hear and see us in the driveway. I couldn't say anything else. I wanted to tell you. I just didn't know how to."

He shook his head as if reeling from everything I was saying. "I was so fucking angry at you."

"We need to help your mother." Sobs tore out of me and there wasn't a thing I could do to stop them. "It was so hard to leave you—especially since I didn't know what was happening at the manor while I was gone. I've been terrified."

Seren moved toward me and wrapped his arms around me, holding me tightly. "It's okay, baby. You're here now."

I could barely catch my breath. I was home in his arms with his scent and body wrapped around me, but still so scared. "I've been so alone," I choked out.

"You've got me," he said.

I wanted so badly to believe that, but I'd seen firsthand that he'd moved on in Alabama.

We stood like that for a long time, both of us in our own heads.

"Seren?"

He dropped his arms at the sound of another girl's voice, leaving me feeling bereft. He looked to the girl who'd been in his room.

"I'm gonna head home," she said, her mouth turned down in a frown.

"I'll let DJ know you waited for him," Seren said.

She shrugged before looking at me. "Looks like it worked." Her brows bounced before she walked away.

Seren pulled me back in his arms.

"So, you and her?" I asked, almost scared to let myself believe nothing was going on between the two of them.

"Nope."

I relaxed in his arms, feeling safer than I ever imagined I could feel again. I didn't want him to let me go. I needed him to protect me. And I needed him back in my life. The waterworks began again.

He pulled back and his eyes moved over my tear-soaked face. "What is it, Grace?"

"He threatened to poison you and my mom. I was so scared. So helpless."

"Oh, Grace. I'm safe. And your mom's safe. I can't believe you've been carrying this all on your own."

"It felt wrong to leave everyone with that monster, but if I didn't, he would've hurt you. It was a no-win situation."

He pressed his lips to my forehead, trying to reassure me. "We're together now. We can stop him."

"He's got ears everywhere."

I expected him to respond. But he didn't. Instead, he lifted me up off the ground. I wrapped my legs around his hips and held on. "It's one in the morning. You need to sleep, and I need to figure out who we can trust."

"You can trust me."

He looked me right in my eyes. "I should've known that."

CHAPTER 42

Seren

I left my phone in my room and swapped rooms with one of my teammates for the night because I wanted to ease Grace's fears about Martine bugging my phone and room. Even though her concerns sounded far-fetched, my father had been working on espionage technology before he died. And while Martine mentioned a potential deal with the military, I didn't realize he'd actually finished my father's work. No wonder why he didn't want to relinquish control to an eighteen-year-old who owned more of the company than he did. He was set to make billions when this technology went public. No way he'd want me to reap the benefits. He wanted one hundred percent of the company—by any means necessary.

Grace immediately lay down on my teammate's spare bed since his roommate had yet to move in. I covered her with a blanket I'd brought from my room and lay down beside her, wrapping my arms around her and pulling her back to my chest. She instantly relaxed like she had outside. But, my God, she was skin and bones. She'd been suffering. I knew the second I saw her standing at my door that she wasn't okay. I knew everything that went down in the driveway that night had been a sham. She wouldn't have traveled all the way to Alabama if it hadn't been. Nor would she look like a shell of herself.

I seriously couldn't wrap my head around all she'd been holding in. Martine would pay for it. *All* of it.

And, as much as I wanted to make up for lost time and get lost in Grace for the rest of the night, we'd both been through hell. I tightened my arms around her, careful not to hurt her.

We lay in silence for a long time.

"Do you think I should go home?" I asked her.

Her body went rigid.

"I think I need to be there."

She turned in my arms so we were eye to eye, but fear had overtaken her features. "There's so much at risk, Seren. *So* much. He sees and hears everything."

I tightened my arms around her, needing to calm her fears. I couldn't even begin to imagine what she was going through now that she could finally tell me everything. The motherfucker had scared the shit out of her. He would pay for *all* his sins. "We're in this together, Grace. We'll figure it out together."

"Your mom didn't do it," she said, reminding me of what I'd already figured out.

I'd been such an asshole toward my mother. So cold. So dismissive. So…unfair. I'd fix that *after* I saved her from Martine. "I know."

"She'll forgive you," she said.

"I know that too. Will *you* forgive me?"

A small smile tipped her lips.

I leaned down and captured her lips, kissing her slowly. It was almost two in the morning now, and I knew so much had happened, but I also knew I'd never sleep until I was sure she forgave me.

Grace pulled at the hem of my shirt telling me I wasn't the only one who, despite everything that had happened, still craved more.

"You sure?" I asked.

"Yes," she assured me.

Waves of relief washed over me as I sat up, seized the back of my T-shirt, and peeled it off. I stared at her in amazement. I couldn't believe I had her back. "Are you gonna let me love you?"

Tears glazed her eyes as she nodded.

"Thank fuck. Because I never stopped loving you, Grace." I covered her with my body and captured her lips. I hadn't forgotten how her lips just fit with mine. How they did whatever I wanted them to do. I tore my lips from hers and pulled her shirt off, revealing her black bra. Her ribs were protruding, and the sight broke my fucking heart. I tossed her shirt and leaned down, peppering kisses down her chest, between her breasts, and over her ribs. I brushed my lips gently over them as if that could somehow erase the last month and the pain she'd been through. Her fingers tunneled into the back of my hair telling me she wanted me there. But that wasn't my final destination. I inched down, kissing a path across her stomach while I unbuttoned her shorts. She lifted her ass and I slipped them down her legs leaving her in a thong. I leaned back down and pressed kisses over the material as Grace sucked in a sharp breath. "I've missed you," I said between kisses. "The way you feel…the way you taste…the way your body fits with mine."

Grace's breath became labored, and I loved knowing my words could do that to her—especially after I'd been so sure over the last month that she didn't give two fucks about me.

I moved lower, kissing a path between her thighs. I spread her legs and found a comfortable spot to continue. She gripped my shoulders, holding on tightly. I was fairly certain no one had done this to her before, and I loved that she was letting me. I pulled the strip of her thong to the side and ran the tip of my tongue along her seam.

Grace

My grip on Seren's shoulders couldn't get any tighter. My embarrassment of having him down there quickly dissipated as the tremors began. His tongue licked a delicious path from front to back, repeating the motion until I could barely stay still for him. My thong was in his way so he pulled it down my legs and then his mouth was back. This time, he sucked on my clit. I gasped. His tongue moved, circling it, moving over it, then sucking on it again. Waves of tremors washed over me. I didn't think it could get any better. Then Seren plunged two fingers inside me as he continued assaulting my clit with his tongue. I closed my eyes tightly and dropped my head back against the pillow. "Seren," I pleaded, though I had no idea what I was pleading for.

"Right here, Grace," he said while continuing to lick circles around my clit.

"So…good," I breathed.

"I know, babe. That's why I'm doing it. I want you to feel good."

"I'm close."

He abandoned my clit, leaving me on the verge of the most intense orgasm I'd ever experienced. "I need to be inside you," he said as he pulled off his shorts and dug into his wallet, retrieving a condom and rolling it on. He covered me with his body. I could feel his erection between my legs as he stared down into my eyes. "I love you so damn much."

Tears glazed my eyes. Seren loving me had seemed so impossible over the last month. "I love you, too."

He pressed his lips to mine, and as he parted my mouth with his tongue, he thrust inside me. I gasped, but he didn't stop kissing me. His hips began thrusting, and I yearned to melt into him. To get lost in him. To let him erase everything from my brain. I slipped my hands behind his back, trailing my fingertips up to his neck and through the back of his hair. His scent brought me back to prom night in the treehouse. Our first time together. All he'd done to make the night perfect. I knew it then. And, I knew now. Seren Grayson was it for me. I could feel it all the way down to my bones.

I tore my mouth from his, catching my breath as he buried his nose in the crook of my neck, grunting as his thrusts became deeper and harder. God, he was so strong. He was everything I never knew I needed in my life.

I lifted my hips, meeting his thrusts. With that angle, he brushed my clit relentlessly. I whimpered as the sensations between my thighs began to intensify.

"Are you close?" he asked.

"Yes," I breathed, my eyes pinched tightly as my thoughts focused on our bodies moving as one.

"Look at me, Grace," Seren rasped.

I opened my eyes.

His face hovered inches from mine. "God, you're so damn beautiful."

I closed my eyes, embarrassed by his words in such close proximity.

"Look. At. Me," he grunted with each thrust.

I opened my eyes again.

"I want to watch you let go," he said.

His words acted as a direct line to my clit because it seemed to coil, all the sensations building in that one spot.

"Show me, Grace," he said, his hips still moving and his eyes on mine.

The coil unraveled and tremors shot out, a glorious hum coasting over my skin as I trembled from the inside out. I kept my eyes focused on his as my body continued to quiver. Then, a peaceful calm washed over me, keeping me abuzz with after-tremors.

Seren continued thrusting until his eyes closed and he dropped his head, a low groan coming from the back of his throat as he thrust one more time then stopped inside me. "Jesus," he said as he lowered himself down on top of me. "I missed you."

I wrapped my arms around him, knowing exactly what he meant. Despite our differences, despite our rocky start, despite the month apart, the two of us were meant to be. And nothing—and no one—would come between us again.

CHAPTER 43

Seren

The next morning while Grace slept soundly—probably the first good night's sleep she'd had since that motherfucker kicked her out of the manor—I lay beside her, relishing in the feel of her body as I tried to figure out what the hell to do. If everything was monitored the way she said it was, I needed to watch my every move and stay a step ahead of Martine. He thought he was so clever. The fucker had no idea who he was up against.

There was a knock on the door. I sat up slowly, not wanting to wake Grace. I went to it and took the breakfast I'd ordered from the delivery guy who stood there. "Thanks, man," I said before closing the door quietly and placing it on the desk. My girl needed to eat.

I sat down on the edge of the bed and grabbed Grace's phone off the desk. I'd get my own prepaid phone today so I could contact her and my brothers moving forward. I sent off a quick text. **It's Seren. I need your help. Call me at this number.**

"Seren?" Grace whispered.

"Go back to sleep," I whispered. "I'm figuring some things out."

"Let me help."

"Awwww, babe. You've already done more than enough." I leaned down and pressed my lips to her forehead, never feeling as lucky as I did with her beside me. Last night had been what we both needed. And now I knew for sure that our time apart had not changed a thing. Our feelings were still the same, and no crazy stepfather could change that. "I got you breakfast."

"You didn't have to," she said.

"Yes, I did."

Her phone buzzed in my hand. I recognized the number and answered it. "Hey."

Grace

I lay there, listening to Seren's side of the phone conversation. He shared everything with the person on the other end.

"We can't get the police involved until we have solid evidence," Seren explained. "I'll let you know when the time is right…Just do me a solid and catch up with Sawyer and Saint…I don't know. Probably at the courts. Be sure they're nowhere near their phones then have them call this number from your phone…I owe you one." He ended the call.

"What's going on?" I asked.

He put my phone down on the desk and rolled over, wrapping his arms around me. "We're waiting on Sawyer and Saint to call."

"And?"

"And, that's it. For now."

"Are you at all worried about how Saint will react?"

He chuckled. "Because he's crazier than me?"

"Kind of."

"Nah. He'll do what I say."

We both fell silent.

"Grace?" he eventually said.

"Yeah?"

"I need you to eat."

I shut my eyes, knowing I looked terrible. "I do eat. Keeping it down is another story."

He huffed, but I knew his anger wasn't with me. It was with Martine who'd caused all of this. "I promise you. I'm gonna make sure he gets what's coming to him. And no one else is gonna get hurt."

"How can you be sure?" I asked.

"I'm Seren Grayson," he said, but it didn't hold the humor it once had. "You're sure he has cameras and mics everywhere on the property?"

"Even in the treehouse. He played us…you know… when we were alone…on prom night," I said.

Rage flared in his eyes. "What?"

"He wouldn't turn it off as much as I begged him to."

"I'll kill him," he gritted out.

"Killing him would be too kind," I assured him. "He needs to suffer."

"Oh, I plan on it."

* * *

We sat in a campus café that afternoon after Seren bought his own prepaid phone. I didn't know how to tell him I wasn't hungry for lunch after he'd had a breakfast delivered that could feed ten, so I picked away at the sandwich he'd bought me.

My phone rang on the table. Seren grabbed it before I could and answered it. "Hello?"

He listened for a minute before speaking. "I know, bro. But you can't let on that you know anything. Promise me you won't say a word on the property or around your phone. Everything will backfire if you do."

Given his warning, it had to be Saint on the other end. And the fact that he didn't have to go into detail, told me Saint had already been filled in on the details.

"I have a plan," Seren continued. "I just need you to listen and relay it to Sawyer."

He listened for another minute, closing his eyes tightly in frustration. Saint clearly wasn't following his directions the way he'd hoped. "Dude. Just fucking listen to me!"

A few people scattered around the café looked over to see what Seren was so angry about.

"The bastard threatened Grace," he continued a little quieter, causing the people to get back to what they were doing. "He showed her footage from inside our treehouse. The only time we can speak is when you're away from the manor and on someone else's phone. Do not go rogue on me. It puts everyone in harm's way."

Again, he listened to Saint.

"I need you to come up with an excuse for being down in the dungeon." His eyes cut to mine, realizing what he just called the basement at the manor. He shot me an apologetic look. "Once you're down there," he continued into the phone, "you need to locate the camera so you can avoid it. If for some reason you're caught on it, pick something up like it's what you'd been looking for down there. Report back to me after that."

He listened to Saint, nodding his head like Saint could somehow see him.

"Then we wait for him to leave. He's gotta be going out of town soon. You'll return to the basement—avoiding the camera you already found—and turn off the main power from the breaker."

Oh, good idea. Shut down all the cameras in the house in one shot.

"We've got three minutes before the generator kicks on. So, while the power's off, Sawyer needs to get to the third floor. There's got to be something in Martine's office. Something we can pin on him." Seren's eyes cut to mine. "The stuff he was putting in my mother's drink. What was it in?"

"A small clear tube," I said, knowing if they could get it and there were still some remnants inside, it could be tested.

"A small tube," Seren repeated to Saint. "I need you to let me know when it's going down. I need to be on the phone with you so if anything goes wrong, I can help."

He listened again.

"Give me your word you won't talk about this on the property or around your phone. Grace swears he can hear without the phone being used. Oh, and go buy you and Sawyer prepaid phones so we can talk moving forward. We're gonna take this motherfucker down once and for all." He ended the call and just stared at my phone, a million thoughts clearly running through his mind.

"You okay?" I asked.

"As long as Saint follows my plan."

"You repeated yourself enough for him to know what's at stake," I assured him.

"I think they can handle it," he said, though his words didn't hold much conviction.

"They definitely can," I said, knowing he needed to hear it just as much as I did. They hadn't seen the way Martine switched into someone unrecognizable at the drop of a dime. The man was a sociopath capable of unthinkable things. They needed to be careful.

"I've got practice in an hour," Seren said, glancing at his new phone. "But I don't want you to leave."

"I need to go back," I said, starting to get myself worked up. "He could see that I haven't been there. He could get suspicious."

Seren reached across the table and linked his fingers with mine. "You haven't told me about the dolphins."

He was trying to calm my fears, and I needed to let him or else I'd be right back to where I'd been when I arrived. "I haven't gotten to work with them yet. But I've been training and learning all I need to know for when I do."

"Sounds promising," he said.

"I just wish…"

"What?"

"That I wasn't only there because Martine made a donation to get me in."

He squeezed my hand. "Don't for one second think you don't deserve to be there. It's your dream."

My eyes flashed down, knowing I wouldn't have gotten the spot without Martine's unwanted assistance.

My phone rang again. Seren released my hand and grabbed it. "Hello?" Worry filled his eyes. "I'm sorry you had to find out like that, little brother. Saint should've used better judgment." His lips twisted, clearly pissed by the way Saint must've delivered the news to Sawyer. "I promise we're gonna take care of him. All three of us. Just keep your distance so you don't do anything rash. We can't afford a slip-up that lets him know we know. Keep your eye on mom. Hang out in the kitchen so he can't get her a drink without you seeing. Right now, that's all we can do. Did Saint tell you the plan?"

He listened for a long moment.

"Yeah. I need you to be stealthy," he said. "Get in that office and find what we need to get this motherfucker thrown in jail. You won't have much time, but I know you'll find something. Just get out before the lights go on and the cameras start up." He ended the call and looked at me.

"All good?"

"Time will tell," he said, exhaustion clouding his eyes.

I knew the feeling. Carrying the truth was like a heavy weight. "I'm gonna stream your first game," I said, trying to redirect his thoughts.

His eyes lit up. "Yeah?"

"I need to see what all the hype's about."

"Hype?"

"So, you've told me."

He chuckled. "We'll see if I get any playing time."

"You will."

His eyes narrowed. "How do you know?"

"You're Seren Grayson."

His head dropped back and he laughed. "Damn straight I am."

Leaving him again would be difficult, but this time I knew it wouldn't be forever. "I never thought I'd hear you laugh again."

"Come here." He took my hand, urging me to my feet and onto his lap. He wrapped his arms around me. "I'm not going anywhere."

My lips twisted, not really sure what to say because *I* was going somewhere.

"Do you know how hard it was to get you to trust me?" Seren asked. "There's no way I'd *ever* blow my shot."

I laughed, and he tightened his arms around me.

"I'm yours, Grace."

My belly dipped.

"For as long as you'll have me," he continued.

"Forever," I whispered.

He pulled back, examining my face for the punchline. "Promise?"

I nodded, loving that I could still surprise him. He closed his eyes, and relief washed over his features as if he needed that assurance. Martine had taken a month away from us. He'd never take another day.

CHAPTER 44

Seren

It had been a long week with Grace back in Tampa, football practices kicking my ass, and my brothers calling me from everywhere but the manor. My prepaid phone buzzed as I crossed campus after practice on Friday night. Grace's name filled my screen. "Hey, babe," I answered.

"Hi."

"You sound excited. What's going on?"

"I got to assist with a dolphin rescue today," she gushed. "It was amazing."

"That's awesome."

"I learned so much about how to carry out a rescue and then how to transport them safely back to the rescue center. And, oh, she's going to be okay. She's such a fighter."

"Just like you," I assured her, loving her excitement over her internship. She was totally in her element.

She laughed. "Only with you."

"I'm really happy for you, Grace," I said. "You're getting everything you wanted."

"What's going on with *you?*" she asked.

"I've got good news too."

"Tell me."

"Tomorrow's the day."

She went silent. I waited her out, but she didn't speak.

I stopped walking and sat on a bench. "Grace?"

"I'm here."

"Stop worrying," I said.

"I'll stop worrying when they find something," she said. "Where will Martine be?"

"He and my mother are going to a fundraiser," I said.

"There's no chance they'll skip it?" she asked.

"I guess there's always a chance, but for now, the plan is set for after my game."

"Sawyer and Saint know what they need to do?" she asked.

"Don't worry. They're all set. And, they're gonna find something to nail the fucker to the wall." I didn't dare tell her I wasn't sure at all that they'd find something. But, the more I said it, the more I hoped it became a reality. Because if I wasn't confident in their success, they wouldn't be confident. "Trust me."

"I do."

A knot twisted in my gut. There was a hell of a lot riding on this plan. With no plan B, this had to work. It just had to.

* * *

I'd been to a game in Alabama before when I was a kid. I'd been seated in the sea of red shirts. I'd been privy to the booming sound of a hundred thousand fans. But never before—not even in my wildest dreams—had I ever had every eye in the stadium focused on me. Kenyon had started. He'd been sacked three times in the first quarter, fumbling once. Coach pulled me off the sideline and put me in. I tried to tune out the deafening roar of the crowd and focus on the play. "Eight night space," I yelled, barely able to hear my own voice.

My teammates clapped once and jogged to their positions. I bent, called hike, and grasped the ball. I backpedaled, looking to my far right for my receiver who cut left then right. I released the ball, holding my breath as I watched it sail through the air and land right in his arms. The defense brought him down at the thirty-yard line.

The crowd exploded.

I glanced to the sideline where Coach punched his fist in the air. Only then, did I exhale. And, only then, did I feel like a leader on the field.

I jogged to the thirty as I heard the play relayed to me in my helmet. I stepped into the huddle. "Seventeen burning house."

My teammates clapped once and jogged to their spots on the line of scrimmage. Again, I bent, called hike, and grasped the ball between my hands. This time my offensive line held off the defense, giving me time to hand off a quick pass to the running back who made it ten yards before being brought down on the twenty.

The crowd roared.

I jogged to the twenty hearing the play called into my ear. I motioned for no huddle. The guys knew to line up. I shouted to my right then to my left. "Seventeen burning house." We were running the same play. I bent, called hike, then quickly grasped the ball and handed it off to the same running back who took off, weaving around defenders until he took it into the end zone. I pumped my fist in the air as the crowd exploded. The running back celebrated in the end zone and the rest of the offense joined him. I jogged over, meeting him as he broke free from their embraces and pounded his fist. "Nice, man."

He smiled under his helmet, and I knew if I kept getting him the ball, he'd keep scoring me touchdowns. I looked to the rest of the offense as they jogged off the field, bumping their fists as well. "Nice job."

Once I was back on the sideline, I dropped down onto the bench, knowing my girl and my brothers were watching. I just wished it wasn't my father's murderer who was on my mind. Sawyer and Saint were undoubtedly getting ready to move to their spots in the manor. Saint had staked out the cameras and had a pretty good plan for avoiding them before cutting the power. They were just waiting for my game to end so I could be on the phone and know exactly what was going down.

A few more hours and we'd have what we needed.

* * *

I hurried out of the locker room after having to sit in on interviews with Coach. Our first win of the season was big news given the team was led by a freshman quarterback—me. Reporters had lots of questions, but I just wanted to get the hell out of there so I could get to my room and be there for Saint and Sawyer.

My phone buzzed as I exited the locker room. My mother's name lit up the screen. I hadn't spoken to her since I'd learned the truth and now I didn't know how to act. My coldness toward her seemed unwarranted now, but anything else would've been odd coming from me. "Yeah?" I answered, hoping to God she was at the fundraiser.

"Your father would've been so proud of you today, Seren," she said.

A tinge of remorse twisted in my gut. "You watched?"

"Of course I watched. Martine and I are on the way to a fundraiser, so we had to stream the last quarter in the car."

Relief whooshed through my lips knowing they were away from the manor.

"Great job, Seren," Martine said on speaker. "You played a hell of a game."

"Thanks," I said, wanting to add, 'My dad would've loved to see me play, but his life was cut short because of you.' Instead I said, "I appreciate you guys watching."

"After that showing, it looks like you'll be starting next week," Martine said.

It took everything in me to keep my voice steady. "I hope so."

"Oh, Seren, we're pulling up at the fundraiser right now," my mother said. "We've got to go."

"No problem. Thanks again for watching." I hung up the phone and trekked across campus, trying to avoid all the people who suddenly wanted to call out to me.

"Nice game, Grayson," a guy called.

"You looked great out there," a girl called.

"Thanks," I muttered, keeping my head down and walking faster. I had important shit to do.

"Hey, Seren," a girl called, hurrying to keep pace with me.

"Hey," I said, trying not to be rude but desperate to get to my dorm.

"My friends are having a party tonight if you'd like to come with me," she offered.

"Thanks, but I've got plans," I said.

"With a girl?" she asked.

"Nope."

"So, you're single?" she pried.

"Nope."

"I don't mind," she said.

"I do."

She huffed and stopped walking with me.

Brooks had been right. People would suddenly like me for the wrong reasons. But I wouldn't get caught up in all that bullshit. I was here to play football. *And*, I had a girl who loved me who I wouldn't risk losing again.

I reached the front door of my dorm and sprinted inside, taking two steps at a time until I was in my room. I dropped onto my bed, needing a minute before calling my brothers. This had to work. There really wasn't any other option. After a long moment, I slipped my phone out of my pocket. Being overly cautious, I stood and moved into the hallway. Only then did I click on the Zoom link we were all joining. Grace was already on the group video call when I appeared on the screen. "Hey,"

I said, sitting down on the floor with my back against the wall.

"You looked amazing out there," she gushed, her pretty smile beaming with pride.

"Did you expect anything less?" I asked.

"Honestly?" Her nose wrinkled like she had to think about it. "No, because you're awesome."

"Damn straight I am."

Even though we were joking around, a silent moment passed between us. We both knew what was about to go down, and there were so many things that could go wrong with me in Alabama and my brothers at home. And, as much as I wanted to trust them to see this thing through, I had my doubts.

"You ready?" she asked.

"No. You?"

"No."

Another silence passed between us. I really wished she was there with me because there was so much on the line. If Martine knew they'd been in his office looking for evidence that he was a cold-blooded killer, he'd try to pin it on Grace's mom or me. "They can handle it," I said.

"I know," she said, but her tone was just about as convincing as mine.

Saint appeared in a box beside Grace on my screen. "Hey. Great game."

"Thanks."

"'Sup, Grace," Saint said.

"Good luck," she said.

"I don't need luck. Sawyer does," he said.

"Is he upstairs?" I asked just as Sawyer appeared on the screen. They were in three boxes now with Saint and Sawyer at the top and Grace down below.

"'Sup, brothers?" Sawyer said, before noticing Grace on the screen too. "Hey, girl. Looking hot as ever."

Grace laughed. "Miss you, kid."

"You too. Thanks for trying to save our mom," he said.

Her eyes lowered and they were likely filling with tears. I hated seeing her cry. It just showed how much she'd been holding in. And as much as I knew what we were about to do was for my father and my mother, it was also for Grace. It was going to take a lot of time for her to get over the guilt and fear Martine had instilled in her. But once we found the proof we needed, we'd all be able to begin to heal and hopefully move on.

"We ready to do this?" Sawyer asked, always the excited and eager one.

"Are *you* ready?" I asked him.

"You can trust me," Sawyer assured us. "Killer game, by the way."

"Thanks."

Saint's screen was jumping all over the place which meant he was moving. "I'm almost there," he whispered, knowing there were cameras and mics all over the manor.

My heartbeat began to accelerate. "You've got three minutes once everything goes dark before the generator kicks on," I reminded Sawyer.

"I've got a screwdriver and my phone as a flashlight," he assured me.

I hoped to God that's all he needed.

"I'm here," Saint informed us.

"I'm ready," Sawyer said.

Within seconds, their phones turned dark and all I could hear were Sawyer's sneakers pounding up the stairs until he reached the soft hallway rug where he ran to Martine's office. The door flew open.

"I'm in," he panted. The light of his phone switched on and then I heard papers being shuffled around. "The drawers are locked," he said.

"Can you open them without destroying anything?" I asked.

"No idea."

He lay his phone down. All we could hear was banging as he tried to force open a drawer.

"It's been thirty seconds," Grace said.

"Fuck," Sawyer cursed.

"Keep going," I urged. "Find something."

"I'm trying," he said.

"Grace said the container was small, so it could be anywhere."

A drawer opened. More shuffling. Banging. Swearing.

"Try the middle drawer," I said. "There might be a button to open the cabinet or other drawers."

"I'm feeling for one. But nothing. *Dammit.*"

"One minute," Grace said.

"Fuck," Sawyer cursed.

"You've got this," I assured him.

"I'm looking, but there's just papers and folders," Sawyer said. "And a copy of Mom's will."

"Take a picture of it," I said, wanting to know what Martine was up to. My mother's will appeared on Sawyer's screen as he rushed to snap pictures of each of the pages before he was using it as a light again.

"Seren, there's nothing else in here," he said.

"What about the garbage? Or the bookshelves?" I asked, knowing the sudden fear in my voice was difficult to disguise.

More shuffling.

"Two minutes," Grace said.

"God, dammit!" I yelled.

"Seren, relax," Grace said. "Sawyer will find something."

"Anything important is probably in his safe," Saint said.

"Get to his closet. Check in there," I said, knowing time was running out. "Saint, don't you dare put the power back on yet."

"Copy," he said.

Sawyer's footsteps pounded down the hallway and stairs to the second floor.

"Check drawers and pockets," I said.

"He's got so many damn suits," he said over the rustling of him going through them.

"Only thirty more seconds," Grace said, the fear now evident in her voice.

I tunneled my hands through my hair, desperately needing him to find something.

"Check his sock drawer," Saint chimed in. "I hide everything in mine."

"Noted," Sawyer said.

I scrubbed my hands up and down my face, knowing our plan had been destined to fail.

"Nothing but his underwear," Sawyer said.

"Get out of there," I said.

"What?" all three of them said.

"Get out. Saint, wait for him to be in his room then turn the power back on."

"Ten more seconds," Sawyer pleaded, still fumbling through drawers.

"Get back to your room!" I ordered.

"I'm so sorry," Sawyer said.

"You didn't do this!" I snapped. "*He* did."

Everyone was silent.

Grace's eyes were down. Lights switched on and Sawyer and Saint looked just as pissed as me.

"Goddamnit!"

One of my teammates poked his head out of his room. "You all right, man?"

"Fine," I said to him. "I gotta go," I said to Grace and my brothers before hanging up on all three of them.

They'd looked to me for answers. They expected me to be able to fix any situation. They relied on me, but I failed. We had one shot. And I blew it. How had my father ever expected me to run his company? I couldn't even bring down the man who killed him.

My phone pinged and I looked at my screen. Sawyer had sent me the photos of my mother's will. I tucked my phone into my pocket in no mood to deal with that shit tonight. She likely left everything to Sawyer anyway. He was her favorite. All I'd been over the past three years was an asshole who treated her like crap. Now, I couldn't even save her when I knew I was the only one who could.

CHAPTER 45

Grace

Yesterday had been a disaster. Now, we were no closer to exposing Martine, *and* Seren had gone MIA. I knew he was disappointed. We all were. But we needed to stick together—not avoid each other.

"Grace, would you mind helping with Otto?"

I glanced to Jose, the trainer in the water where I stood with a bucket of fish. "You bet," I said, hurrying toward him.

"You okay?" he asked.

"Yes. Absolutely," I lied.

"Climb in," he said.

"Seriously?" I asked.

He laughed. "Yes."

I climbed into the water in my wetsuit.

"Are you planning on interning here when school starts?" he asked as he showed me where to hold my hands so Otto could rest in them.

"I sure hope so. It's my dream to work here when I graduate." I laughed as Otto spun in my arms, stopping once he lay belly side up.

"Good, boy," Jose said to Otto, before checking out a small wound he'd suffered. "Well, keep interning. It's how I started, too."

"It is?"

"They like to hire people they know. People who've invested time here. So, stick around, and you're almost assured a job."

"Thanks for saying that."

Otto clicked.

"I think he likes having you here," Jose said.

"I like being here," I said, smiling down at the gorgeous dolphin in my arms. If my dad could only see me now.

On my way home from interning, I called Seren who didn't answer. I tried again after I ate dinner. But still, he didn't answer. The next morning on my way to the rescue center, I tried again but still no answer. "Hey, it's me again," I said to his voicemail. "Call me when you get this. I'm worried about you." I ended the call and stared down at my phone, willing him to call me back. I was just as disappointed as him that the plan failed. But if I was going to begin to heal after what I'd been through, I needed to let go of some of the pain I'd been carrying. Seren, Sawyer, and Saint now shared the burden of carrying it with them. It wasn't all on me anymore, and while that sucked for them, it had taken some of the pressure off me. And though we may have failed at our first attempt, I had faith they would come up with another plan. And then, Martine would pay for what he'd done.

* * *

Jack and Rya, a couple of the other interns, invited me out after our shift that evening. If I was going to stay in

Tampa, I needed friends. And since we all shared a love for dolphins, they were the best type of friends to have.

"I can't believe you're out with us," Jack said from across the table in the dive bar they'd picked.

"Why?" I asked.

"You just said no so many times, we were about to give up," Rya said.

"And, you're so quiet all the time," Jack added. "Like you're always thinking about something."

"Oh, I just left home kind of abruptly. There were a bunch of loose ends I needed to tie up."

The waitress came over with our pitcher of beer. They definitely didn't card in this type of place.

"I'm sorry I've been distracted because I love being here," I said. "And everyone's so nice."

"Say no more. We all understand what it's like to leave home," Jack said as he poured our beer into plastic cups. "It's never easy."

After returning from Alabama after making things right with Seren, I'd been so much more hopeful. I'd gotten to work with the dolphins, and I'd met new people who I could finally begin to let in. I'd been closed off my first month in Tampa—with good reason.

"Did you leave a guy behind?" Rya asked as she sipped her beer.

I nodded. "And it wasn't on good terms."

She cringed. "Bummer."

"We're all good now," I explained as I sipped the cheap beer. "At least I think we are."

"Well, that's good," she said. "Is he still back home or heading to college too?"

"He's in Alabama playing football."

"*The* Alabama?" Jack asked.

I nodded.

"He must be good to play there."

"He's really good. He's actually the starting quarterback."

"No shit?"

My prepaid phone buzzed. I lifted it and glanced at the screen. There was a link in a text from Seren. I clicked on it. It was a plane ticket for a flight to New Hampshire leaving at seven tomorrow morning. My stomach dropped. Why was he sending me a plane ticket? I wasn't supposed to go back there. I sent off a text. **I can't.**

I need you.

After twenty-four hours of radio silence, he couldn't even call me? What was going on?

"You look like you just got some bad news," Rya said.

I glanced up. "Oh…I…"

"The guy?" she asked.

I nodded. "He needs me to fly home tomorrow morning."

"Are you working tomorrow?" Jack asked.

"No. But…" How did I explain that I'd been blackmailed to leave the state? I guess if I wanted to keep these friends, I didn't. But could I actually go back to the manor? How could I be sure Martine wouldn't do something to me or the people I loved? Had he found out they'd been in his office? Had something already happened?

I reached in my bag and pulled out my other phone, sending a quick text to my mom. **R u ok?**

"Are you cheating on your man?" Jack asked.

I glanced at him. "What?"

He lifted his chin in the direction of the phone in my hand. "Why else would you need two phones?"

Dammit. "Oh…I…"

"Leave the girl alone," Rya chimed in. "We're allowed to have secrets, ya know?"

Oh, if they only knew….

CHAPTER 46

Grace

A driver, holding a sign with my name on it, waited for me as I stepped off the plane a little after ten the following morning. I still hadn't heard back from my mom or spoken to Seren. I prayed he knew what he was doing by bringing me back home. My legs bounced nervously as we drove through the familiar streets of Windham, nearing the manor. My heartbeat hastened and my palms dampened. Was my mother okay? Had she been hurt? Is that why he brought me home? Had something so bad happened that he couldn't risk telling me over the phone? My frantic mind spun. I needed to get into the manor.

When the driver pulled up to the front gate, Sawyer stood there, opening the gate for us. He didn't wave or even try to look through the blackened car windows.

What was going on?

I texted Seren one more time hoping this time he responded. **I'm here.**

Stay in the car.

I twisted my shaking hands as we made the trek up the long driveway. "You can pull up to the side door," I told the driver. When the car came to a stop, I peered out the window, knowing no one could see me through the windows. But this was Grayson Manor. Cameras were everywhere.

The backseat door swung open. I sucked in a sharp breath, only releasing it when Seren scooted in beside me. Before I could say a word, he pressed his lips to mine, devouring mine in a desperate kiss. He pulled back with an anxious look in his eyes. "Thanks for coming."

"Is my mom okay?"

"She's fine. I sent her to the store to get groceries."

Relief whooshed out of me. "What am I doing here? And why haven't you called me back?"

He cupped my cheeks, his eyes riveting between mine. "There's a lot at stake. And you're my ace in the hole."

"I don't understand."

His eyes drifted over my face as if he'd forgotten what I looked like. "The fact that you dropped everything and showed up here with nothing more than my need for you tells me one thing."

My brows scrunched together. "What?"

"I'm gonna marry you one day, Grace." Again, he gave me no time to respond. His lips captured mine. This kiss was hard and quick before he pulled away. "Wait in here. Do not open the door for anyone but me. I need you in Martine's office at noon with your rubber gloves from the kitchen and a bottle of water."

"What?" I said, dread washing over me.

"You'll be safe. I'll be there," he assured me.

Though I trusted him, the thought of walking the halls of Grayson manor alone still terrified me. "Okay."

"Okay, you'll be there at noon?"

"Okay, I'll marry you someday."

He smiled, and when he smiled like that, all big and excited, I knew everything was going to be okay. "Wish me luck," he said as he pushed open the door and disappeared from the car as quickly as he arrived.

Seren

"What are you doing home?" my mother asked as I stepped into the kitchen.

"Hello to you too, Mother."

"I didn't mean it like that. I'm just surprised. You didn't let anyone know you were coming."

"I like the element of surprise," I said.

"Did you get kicked off the team?" she asked.

"What? No. I just had some stuff to take care of here. I plan on heading back tomorrow," I explained.

"Well, I'm happy you're home," she said, turning to the refrigerator.

"You look better," I said, knowing that Sawyer had been keeping a close eye on her—and Martine—in an effort to stop any attempts to hurt her.

She spun back around. "Excuse me?"

"When I left for school, you looked weak. You look more like your old self."

She tilted her head, and instead of glaring at me like she usually did because of something I said, she smiled.

"Stop shooting that shit into your forehead and lips. Age gracefully. You're hot."

Laughter burst out of her. "Did you really just say that?"

"I did. So, listen to me."

Her lips pursed in contemplation. "Maybe I will."

"Good."

"Good," she repeated, and for a split second I noticed that sparkle in her eye she used to have when my father was alive.

"Where's Martine?" I asked.

"His office. He said he had a meeting and was not to be bothered."

"I'd like to say hello," I said.

"Say hello? Since when do you care to say hello to him?"

I shrugged. "Maybe I've changed since being away from this place."

"Well, for what it's worth, I like the change."

I grabbed an apple from the fruit bowl in the center of the island and bit into it. "Noted." With that, I walked out feeling a little lighter.

CHAPTER 47

Seren

"Hey," Saint said, greeting me in the hallway. "Welcome home."

"I'd like to say it's good to be home, but…you know."

"You see Sawyer yet?" he asked.

"Heading there now," I said as we climbed the steps together to the second floor. I knocked once before pushing open his door.

"Hey," Sawyer said, stepping out of his bathroom.

"You ready for this?" I asked the two of them.

"Damn straight we are," Saint said.

"Just follow my lead," I said.

"You got it," Sawyer said.

We climbed the stairs to the third floor. The door to Martine's office was closed. I pounded with the side of my fist.

"I'm in a meeting!" he bellowed.

I threw open the door, letting it slam against the wall behind it.

Martine sat behind his desk. His eyes stretched wide with confusion as the three of us stepped inside. I didn't realize how hard it was going to be to see him after what I'd learned. Self-control in this situation was key, but I was now more determined than ever before to take down the man responsible for my father's death.

"Martine? Are you there?" a voice asked from his computer screen.

"I've gotta call you back," he said before clicking a few buttons then looking back at me. "Seren? When did you get home?"

"A few minutes ago," I said, dropping into one of the leather chairs across from him.

Martine watched in confusion as Saint walked to the bookshelf at the side of the office and leaned his ass against it, while Sawyer took a seat in the chair beside me. "To what do I owe this pleasure?" he asked us.

"Time's up," I said.

"I beg your pardon?" he asked, his brows drawn in puzzlement.

"No need to beg yet, Martine," Saint chimed in. "There will be plenty of time for that."

"Boys, I'm at a loss. What's going on?" he asked, his eyes shooting among us.

"I've decided I want the company," I said.

"Come again?" Martine said, clearly caught off guard by my words.

"I'd like to sign the papers to put fifty-one percent of Grayson Industries into my name."

"But…I thought…what about football?"

"Saint will step in for me while I'm away, and then when I'm home, I'll take the helm like my father always wanted."

"Knock, knock," Arthur, my father's lawyer, said as he stepped into the doorway. "Am I interrupting?"

"Not at all. You're right on time," I said, as Sawyer stood to offer his chair to him. "I was just breaking the news to Martine that I will be taking my seat at Grayson Industries."

"That's wonderful news," Arthur said as he sat down in the chair beside me. "It's what your father always wanted."

"So, when is all this happening?" Martine asked.

"Well, today if you'd like?" Arthur said, glancing to me for confirmation.

"Absolutely," I said with a shit-eating grin.

Arthur slipped his laptop out of his briefcase and opened it.

"Wait," Martine said.

We all looked at him.

"I'm gonna need my lawyer to look over any documents," he said.

"Oh, that'll be unnecessary," Arthur said. "There's nothing for you to do. It's all Seren."

I looked at Martine. "All me."

"But—"

"What's wrong, Martine? You seem unhappy with my decision," I said.

"Oh…no…it's just…"

"It's just, what? The stipulation in my mother's will said my fifty-one percent of Grayson Industries would go to *you* if I'd yet to accept it by my nineteenth birthday and something were to happen to her."

"*What?*" he said, acting as if he hadn't made her add that addendum to her will.

"I've seen her will," I said. "I didn't want to lose my chance given that my nineteenth birthday is in a couple of weeks."

There was another knock on the door.

We all turned our attention to it. My buddy Clay, the cop who'd fucked with Grace and her friends, stood there in his uniform with two more uniformed cops behind him. "You're just in time," I said with a grin.

"Martine Giovani, we have a warrant to search your office," Clay said, holding up the warrant.

"What?!" Martine cried.

"That includes his computer and safe, right?" I asked, linking my hands behind my head and enjoying the show. Martine looked ready to jump out of his skin.

"It does," Clay confirmed.

"I want my lawyer," Martine demanded.

"I'm a lawyer," Arthur said. "And I wouldn't be able to help you once the warrant has been served."

The other cops moved into the room, standing with their arms crossed in different corners.

"Please stand from your desk," Clay said to Martine.

His mouth twisted in fury as he slowly stood up, glaring at me.

"I'm going to need password access to your computer," Clay said. "And your safe."

"Make me," Martine growled through gritted teeth.

Clay grabbed his arms behind his back and threw him down chest first onto his desk like a ragdoll.

"What the hell?" Martine cried.

Clay grasped his wrists and cuffed him. "You are going to comply or I'll have you on resisting arrest and interfering with a police investigation."

"Don't forget there'll be a media storm outside the manor," I said.

Sawyer aimed his phone at Martine, recording everything. "Just give me the word, and this shit goes viral."

"Now, either you're going to give us your passwords to your computer and safe," Clay said into his ear. "Or, we're taking both down to the station for forensics to search."

"No one uses passwords anymore," Saint chimed in. "Everything's facial recognition."

"Great," I said, standing and rounding Martine's desk. "Let's make this easy on you." I yanked Martine over to the screen that awoke once his face was in view. He fought to turn his face away, but I braced his head on both sides and held it there long enough for the screen to open to all of his apps. "Now the safe." I moved to a portrait on the wall and pulled it so it swung open like a door. My father's safe was still there, only now Martine used it.

"I got it, Seren," Clay said before pushing Martine toward it.

Martine dragged his feet, but the other cops moved to him, carrying him by the arms to it. Despite his attempts to move his face away, Clay did what I did and held Martine's face in front of it until it unlocked and the door clicked open.

Someone cleared their throat in the doorway.

All eyes moved to Grace standing there looking like the vision that she was. My eyes cut to Martine. The color drained from his face.

"Yes, Martine. She had quite the story to tell," I said to him before looking to Clay. "Keep him away from Grace and bring him in the hallway."

Clay motioned to the other officers who dragged Martine toward the doorway.

"You won't find anything!" Martine cried.

"You might want to stick around for this, Arthur," I said as Grace moved into the office and far away from Martine who was escorted out.

"Allow me," Saint said, moving behind Martine's desk. He sat in Martine's chair and began going through the apps.

"Since when do you know about this stuff?" I asked.

"You think Dad was the only one good with this shit?" Saint said.

"He sent Grace away on the eighth. We need video footage from that day in the kitchen," I explained to Saint.

Video footage from all the rooms in the house filled the television screen like a checkerboard so everyone in the room could see.

"What time?" Saint asked Grace.

"Around five, I think," she said, her voice shaking with the nerves we all felt.

The videos on the screen moved in triple time as Saint flew through the footage from that day, stopping around five o'clock.

"Right there," Grace cried, pointing to a box in the bottom corner of the screen.

"Click on it," I said.

Saint did and that particular footage filled the screen. Martine stood in the kitchen at the island. A cup of something hot sat in front of him. He slipped something small out of his pocket. We all gasped.

"Can you zoom in?" I asked.

Saint did. The small container in Martine's hand contained something white. Saint zoomed out, and we watched as Martine glanced around before pouring the white substance into the cup. Something spooked him and he spun around, quickly tucking the container into his pocket. Grace entered the screen and her startled expression said what we all now knew. He was trying to kill my mother to get full control of Grayson Industries.

"Bingo," Sawyer said.

We all turned to him standing at the wide-open safe. The same container was in there but beside it was an unlabeled clear container of white substance.

"Don't touch it!" I ordered Sawyer before turning to Clay. "Bring the bastard in." Rage pricked my skin. *Knowing* what Martine was trying to do was one thing. But *seeing* it for myself flipped a switch.

"Dude, let me bring him to the station," Clay said, trying to calm me down. "We have enough evidence to hold him."

"Bring him in here," I repeated, my voice now low and menacing. He needed to pay.

"Listen to him, Seren," Arthur urged.

"I'm gonna need you to step out now, Arthur," I said, needing time alone with Martine.

Arthur stood, and despite his reservations about allowing me to do whatever I had planned, he hurried out of the office.

"Grace?" I said, holding out my hand to her. "Gloves."

She moved to me with the rubber gloves. I took them and slipped them on. I moved to the safe and grabbed the container of white substance, checking for a label that wasn't there. Anger bubbled inside of me.

Clay walked Martine in, though everything on his face told me he knew it was a bad idea.

"What's this?" I demanded.

Martine said nothing, his lips remaining in a tight line.

"Grace," I said, "can I have the water?"

She walked toward me with the water bottle. Her smile told me she knew what I was up to and was completely on board.

"Thanks, babe," I said.

"What are you doing?" Clay asked, the nerves in his voice indicating he was torn between having my back and following the oath he'd taken when he became a cop.

"The same thing he did to my father and was now doing to my mother," I explained as I set the container and water bottle down on Martine's desk, twisting off the covers on both.

"Careful, Seren. If that's what I think it is, it can poison you through your skin," Grace warned.

"No need to worry about me. It's him you need to worry about." I took a pinch of the white substance and dropped it into the water. It barely did anything to the water. No wonder why it couldn't be detected. "That doesn't seem like enough," I said as I pinched more of the substance and dropped it into the water. "That's better." I turned with the water bottle now in my gloved hand. "Here," I said moving up to Martine who was held in place by the two officers grasping his arms. "Drink it."

"Seren," Clay warned.

"I said, '*Fucking drink it*!'" I screamed in Martine's face, my voice echoing through the room.

Martine's eyes shot away from me.

"Here," I said, lifting the bottle toward his lips. "I'll hold your mouth open and you *will* drink it."

His lips stayed pressed firmly together, and he moved his face away.

"What's going on in here?" my mother asked.

I looked to the doorway where she stood taking in the crazy scene that was transpiring in her husband's office.

"You tell her," I ordered Martine.

"Tell me what?" she asked, the desperation in her voice there for all to hear.

"There's been a mistake," Martine said.

I scoffed. "He killed our father."

She clasped her hand over her mouth.

"And he's been slowly poisoning you," I explained.

Her hand remained over her mouth as tears glazed her eyes.

"He's lying," Martine argued.

"Prove it! Drink the fucking water!" I pushed it toward his mouth.

"Martine?" my mother finally said. "Is this the truth?"

"No," he snapped.

"Then do what he's asking. Prove it," she said.

He looked away from her, and that's all I needed. I placed the water down on his desk, pulled off the rubber gloves, and looked to Sawyer. "Turn off your camera now."

He did.

I pounced, grabbing Martine by the front of his shirt. The cops stepped back as I slammed him into the closest wall, his head bouncing off it. They would've done the same thing if someone killed their father.

I heard my mother scream, but I blocked it out.

"What are you doing?" Martine cried.

"You know exactly what I'm doing."

And as if he were Jekyll and Hyde, his lips twitched and a devilish sneer swept across his face. "Your father always said you were the smart one."

At the mention of my father, I slammed my fist into his stomach. He made to bend, but my forearm held him at his throat. "Don't you dare mention him in this house, you sick son of a bitch."

"What are you gonna do? Kill me?" he asked with an air of arrogance.

"An eye for an eye," I said, pressing my forearm harder against his neck.

Sardonic laughter erupted from somewhere deep inside of him.

"You think this is funny?" I said through gritted teeth.

"I'll be out on bail by morning," he struggled to utter with my arm against his throat.

I slammed my fist into his face. Blood sprayed from his nose.

Everyone was quiet.

"Did you see what he did?" Martine demanded of Clay. "I want to press charges."

"It's unfortunate that you slipped when we were walking you out of the manor," Clay said.

"Saint? Sawyer? Would you like a piece of him?" I asked and they both eagerly stepped forward.

"I would," my mother said, stepping forward and moving in front of Martine. "Look at me."

He wouldn't.

She snapped. "Look at me, Goddamnit!"

He begrudgingly met her gaze.

"I don't want you to think for one second you replaced my husband. He was an extraordinary man who didn't deserve what you did to him. He had my whole heart even when I said 'I do' to you." She raised her hand and smacked him across the face, the *thwack* silencing us all. "Take him away," she ordered Clay as she wiped Martine's blood from her hand onto the leg of her expensive pants.

The cops moved Martine out of the office.

My mother walked over to me and wrapped her arms around my waist, twisting into me and sobbing. I held her as she cried. It would take time for her to understand why he'd done what he'd done. Time to get past the fact that she'd slept in the same bed as a murderer. Time to trust people again.

I glanced to Grace who nodded her approval at my attempt to ease my mother's pain. "I love you," she mouthed.

Even in a moment like that, her words warmed the emptiness I'd felt inside of me for the past three years. "I love you," I mouthed back. Without Grace, I would've lost the only parent I had left.

"They'll be back up to help me collect all this evidence," Clay said, pulling my attention from Grace. "You did good today. I don't think I could've handled it as well as you did. Though, if he drank the water and you killed him, I would've had a hell of a lot of paperwork to fill out."

I tried to smile, but I couldn't as my mother was sobbing in my arms. Saint and Sawyer moved over to us and threw their arms around me and my mother. Grace stepped back to give us space. I waved her over and took her hand as she stood outside our embrace. She may not have been a Grayson yet, but I'd been honest with her when I said I'd marry her one day. Because when Seren Grayson set his mind to doing something, he always did it.

EPILOGUE

Five Months Later
Grace

The roar of the Texas stadium overwhelmed my senses. The last time I'd been in a place that rumbled so loudly, it had been a Savage Beasts concert and I'd been one of the people screaming. I mean, the lead singer Z. Need I say more?

Seren had led his team to an undefeated season. They'd won the Conference Championship game and were now at the National Championships in Arlington, Texas against Georgia. Maureen had paid for my friends and me to attend the game, springing for front row seats on the fifty-yard line. She'd really changed since the truth about Martine was revealed. She'd stopped having work done on her appearance—per Seren's request—and she was beginning to look like a normal person and not some fake Barbie doll. She'd also kept Grayson Industries. It gave her something to do and gave her a purpose. And while she was doing a great job running the company, she assured the boys it was only temporary and would be there whenever Seren—or one of his brothers—wanted it.

She was currently off schmoozing with other rich people up in the boxes with my mom. Yup, Maureen had even been spending time with my mom, promoting her to her personal assistant—which was ultimately a paid friend position. They'd begun doing all the things they should have been doing all along as best friends—shopping, getting manicures, going out for lunches and dinners. And, my mom would be there for her when Martine's trial began next year.

My mom had even become #TeamSeren. She understood why he'd acted the way he had since his father died, and she respected the way he'd been trying to make up for lost time with his mom.

"His ass looks so hot in those tight pants," Holly said from the seat on my left.

"*Holly*," Laney admonished from my right. "That's Grace's man."

I laughed. "He does look hot in the pants."

"That's my brother," Sawyer chimed in from beside Laney.

"I always knew she wanted him," Saint grumbled from beside Sawyer.

I rolled my eyes knowing that could not have been further from the truth. I hated Seren Grayson at one time. *Wholeheartedly.*

"Can he hook us up with some of his teammates?" Laney asked, redirecting my attention to the field where Alabama's offense ran out onto the field. Seren got them into a huddle.

"Maybe," I laughed as I stood up and straightened out my Alabama jersey.

Being away from Seren during the first semester sucked. Luckily, we video chatted daily, and I streamed his games every weekend. I was able to go to a few over winter break, so this wasn't the first time I was getting to see him play in person. And he definitely lived up to the hype.

Though I was loving my time in Tampa, I couldn't wait for summer. Seren planned to stay with me so I could continue interning at the rescue center, and we could spend all my free time together. He'd have to head back for summer football practices—being the team's starting quarterback and all—but we'd still get to spend quality time together like we'd done over winter break.

On the field, Alabama was down by three with under three minutes remaining. Seren would be heartbroken to have taken his team this far only to lose in the national championships. The ball was snapped and Seren shuffled back, looking to go long to one of his receivers. The crowd grew louder, willing the receiver to get to his intended spot faster. Seren dodged a defender and then released the ball. The ball soared in a perfect spiral and the receiver nabbed it over his head, bolting toward the end zone but was tackled at the forty-yard line.

"Dammit," Sawyer cursed, despite the crowd's cheers.

"What's wrong?" I asked.

"The clock doesn't stop if they get tackled inbounds," Saint said.

Right. Seren told me that. I didn't know much about football before dating him, but since I'd been watching his games and getting play-by-plays after the games, I'd been picking up the basics.

On the field, the ball was tossed back by the ref. Seren didn't call for a huddle this time, and his offense moved to their spots on the line of scrimmage. He called something to the right then to the left. The ball was snapped, and everyone was on the move. Seren took a few steps back, and a running back crossed behind him. He handed off the ball to him. The running back took off, but the defense was there and tackled him, not allowing for any yards.

"They may not score," Saint said.

"Don't jinx them," Sawyer and I snapped at the same time.

With the clock stopped, Seren called his teammates into a huddle before they lined up. The ball was snapped and again Seren handed it off to a running back. This time the running back found a hole and bolted down the field. The crowd became deafening as they willed him into the end zone, but he didn't make it that far, getting tackled at the twenty-yard line. The crowd went wild. Victory was so close we could all taste it.

My eyes jumped to the clock. "Why'd the clock stop? I thought it only stops when they go out of bounds?"

"Two-minute warning," Sawyer explained.

"I can't believe Seren dates someone who knows so little about football," Saint sneered.

"Screw you, Saint," I snapped.

He cursed under his breath and took off, leaving us to watch the remainder of the game without his unwanted comments.

"He's just worried they're gonna lose," Sawyer assured me. "Don't take his ignorance personally."

My body buzzed with nerves. Two minutes to bring home a victory. If anyone could do it, Seren could. I mean, he wouldn't allow it to happen any other way.

Seren and his teammates lined up. This time when the ball was snapped, he backpedaled, avoiding one defender and getting into an open spot. Out of nowhere, another defender charged him, but somehow, he sidestepped him. He needed more time to find an open receiver. He, along with the rest of the stadium, spotted one cutting left in front of the end zone. Every breath was held as he released the ball. It seemed to float in slow motion forever until it landed in his teammate's hands. Instantly, he was tackled on the two-yard line.

The stadium exploded. Two. More. Yards!

I looked to the clock which was still ticking down. Fifty, forty-nine, forty-eight…

"Can't they call a timeout to stop the clock?" I asked Sawyer.

"No timeouts left," he said.

Seren huddled with his teammates as the seconds continued ticking down.

With forty seconds to go on the clock, they lined up. I chewed on my bottom lip, so damn nervous yet excited at the same time. The ball was snapped. Seren didn't reel back with it, instead, he plowed forward, jumping over the defense who was charging at him. He landed with a roll in the end zone.

The crowd erupted, the cement beneath my feet rumbling like an earthquake had hit. My friends and Sawyer sandwiched me and we jumped up and down together. There wasn't a person seated in that stadium. Seren ran to the sideline, and his teammates jumped all over Seren, celebrating his amazing play that hopefully secured their final win of the season and a national championship.

I watched Seren get swept up in the arms of all of his new friends. This was where he belonged. He never fit in back at Windham. He'd been surviving, but not living. I'd like to think I had something to do with the change in him, but I knew it was because all the anger toward his mother he carried for three years had been lifted from his shoulders. He also gained more confidence—if that was even possible—by winning the starting position. He clearly deserved the position, and there wasn't a fan out there who could deny that.

Alabama scored the field goal, getting them the extra point. With seconds left, Georgia attempted a Hail Mary which resulted in an interception.

The game-ending cheers and celebration lasted for a good ten minutes before the stadium began to clear out. Sawyer and my friends opted to wait in the parking lot where there was bound to be a raging tailgate party. I stayed at my seat, watching as reporters interviewed Seren who was completely in his element. He ran his hand through his sweaty hair as he laughed at something a reporter had asked him. I beamed with pride knowing he got his dream. Not his dad's dream. But his dream. Though, there wasn't a doubt in my mind, his dad was looking down and so incredibly proud of the man he'd become.

I couldn't help but relish in the fact that the Seren Grayson all these people were just getting to know wasn't the Seren Grayson I knew. They didn't know all the things he'd been through. Or, all the things he'd done to get me to fall for him (and hate him at the same time). They knew the superstar. The guy with the heart to take his team to a national championship.

"Grace?"

Goosebumps popped up all over my body at the sound of his deep voice. I glanced down, not even realizing he'd finished with his interviews. "You did it!" I gushed.

He climbed up the wall between the field and me and pulled himself over the railing. He wrapped his sweaty body around me. "Can you even believe it?"

"Your dad would be so proud of you," I assured him.

"Are you proud?"

"Yes!"

He chuckled and pulled back to look at me. "This night couldn't be any more perfect. We won. My whole family's here. And you're gonna marry me."

I laughed. "I said someday."

He released me and stepped back, dropping down onto one knee.

My eyes widened. "Don't kid around like that."

He stared up at me with flushed cheeks and sweaty hair. "Grace, I know we're young and we live in different states right now, but I've loved you since the night you pulled into my driveway. It was like a rush of adrenaline coursed through me, and I knew you were gonna change my life. And you have, Grace, in so many ways."

Tears glazed my eyes and my bottom lip began to quiver.

"It doesn't have to be tomorrow or even next year, but say what we have is forever and say you'll marry me." His eyes shifted behind me and he held his hand out to the side as if to catch something.

I glanced over my shoulder. My mom and Maureen stood a few rows back with their arms linked. Holly and Laney grinned like fools beside them with their phones recording everything. Saint sat alone in a seat playing on his phone, not the least bit interested. And, Sawyer eagerly tossed something down to Seren.

My attention returned to Seren who held a ring box.

He opened it and a gorgeous Tiffany-cut diamond ring sparkled inside. "What do you say, Grace?" he asked, the vulnerability of a child softening the areas around his eyes. "Will you spend forever with me?"

My eyes moved from the ring to Seren who anxiously awaited my answer. He'd come into my life so unexpectedly and turned it on its head. But, oddly, now when I looked at him, everything else just faded away and I only saw love in his eyes. Yes, we were young. And, yes, we lived in different states. But Seren Grayson was it for me. And I knew, with much certainty, I was it for him. "Yes."

"Thank God," he said like he actually thought I'd say no.

I held out my shaking hand, and he slipped the ring onto my finger. I had no time to admire it because he stood and pulled me into his arms, kissing me in front of our audience who broke into applause. The amount of happiness I felt in that moment took over my body, and I knew there was nowhere in this world that felt more like home than Seren's arms. I don't know who pulled out of the kiss first, but when we did, we didn't look to our audience. We looked up at the night sky. Our fathers had something to do with bringing us together, and I think deep down, we both knew it.

The End

ACKNOWLEDGEMENTS

Thank you so much for taking the time to read Seren and Grace's story. I hope you enjoyed it as much as I enjoyed writing my first high school bully romance!

To all the bloggers, bookstagrammers, booktokers, and readers who have continued to share my books. I say it every time, but it's the truth. I could never do this without you! Thank you so very much for taking the time to read, review, and share my books!

To my wonderful ARC team who read and reviewed *Seren*. I am so lucky to have such a wonderful group of readers on my team! Hugs to all of you!

To my reader's group, *J. Nathan's Book Boyfriend Lovers*. Thank you so much for interacting and for loving my books!

To my wonderful beta readers: Dali, Megan, Maria, and Jill. Thank you for always giving me feedback I can work with! I know I can depend on you all. Thank you so very much!

To my editor Stephanie Elliot. Thank you for always giving me such honesty. And for making me laugh when you totally don't like something. I feel so lucky to have had you in my corner since day one of this journey.

To my wonderful proofreader Peggy. You may be the last one to read my books, but you are one of the most important people on my team. Thank you for being so good at what you do!

To my wonderful PA Renee. What would I do without you? Is it strange that I can hear you answering that in my head as I type this? LOL! Thank you for being you! I'm so lucky to have you!

To Kate at Y'all. That Graphic for creating another beautiful cover and amazing teasers! I always know I'm in good hands when you get my cover photo. Thank you!

To Migelanxo for the amazing cover photo of the gorgeous Sergio. I hope you love the cover as much as I do!

A big thank you to Grey's PR for your assistance with this release! You are so wonderful to work with! Thank you, Josette for the gorgeous graphics!!

And, last but not least, thank you to my family and friends. I am so lucky to have your love and support! NayNay, thank you for your assistance with the twist in this book. You are going to make an amazing author one day with all of your creative ideas! Love you!

MORE FROM J. NATHAN

For You Standalone Sports Series:
Book #1 *For Finlay*
Book #2 *For Forester*
Book #3 *For Crosby*
Book #4 *For Emery*

Savage Beasts Standalone Rock Star Series:
Book #1 *Kozart*
Book #2 *Treyton*

Standalones:
All Your Tomorrows
Something About You
I Just Need You
You're the Reason
Until Alex
Before Hadley
Since Drew

ABOUT THE AUTHOR

J. Nathan resides on the east coast with her husband and twelve-year-old son. She is an avid reader of all things romance. Happy endings are a must. When she's not curled up with a good book, she can be found spending time with family and friends, at baseball games, and working on her next novel.

www.ingramcontent.com/pod-product-compliance
Lightning Source LLC
Chambersburg PA
CBHW021217310726
48971CB00006B/1594